# THE RAGE WAR BOOK 2
# ALIEN™
## INVASION

Yours to Keep
Withdrawn/ABCL

THE RAGE WAR BOOK 2

# ALIEN™

## INVASION

TIM LEBBON

**TITAN** BOOKS

## ALIEN™: INVASION

Print edition ISBN: 9781783296095
E-book edition ISBN: 9781783296101

Published by Titan Books
A division of Titan Publishing Group Ltd
144 Southwark Street, London SE1 0UP

First edition: April 2016
10 9 8 7 6 5 4 3 2 1

A CIP catalogue record for this title is available from the British Library.

Printed and bound in the USA.

**Did you enjoy this book?**
We love to hear from our readers. Please email us at readerfeedback@
titanemail.com or write to us at Reader Feedback at the above address.

To receive advance information, news, competitions, and exclusive
offers online, please sign up for the Titan newsletter on our website
**www.titanbooks.com**

*For Lemmy.*
*Born to lose, lived to win.*

# THE RAGE WAR: BOOK 1

## PREDATOR: INCURSION

When Yautja attacks across the Human Sphere of space grow in frequency, Colonial Marine units are put on high alert. Soon, an invasion is feared.

Meanwhile Liliya—an android—escapes from the Rage. Originally known as the Founders, the Rage are humans who have fled beyond the Human Sphere over the course of centuries. Now led by Beatrix Maloney, they are on their way back, bearing alien-inspired technology and weapons far exceeding those possessed by the Colonial Marines or Weyland-Yutani. Maloney's aim is the subjugation and control of the Human Sphere.

When Liliya flees, she carries with her a sample of their technology that might help humanity fight back. Maloney sends Alexander, one of her best generals, in pursuit.

Isa Palant is a research scientist fascinated with the Yautja. Slowly learning their language, she is almost killed in a terrorist attack on the base where she is stationed. It's one of many such attacks instigated by the Rage across the Human Sphere in preparation for their return.

Johnny Mains is leader of an Excursionist unit,

a Colonial Marine outfit created to keep watch on a Yautja habitat beyond the Sphere. When someone—or something—attacks the habitat, Mains and his crew crash-land there. What they discover is beyond belief.

The Yautja aren't invading the Human Sphere. They are fleeing an assault by weaponized Xenomorphs.

This is the army of the Rage.


*At the end of Book One:*


Isa Palant and Major Akoko Halley, the Colonial Marine sent to rescue her, confront the Yautja elder Kalakta and broker an unsteady peace between humans and Yautja.

Liliya, taken into custody on a Yautja ship and tortured at the hands of the warrior called Hashori, escapes with her captor when the Rage general Alexander closes in and attacks.

Lieutenant Johnny Mains and his surviving crew member, Lieder, are trapped on the Yautja habitat UMF 12. They have witnessed and fought the weaponized Xenomorphs, and a Rage general, Patton, is also aboard, seriously injured. Mains and Lieder have witnessed evidence of ancient human colony ships, returning from the dark depths of unexplored space. They theorize that these could be used as birthing grounds for tens of thousands more Xenomorph soldiers.

The Rage are coming...

# 1

## JOHNNY MAINS

*Yautja Habitat designated UMF 12, beyond Outer Rim*
*September 2692 AD*

General Patton was laughing, and Lieutenant Johnny Mains, leader of what was left of the 5th Excursionists, the VoidLarks, knew that he was going to die.

He refused to go without a fight.

The scratching, scampering sounds of the approaching Xenomorphs grew louder. They were nearing the bridge of this strange ship, perhaps called by their android master, or attacking of their own volition. Either way, it would mean the end. Mains and his one surviving Excursionist, Lieder, were low on ammunition. Their combat suits were depleted. They had fought well and lost many good friends along the way, but this was their last stand.

"We stay together," Mains said. "Concentrated fire. Keep them at the doors—once they're onto the bridge they'll spread out and take us down. Ammo?"

"Com-rifle has some nano, low laser charge, one plasma shot. Sidearm. You?"

"Shotgun. Couple of grenades."

"We might as well spit at them."

"We'll take a few. Last grenade's for us."

Lieder glanced at him as she drew closer. No objection there, and he was glad. They'd watched too many people die beneath a Xenomorph's attack to have any intention of going that way. At least hugging a grenade between them would ensure they'd die together.

The android Patton chuckled again, a wet, mechanical sound that grated on Mains's nerves.

"Can't I shoot him?" Lieder asked. She knew the answer. It would be a waste of ammunition.

Patton remained pinned to the rear wall of the ship's bridge by a Yautja spear. Splayed at his feet were the bodies of a single Yautja and innumerable dead Xenomorphs, their slick carapaces burst apart from when they'd self-destructed at the moment of death. Countless acid burns splashed and scarred the walls and floor, and the acrid stench still hung on the air.

Mains had never heard of a Xenomorph doing that before. *Suicide is a Yautja trick,* he mused. *Just another mystery.*

"They're close," Lieder said.

Mains didn't need telling. His suit's systems were low on charge and glitching, after all he'd been through, but they still projected a motion image onto his visor. The trace was large, and close.

Patton made a strange, new sound. Straining, groaning, electrical clicks and ticks rattling behind his inhuman voice. Mains had the nagging urge to communicate with the android, get some answers. That he commanded the Xenomorphs was clear—his name was stamped on a patch of exoskeleton at the back of each of their heads. How did he do it? What did he want? Where had he originated, and why had he attacked this huge Yautja habitat?

Mains hated the idea of dying without knowing.

"Been an honor, Johnny," Lieder said, squeezing his hand.

"Fuck sentimentality, Private," Mains said, but he squeezed back.

"Here they come."

The first Xenomorph darted through the doorway and onto the bridge. Lieder sliced it neck to crotch with a laser blast, and it thrashed across the floor and against the wall, body bursting and acid blood spraying as it self-destructed.

Two more followed. Mains fired his antique shotgun three times at the first. It dropped from view behind a control panel, then leapt again, leaking corrosive blood and coming right for him. Another shot put it down.

Lieder killed the third creature with a nano burst, the specks flowering in a thousand explosions across the entrance to the bridge. It caught another couple of Xenomorphs down in the approach corridor, and when the first detonated it must have killed the second, their death throes thudding through the ship.

Patton was becoming more agitated, writhing on the wall, grasping at the heavy Yautja spear that pinned him there, attempting to tug it away. He would not succeed. Sparks danced at the spear's entry point in his chest, miniature lightning storms arcing between android and weapon and back again. He scratched at the shaft, and then tried to force his fingers inside the wound.

"Plasma!" Lieder shouted.

Three more Xenomorphs were coming through the entrance to the bridge, two on the level and one crawling across the ceiling like a monstrous spider. Mains's visor darkened automatically as Lieder unloaded her last remaining plasma charge in their direction. The blast struck the one on the ceiling, and it disintegrated in a sun-hot eruption, melted flesh and sinew blazing as it showered across its brethren below. They screeched in agony, scampered further onto the bridge, slumped down and burst apart.

The air filled with a haze of superheated gas. Their combat suits filtered much of it from view, but it still seemed to Mains that his visor was misting up.

Patton wailed, a horrible, high sound that descended into something like laughter. It was a strange android, features bland and only superficially human, with no apparent attempt to convey a personality or make it in any way distinctive. That served to render its very human sounds of distress and frustration even more haunting.

*Maybe I* should *have put a shotgun blast in its head*, Mains thought.

The plasma burst had set a white-hot fire around the entrance, and for a few seconds the attacking Xenomorphs held back.

"They won't wait long," Mains said.

"Don't want them to," Lieder said. "I'm all fired up. What the hell is *he* doing?" She nodded at Patton. Both of his hands were now pressing into the wound in his chest, fingers-deep in his fleshy outer layers, silvery charged arcs dancing from knuckle to knuckle.

"Doesn't matter," Mains said. "Our Yautja friends have already taken care of him."

The Yautja were not their friends. Far from it. For more than a year Mains's unit—the 5th Excursionists, nicknamed the VoidLarks—had been shadowing the massive Yautja habitat designated UMF 12, keeping a careful eye on the strange aliens and ensuring that they launched no ships toward the Outer Rim. Just recently there had been a spate of Yautja attacks across the Rim, incursions that resulted in hunts and deaths. The

VoidLarks had been involved in one of these, called to Southgate Station 12 while on a rare resupply run. They'd lost two of their crew of eight taking on the Yautja there, and that had seemed like a huge loss.

Upon returning to station a million miles from UMF 12, they'd soon become involved in more fighting as Yautja ships launched back toward the Human Sphere. Damaged in a deep space contact, they'd crash-landed their Arrow ship the *Ochse* on the huge habitat, then survived for a month with only occasional contacts. Running, hiding, it had been the sighting of this large, mysterious ship that had steered events toward a bloody end. Neither recognizably human nor Yautja, the ship had become their objective, and it would be their resting place.

That end was now close. With only two of them left out of the original eight, the VoidLarks were fighting their last.

Patton chuckled again as he noticed them watching him. It was a haunting sound, filled with humor yet coming from an expressionless face. His eyes were deep and dark, giving away nothing. His blood was too white, skin too pasty and pale.

"L-T!" Lieder shouted.

Mains crouched and fired as more Xenomorphs surged through the plasma flames and the remains of their kin. There were six of them, then eight, and he primed and heaved one of his two grenades toward the bridge's lower level.

He and Lieder ducked, the explosion tore through control panels and Xenomorph skin, and as they stood and started shooting again three more aliens were spitting and melting on the floor.

"Back up," Mains said, his voice raised over the hideous sounds. "Toward the end wall, both of us together."

"I'm not retreating anymore," Lieder said. Through the explosions, shrieking, and chaos, her voice was transmitted directly into his ear through his combat suit's headset. Her determination and fury made him proud.

"It's not a retreat," he said, and when she looked he showed her his last grenade. "We press this between us and the wall and it might just vent the ship to space."

The alien ship was secured to one of the long mooring towers protruding from the end of the Yautja habitat. Its atmosphere was thin but breathable, and the habitat maintained an artificial gravity that meant they could move from one place to another without having to float.

But one hole punched through the ship's hull, and everything would be sucked out into the void. The remains of their bodies, twisted together in death, mingling with the corpses of Yautja and the shreds of Xenomorphs scattered across the bridge—and anything else left alive.

"What a way to go," Lieder said.

"Spin!" Mains shouted.

Lieder reacted instantly, finger closing on her trigger as she crouched and spun. She had her laser set on widest spread, and she took down two Xenomorphs with one burst. Another barreled into her, knocking her from her feet, crushing her down to the floor, its arms slapping her weapon aside as its head dipped down.

Mains saw her eyes go wide, and she turned to look at him.

He stepped forward and fired his last shotgun shell into the side of the Xenomorph's head. Its acid blood sprayed, spattering across his hand and forearm and dropping onto Lieder's chest. Their suits hardened against it, repelling the acid, but their charges were dangerously low, and he soon started to feel the burn as the toxic fluid ate into the weakened material.

He threw the shotgun aside, sorry to lose it. An antique, and hardly standard issue, it had saved his life on more than one occasion. Now it had saved Lieder's, just in time for both of them to die.

She scrambled to her feet and they locked arms, backing quickly across the bridge. Much of the equipment was mysterious, but there was enough here to recognize. This ship looked to have been built and sent by humans, its purpose to attack a huge Yautja habitat with weaponized Xenomorphs, their leader a mad android. Once again Mains was struck by regret, that they'd die without uncovering what this all meant.

More Xenomorphs appeared and stalked them. Moving slowly now, seeing their prey defenseless, perhaps even now they were somehow listening to Patton's command.

The android twisted and tensed on the wall, still trying to delve into his own ruined chest. Reaching for something. Trying to fix something that was broken, perhaps.

Mains held the grenade behind his back and pressed it to the wall. Behind him, less than a hand's width away, was cold dark space. He would meet it soon.

Lieder stepped in front of him, face to face, and pressed herself to him. More of the grenade's blast would be forced against the wall that way. It also meant that they could kiss. The clear suit masks meant that it was not real, but the thin material flexed, and Mains imagined he could taste her breath and feel the heat of her against him.

"Private, you're crossing a line," he muttered.

Lieder smiled.

His thumb stroked the grenade's priming button. One more press and they'd have five seconds.

He pressed.

She knew.

*Five…*

His comms unit crackled and whistled. "Johnny Mains, you bastard, hold onto something!"

*Four…*

"What the hell was that?" she muttered.

*Three…*

Mains knew that voice.

The Xenomorphs, perhaps sensing that something had changed, surged toward them. There were six of them leaping the control panels, limbs skittering and scratching.

*Two…*

"Hold onto me as tightly as you can!" Mains shouted. He lobbed the grenade across the room and fell sideways, kicking his way beneath a control panel and dragging Lieder with him.

*One…*

"Grapple and harness!" For a split-second he thought his combat suit was out of charge, and couldn't obey his command. Then he heard the faint hiss of his waist pack firing the small grappling hook. It bounced against the heavy panel behind his back, then burrowed inside, barbed hooks splaying and holding it tight.

The grenade exploded. A Xenomorph shrieked. Mains and Lieder held each other. The blast whistled in his ears.

"Don't you fucking *dare* let go of me," he said.

"Johnny, what the hell's happening?"

An alien blocked out the light. Its shadow was sharp and vicious, teeth dripping, limbs reaching for them as it hissed in victory.

"Durante is happening," he said.

The second explosion was much larger than the first. The floor bucked beneath them, light bloomed and flashed, and then the whole world was screaming. Mains kept his eyes open, though his suit had shaded its visor to protect his eyes from the glare. Something tugged at him and Lieder and he squeezed her tight, locking his limbs around her, determined that if she went, he would go too.

*It'll tear us apart*, he thought, *pull off our limbs, open us up and—*

It wasn't the Xenomorph pulling them.

Atmosphere was venting. A hole had been blown in the ship's hull, somewhere out of sight, and air was being expelled into the vacuum, screaming across the bridge and carrying with it anything that wasn't screwed down. That included the dead aliens and Yautja, tumbling and colliding as they went, as well as the living Xenomorphs that had been coming at them across the wide space.

His suit's wire and grapple strained tight, but held fast.

He only hoped it would last.

As Mains's visor cleared he adjusted position, turning onto his side so that he and Lieder could see beneath the control panel and across the room. The hole was small, the size of a normal door, but constantly expanded as heavy objects smashed through. Two Xenomorphs flew straight out, then a third grabbed hold of the hole's edge, spidery fingers digging into the damaged superstructure. Detritus struck it several times. It held on, pulling, actually hauling itself against the flow.

A human corpse crashed into the alien and they both disappeared into the void. Faulkner had been Mains's friend. He'd died bravely, and now he was out there forever, tumbling into infinity.

The flow of venting air lessened. Somewhere in the strange ship blast doors must have been closing. Sound retreated, and a few seconds later they found themselves subsumed within a haunting, threatening silence.

Lieder stood first, helping Mains to his feet. They now

carried only a sidearm each, and Mains knew that his laser pistol's charge was down to just one or two swift shots.

The android, Patton, was dead at last. Whatever he had been attempting had failed, when the blast had driven a fist-sized chunk of metal into his face. His head was a bloody mess of flesh, titanium skull, and ruined insides, his unimaginably complex computing power destroyed in an instant. Artificial he might have been, but in reality the android was as frail as any human.

"Johnny!" Lieder said. She slapped his shoulder, reaching for her sidearm with her other hand. He spun and peered in the direction she was facing.

There was movement at the ragged hole in the ship's hull. As he saw what it was, he thought for a moment he might be dreaming.

Maybe he was already dead.

"Wait," he said, holding her arm.

"Holy shit," Lieder said.

Two shapes entered through the hole, safety lines extending behind them and out into space. They were heavily armed.

"*Oxygen levels critical*," his suit said. He might have ten minutes of air remaining.

"What the hell sort of trouble have you been kicking up?" a voice asked.

"Durante," Mains said. "Eddie… really?"

The man who stepped forward must have been almost seven feet tall, broad and powerful, his combat suit straining at the seams even though it would have been specially made for him.

"Always said you'd need rescuing one day," the huge figure replied. He grinned at Lieder. "And who are you?"

"Hitting on her already?" Mains asked.

Durante shrugged.

Mains laughed. "She'd have your balls for dinner."

Durante looked around the smashed ship's bridge as another shape dropped through the hole behind him from above.

"Seen some action, Johnny."

"It's been a tough few weeks."

"Tell me about it."

"What does that mean?" Mains asked.

Durante looked at him strangely.

"We've been cut off here. No communications in or out, other than a signal we sent a few minutes ago."

"So you don't know anything that's been happening?"

"No. Why?"

"I'll tell you on board the *Navarro*. You all that's left?"

"Yeah. How did you know about us?"

"Picked up a distress signal from the *Ochse*. Where is it?"

The *Ochse* had exploded minutes after crash-landing them safely on the habitat, following a tough contact with some Yautja ships departing UMF 12. Frodo, the ship's computer, must have broadcast a distress signal seconds before being blasted into memory.

"It's toast," Mains said. He'd grown close to Frodo. The ship's computer had developed a personality, and they'd all thought of it as another member of the crew.

Durante grunted, then gestured for them to follow.

"Unless you've grown to like this place…"

"Get us the fuck out of here," Lieder said, "and have your ship prep a channel to Tyszka Star."

"Sounds like we've both got plenty of news to share," Durante said as they prepared to leave.

Mains and Lieder held onto each other as they crossed the bridge under the watchful gaze of Eddie Durante and his fellow members of the HellSparks.

Mains hadn't seen the big man in over six years. A fellow Excursionist, he'd been in command of one of the other Arrow-class ships tasked with patrolling beyond the Outer Rim. They'd done some training together at Tyszka Star, and years before that they'd shared time in the same Colonial Marine regiment. They hadn't been close friends back then, but when they'd both been selected for Excursionist training, they'd grown to like each other. Still, Mains had never expected to see Durante again. Such was the life of an Excursionist.

"Thanks for coming by," he said as they approached the smoking hole in the hull.

"Wasn't busy," Durante said. He and Mains stared out over the huge, curved surface of the Yautja habitat, and into the impersonal void of space surrounding them.

Mains did not believe in God, but as he and Lieder were helped over to the *Navarro*, he gave thanks to Eddie Durante.


Like all Arrow-class ships, the *Navarro* had been customized on the inside by its HellSpark crew. It maintained a similar layout to the *Ochse*, but it still felt like a strange ship.

As they passed through the airlock and their combat suits cycled down, Mains and Lieder pulled themselves into flight seats while Durante's medic gave them the once-over.

A small, elfish woman, Radcliffe accessed their suits' CSUs to assess current physical condition and medical needs.

"Hell, what have you guys been doing down there?" she asked. Checking the readouts on a floating holo frame, she glanced at Lieder with what might have been awe.

"Relaxing," Lieder said. "Few drinks in the evening, game of backgammon, nice slow screw before bed."

"Right," Radcliffe said. "Well, I'll concoct a stew of shit to pump into you both, might make you feel a bit better."

"Worse wouldn't be possible," Mains said. "Thanks."

"Not a problem." Radcliffe called over a medical unit and connected it to the holo frame, stroking controls and watching as a selection of medicines were selected. While she worked, Durante slouched down in a seat across from them.

"We're getting outta here," he said. "Sensors indicate that weird ship's still got nasties roaming beyond the blast doors."

"They'll break through and come at the ship, if they can," Mains said.

"Into vacuum?" Durante asked.

"They were controlled," Lieder said. "The android you saw, dead now, but he called himself Patton—and somehow he was giving them orders."

"Weaponized Xenomorphs?" Durante's eyes widened.

Mains nodded. His head swam, and he felt sickness rising. He swallowed it down. Now was not the time.

"Patton... Patton..." Durante said, frowning.

"Twentieth-century general," Lieder said.

"Just what the hell?" Durante said. "How can this have anything to do with the Yautja incursion?"

"The what?"

Durante told them. About the contacts across the Outer Rim, battles, and Yautja incursions deeper into the Human Sphere, as well as the various instances of sabotage against Weyland-Yutani and Colonial Marine bases. Death tolls were huge. Excursionists were being called back in from beyond the Rim to patrol the borders, and even though some sort of ceasefire had apparently been established, they were still on a war footing.

"Yautja don't invade," Lieder said.

"That's what makes it so worrying," Durante said.

"It's not that." Mains shook his head. The sickness rose again, and this time he had to lean to the side and bring it all up. Feeling dreadful, he heaved several times, spattering the floor and the seat's legs. He was only thankful that the *Navarro*'s artificial gravity had been engaged. He wished he could expunge every awful memory of the past few weeks, of all his friends he had seen die.

"You puked on my ship," Durante said.

"Yeah." Mains wiped his mouth. "Sorry 'bout that. But Eddie, I need to send a message back to Tyszka Star. It's not where the Yautja are going we've got to worry about. It's what they're running from."

Mains knew it would take General Wendy Hetfield, the leader of the Excursionists, some time to receive his broadcast and send a response. He also knew that Durante was getting edgy, eager to leave UMF 12 behind and continue his journey back to the Outer Rim.

Nevertheless, he persuaded his friend to maintain a steady orbit around the habitat while he sent the brief signal. It was important, he said. It might be the most important message he'd ever send. When Durante asked him what it was about, Mains invited him to sit in and listen.

In fact, he invited all the crew. They came and watched, all eight HellSparks, him, and Lieder cramped onto a bridge designed for eight. Durante took up enough space for two of them.

Mains and Lieder were feeling better, systems awash with a cocktail of drugs courtesy of Radcliffe. Their various injuries would be treated, and soon, but the effects of several weeks of constant combat, dehydration, and borderline starvation would take longer to recover from. The drugs could only act as a buffer.

He sat silently for a moment as he composed the message. As he did so, he had the feeling he might be defining all of their futures. Then he began.

"This is Lieutenant Johnny Mains of the 5th Excursionists, VoidLarks. After thirty days aboard the Yautja habitat designated UMF 12, we've been picked up by Lieutenant Eddie Durante and his 19th Excursionists. Six of my eight crew are dead, myself and Private Lieder the only survivors. Our ship the *Ochse* is gone. During our time on UMF 12 we've discovered some troubling information.

"Initially we were fighting the Yautja. As usual with their species, more often than not they attacked individually, and we made several attempts to board Yautja vessels with the intention of stealing one to escape, but we couldn't fly any of them. Then we discovered a strange ship docked at one end of the habitat. We started finding Yautja corpses that looked as though they'd been ripped apart. We suspected some sort of internal feud, but we were proved wrong.

"Xenomorphs were present on the habitat. They had arrived on the strange ship, which although largely mysterious to us was almost certainly of human origin. There was an android on board calling itself Patton, named after a twentieth-century general, and it seems that Patton was in control of the Xenomorphs. Someone, somewhere, has weaponized the species.

"When mortally wounded the Xenomorphs self-destruct, sometimes exploding, sometimes melting down. Parts of their exoskeletons can survive, and in several instances we found Patton's name stamped on them, on the carapace at the back of the head. It was a mark of ownership."

Mains looked around at the *Navarro*'s crew. Some seemed shocked, while a couple looked at him as though he were mad. He could understand their skepticism. Thin, weak, battered, he'd obviously been through a lot. Perhaps they suspected him of space sickness.

Yet Lieder sat beside him, silently supportive, and no two people could suffer the same delusions.

"There's more," he said. "We reached the ship's bridge, and moments before the Xenomorphs launched a final attack, and Lieutenant Durante and his HellSparks came to our rescue, Private Lieder detected some strange signals registering on one of the ship's deep space scanners. I'd do best to let Lieder tell you what she saw."

Mains nodded at Lieder. She leaned forward and spoke into the holo frame, her image and words being stored ready to be sent across light years of space. Mains knew that they would have great effect.

He still found it difficult to believe them himself.

"I detected traces of ships approaching the Outer Rim, way beyond even where UMF 12 is drifting. My combat suit has… modifications. I've got access to certain forbidden quantum folds that the Company might not… anyway, that doesn't matter. What matters is that at least seven of these traces indicated that they were human. Fiennes ships."

A murmur passed through the crew. Durante raised his eyebrow at Mains. Mains nodded.

"They were traveling at incredibly high speeds," Lieder said. "Certainly faster than any Fiennes ships were ever designed to travel, and perhaps even faster than Arrow ships. My suit CSU identified two of these ships as the *Susco-Foley* and the *Aaron-Percival*, both of which left the Sol System centuries ago. None of these ships were ever meant to return, and each of them carried tens of thousands of colonists in cryo-suspension. With Xenomorphs involved, our fears are…" She trailed off.

"Nurseries," Mains said, leaning in again. "We're afraid that whoever the android is working with, or for, has weaponized the Xenomorphs, and is about to launch an assault on the Human Sphere using old Fiennes ships as nurseries for their new weapons."

The bridge fell silent. Mains knew that this was pure speculation, and that he and Lieder had gone beyond fact and into the arena of supposition, but the facts spoke for themselves.

"Awaiting orders," he said, then he nodded at Durante's comms officer, who turned off the holo frame.

"Fuck," someone said.

"You good to send?" Mains asked. The comms officer nodded, then looked to Durante for confirmation.

"Let it fly," Durante said. "Then we'll fill in our friends here on what's been happening while they've been on vacation with the Yautja. Seems to me our lives are about to get interesting."

# 2

---

# ROMMEL

*Drophole Gamma 123, Outer Rim*
*October 2692 AD*

*Mistress Maloney:*

They have designated it drophole Gamma 123. For the honor of the Rage, once it is taken I will pronounce it as Drophole One. We're closing in, mere hours away from our target, and now our war truly begins.

All my troops are ready. More than two thousand are hatched, with ten times that many in reserve. They're vicious and fearless, deadly and expendable, and that's why we are unbeatable and unstoppable. No one has ever had an army like this.

Today we make history.

Tomorrow we begin to rewrite it.

Your General,
Rommel

Another one completed.

Captain Nathan McBrain was a record breaker. At seventy-seven years old, he was at an age when most people might consider easing back on their work and taking on other ventures. Some might choose exploring.

One such group was called the one-wayers, elderly space travelers who cashed in all their credits and sold any possessions to purchase a ship of their own and blast off into the void. A class of ship had been manufactured especially for these people. They were cheap and flimsy, not necessarily built to last, but liable to outlast their new owners. Much of the cheapness came from their drives, solid-fuel boosters lacking any real control systems.

Choose a target area in the sky, aim, burn the fuel until it failed—which usually took less than a standard day—and then cruise at that speed forever. Many saw it as a form of suicide, but for those one-wayers who chose this life, it was the bravest form of space exploration, because there was no way back. A true voyage of discovery.

Others settled somewhere out in the Sphere, buying an apartment on a commercial station or settlement, often spending time writing of their adventures or staring at the stars and dreaming of new ones. It was a way of slowing their pace, almost shutting down, settling at last and letting death catch up with them.

A few might decide to return to the place of their birth, but McBrain hadn't been back to Earth in over sixty years, and he had no intention of returning there now. If anything, and if the Company sanctioned it, he'd be keen to travel another five years beyond the Rim to build, commission, and activate drophole Gamma 124.

As captain of the Titan ship *Gagarin*, he was responsible for Gamma 113 to 123, eleven dropholes constructed across a forty-year career. Dedication to his mission meant that he'd never married or had children, though there had been relationships with members of the crews who came and went. He'd spent his whole life working to expand the Outer Rim and further the human desire to explore. He hadn't done it for fame or fortune. McBrain was simply a man who liked to explore, and a captain who loved his job and was proud of what he had achieved.

"Final checks should be complete in two days," Clintock said. He was systems manager, a small, intense man who often surprised with his cutting humor. "But it's looking good. All systems green. Containment fields at max, fuel pods secure, dark matter stable."

"Good, good," McBrain said. Clintock carried on talking, running through a series of checks and reports that McBrain had heard a thousand times before, so he let his attention drift. He allowed himself that, from time to time, and now more than ever he thought he deserved it. He'd built up a superb team around him over the past decade—this was the third drophole they'd completed together—and even though he knew that all of the checks were essential, he also knew that if there was something amiss, they'd have all been made aware of it by now.

Hell, they might have been *dead* by now.

Relaxing back in his chair, he enjoyed looking through the *Gagarin*'s vast bridge window at what he and his crews had achieved. Around him, the murmur of conversations was muted, the lighting low. Each of the fourteen-member bridge crew was lit from his or her screen.

When pulled together for interstellar travel, the *Gagarin* was a huge vessel composed of unique parts that combined to make the whole. But when they were stationary, working in a single location as they had been for the past four months, those disparate sections were spread over twenty spherical miles of space. They ranged from the main *Gagarin* control center—incorporating the bridge, repair port, and the main quarters for most of the scientists and construction staff—to the four small craft that orbited the newly completed drophole structure itself. There were storage vessels, tugs, a hospital ship, welfare centers for the crews, a green dome for growing their food, two recreation blocks, and a score of smaller craft involved in the maneuver and construction processes.

Right now the larger ships were all on station between *Gagarin* and the drophole, smaller ships flitting back and forth carrying crew and supplies to various places. With the drophole successfully commissioned and days away from first drop, it would soon be time to draw the main craft together again. More than forty docking procedures would be overseen by the *Gagarin*'s AI computer Yuri, and then the ship would be whole once more.

McBrain felt the calm satisfaction of a job well done, but also the curious fluttering in his stomach at the prospect of another couple of years' travel to the next proposed location.

Further away, orbiting the site at various points and distances, were the Colonial Marines' ships. There were always two ships on station with a Titan as standard, providing escorts and protection for the vast drophole-building ships. McBrain had been reminded on countless occasions of the value of his charge, running into billions of credits, and he had always felt comfortable with the military presence.

It was rare that Marines and Titan crews ever crossed paths.

There were isolated cases over the past few decades of Titan ships being attacked by pirates, Yautja, or elements of Red Four when the anti-Weyland-Yutani terrorist group had an active presence across the Rim, but the *Gagarin* herself had never been subject to an attack or problem requiring military assistance. Any internal problems were dealt with by McBrain and his supporting officers.

He knew that his career had been blessed. He'd heard of other Titan ships being destroyed when their dropholes went into meltdown at initiation, suffering cataclysmic damage from asteroid impacts, becoming infested with exotic vermin, or even being selected as a staging ground for Yautja hunts.

There had been the case of one ship, the *Peake*, being chased along the Rim by a determined band of pirates, their stolen vessels proving a match for the Colonial Marine escorts. The Titan ship itself was broken down and the constituent parts were used as weapons against the aggressors.

McBrain had read the *Peake*'s captain's famous account, *A Year of Hell*, and although he admired what she and her crew had eventually achieved, he sought no such adventures. The *Peake* had lost half of its eight-hundred-person crew during that year, and many of those left alive were permanently damaged by the events. They were scientists and spacefarers, not soldiers.

So six Colonial Marine ships patrolled around the *Gagarin* and Gamma 123. Over the past couple of months there had been reports of Yautja attacks across this sector of the Outer Rim, and the Marines were constantly on a war footing. There had also been a series of attacks within the Human Sphere—sabotage assaults that had resulted in some horrific disasters and loss of life. He was troubled by this, but comforted by the additional security sent their way. The ships cruised anywhere up to ten thousand miles around Gamma 123, and any aggressors entering the region would be dealt with long before they reached the *Gagarin*.

Beyond the spread of ships and service vessels, the

drophole itself presented a vast, awesome spectacle.

McBrain never tired of viewing the end product of their mammoth efforts.

The drophole was a complete circular unit, more than two miles in diameter and comprising fifty thousand tons of diamond-filament compound. The factory that manufactured the compound was one of the *Gagarin*'s largest units, and he could see the blocky vessel now, seven miles to starboard and buzzing with activity as the decommissioning process was finalized. At its maximum production speed, its output was phenomenal—a thousand tons of the super-hard material spewing from its egress ports each day. The compound was gathered by catcher-ships, then transported to the drophole frame and molded into place.

The drophole glimmered in starlight. Diamond-filament was used because, apart from trimonite, it was the hardest compound known to man. A pleasing side effect of its use was its reflective properties, catching starlight and casting it out again. On rare occasions, and if caught at just the right angle, the entire circular surface of a drophole glowed like a rainbow.

At five locations around the drophole frame were the bulkier containment blocks. These were the real guts of the device. They housed the heavy containment fields behind which science and mystery collided. McBrain had never pretended to truly understand how the dropholes worked. Indeed, he'd heard it said that only a dozen people in the Human Sphere even came close to understanding. What he did know was that the containment fields were the most important aspect of the whole drophole's construction.

If they failed, the anti-matter they contained would interact with matter, and cause a cataclysmic explosion.

Since the early days of this arcane technology, more than a thousand dropholes had been built and commissioned. Around a hundred had failed to initiate, for reasons that were never quite clear. Scores had ended in tragedy. With the accelerated expansion and ever-growing reach of the Human Sphere, a dozen Titan ships had been lost in the last century alone when the dropholes they were building suffered failure.

It was a risky career.

McBrain comforted himself with the idea that if a containment field ever did fail, on a project he was overseeing, he wouldn't know anything about it. He and his entire crew would be vaporized before knowing anything was wrong.

"Boss?"

"Eh?"

"Sorry, boss," Clintock said, "I didn't realize it was time for your afternoon nap."

"Smartass."

Clintock smiled. "I said, we're ready for the first drop." He peered out through the viewport. "Another one bites the dust, eh, Nathan?"

"Yeah. We live to build another day."

They stared at the circular structure in the distance. At present it held nothing within its circumference, and through it they could see stars. But when initiated it would turn dark—black as infinity—and to drop through would be to travel light years.

"Have they told us which will be the first ship to use it?" McBrain asked.

"Not yet," Clintock said. "Probably a Colonial Marine ship, as usual."

"And why not," McBrain said. "They're here to take the risks."

"They're paid a shitload more than us, too."

"Still saving your credits?"

"Of course. I don't want to be out here at the ass end of nowhere when I'm your age, boss." He grinned wryly. "No offense."

"None taken." McBrain stood, groaning as his stiff knees clicked, and then the whole bridge was lit up with the soft blue glow of warning lights.

Other crew members sat up, took crossed feet off of their units, put down mugs of drink, and peered intently at their monitors and screens.

A holo screen unfolded from the ceiling and dropped down in front of McBrain's control suite, and the wide viewing windows around the bridge grew dark.

"What is it?" McBrain asked.

"We've got a ship just dropped out of warp nearby," Ellis said. She was their communications officer, a large, gruff woman who was a priceless part of the team.

McBrain leaned on the back of his seat. Clintock turned off the warning chimes, and the whole bridge went silent. In the holo screen before him, a schematic of their area of space appeared. At first the *Gagarin*, the drophole, and its attendant ships filled the screen, then they rapidly shrank as the surrounding space was plotted. *Gagarin* remained at the center, becoming little more than a green dot, gently glowing.

Blue specks circled farther out, indicating the locations of the six Colonial Marine ships. Two of them were already accelerating across the screen toward the upper right corner, and as they went a red dot appeared.

"Ellis?" McBrain asked.

"Hang on, boss," she said. "I'm getting some info now but it's... er..."

"Spit it out," he said, but he already knew the answer.

The other crew around the bridge gave her their full attention, anxious to hear what she had to say. McBrain knew what they were thinking.

*Yautja? Here?*

The marines guarding Gamma 123 had informed him of the ceasefire agreement that had been reached some weeks ago, but that didn't guarantee that the attacks wouldn't continue. He knew little of the Yautja, other than what was found in the materials provided by the Company. And that wasn't much. As a species they were unpredictable, violent, and still mysterious after all this time.

"Right," Ellis said, breaking the silence. "Well, it's a big ship, dropped out of warp just over one million miles away. Computer has recognized the ship's drive trail but... it doesn't make any sense."

"What doesn't?" he asked, frustration giving his voice an edge.

"Boss, it's a vessel called the *Susco-Foley*."

"Never heard of it."

"I doubt anyone here has. It's a Fiennes ship, launched from Sol orbit in 2216."

"A Fiennes ship?" Clintock echoed. "What the hell's it doing here?"

"Those ships never had warp drives," someone else said.

"It's got to be a mistake," McBrain said. "Yuri, can you confirm?"

The ship's computer coughed as if to clear its throat, an affectation that McBrain usually found endearing, but which now was annoying.

"Yes, Nathan," Yuri responded. "Everything indicates the ship is indeed the *Susco-Foley*, though it appears larger than that original craft, and there are embellishments."

"Embellishments?"

"The warp wave it threw ahead of its arrival seems to suggest it was traveling at warp-30."

A gasp went around the bridge.

"Well that *is* a mistake, then," McBrain said. "No human ship can travel that fast, much less one that was built four and a half centuries ago." Even the Arrow-class Excursionist vessels could only hit warp-15.

He watched the big holo screen before him, as the same image was thrown on other screens around the bridge. Four of the six Colonial Marine vessels were heading on an intercept course, closing on the pulsing red dot that moved closer to the *Gagarin* with every breath.

"Any comms between them and the Marine ships?" he asked.

"Only going one way," Ellis said. "The Marines are hailing, but there's no response."

The four military ships edged closer to the *Gagarin*, forming a protective shield. They would be ready to lay down staggering firepower if the need arose.

"What the hell is this?" McBrain muttered.

"It's not Yautja," Clintock said. "They've never been seen in a ship that big."

"Don't they steal and modify tech as well as building their own?" Ellis asked.

"I don't know," McBrain said. "But it's nothing to worry about. The Marines have got this." Watching the blue specks converging ahead of the mysterious new arrival, he only hoped it was true.

A transmission crackled over their loudspeakers.

"*Gagarin*, this is Blue One. You there, McBrain?"

"I read you, Vicar." Blue One was the Marines' command ship, a destroyer captained by a woman he had never met. Upon arrival, Lieutenant Vicar had told him that he and his crew were safe with her, and there had been very little contact since. That was more than four months ago.

"You'll have seen our new arrival," the voice continued. "We're closing, and attempting to make contact."

"Roger that," he said. "You know that ship's nearly five hundred years old, don't you?"

Vicar didn't reply for a few seconds.

"That has to be a glitch in our computers."

"All of them?"

More silence, filled with the white noise of space.

"Stand by," Vicar said. "Make sure—"

Without warning her voice was cut off. At the same time, one of the blue specks on his holo screen winked out of existence.

"What was that?" McBrain asked, raising his voice without meaning to. "What happened?" His heart was beating faster, not from fear but with uncertainty. He liked to know what was happening. He liked his ducks in a row. "Hello? Lieutenant Vicar?"

"Connection's failed," Ellis said. Then she pointed. "Look."

The second blue dot swerved away from the newly arrived ship. McBrain and everyone else on the bridge saw a dozen smaller red specks separate from the intruder, and give chase.

"More ships?" he asked.

"Think so," Clintock said. "Nathan, what's happening?"

"I think we're watching a battle," he said. His heart fluttered, and his stomach clenched. "Signal all *Gagarin* components," he said. "Tell them to scatter."

"Really?"

"Really! Are you seeing this?" He pointed at the holo screen. The Marine ship weaved and spun, and three of the pursuing red dots blinked out. The other Marine vessels closed around the drophole and the *Gagarin*, and formed a protective shield, but he knew their crews would be witnessing the same events. The marines had just seen their commanding officer killed, along with her crew.

"They're now less than half a million miles away," Ellis said. "Closing fast."

The second blue dot disappeared.

"Oh, shit," someone said. McBrain looked around, catching Clintock's eye and sharing a worried glance.

"Pirates?" Clintock asked. "Red Four?"

"Red Four have never done anything like this," someone else on the bridge replied. "No, this is something else."

More red dots swarmed ahead of the main ship, closing rapidly on the *Gagarin*.

"Screen view," McBrain said. The panoramic viewing windows all around the bridge faded from pale to black, speckled with stars and offering a wide field of vision once more, out toward the drophole.

Two of the Colonial Marine ships immediately leapt into view, closing on the drophole and taking positions either side of it.

*Of course*, McBrain thought. *They'd protect that over us.* He held no bitterness, because he knew that these troops were following Weyland-Yutani orders. The drophole, now established, was far more important than the men and women who had traveled so far and worked so hard to build it.

To the right of the bridge, in the direction of the approaching ship, there was nothing to see.

"Distance?" he asked.

"Two hundred thousand miles," Ellis said.

The last two Marine ships were out there, swinging around to intercept the approaching vessel and the smaller ships that had fallen away from it. McBrain thought they must have been fighter craft or drones.

"Everyone to lifeboats," he said. "Send the signal."

"But we're protected!" Clintock said.

"We've just seen two of our protectors blown to atoms," McBrain said. "Send the signal."

Ellis didn't question. She broadcast the signal to abandon ship, and Yuri took it up and ensured that it was distributed and heard throughout the *Gagarin*'s fleet.

McBrain felt sick. His legs were shaking.

Something an old colleague and lover once said came back to him, as her haunting words had from time to time over the past two decades. Miriam Lane was dead now, killed in a drophole disaster fifty light years around the Sphere. She had always seen their work as pushing frontiers, and one night after a few drinks, lying with her head on McBrain's chest, she'd waxed philosophical.

*"That's the trouble with what we do,"* she'd murmured. *"We're moving so quickly that we don't appreciate what we've passed, and don't fear what might be ahead. One day something will notice us."*

"We've been noticed, Miriam," he whispered, and then they saw the first of the ships.

It must have been the largest vessel, the one identified rightly or wrongly as the Fiennes ship *Susco-Foley*. It began as a speck in the void, just another star, but its slight movement set it apart.

It grew.

"You should go," he said to the others on the bridge, but every man and woman remained there with him, staying at their stations. There was nothing they could do—Titan ships had never been armed, and the *Gagarin* didn't even possess any hull shielding—but it was important that the lifeboats, once launched from the components, were tracked and noted. Yuri would do much of that, but his crew felt that they also needed some element of control.

McBrain's eyes burned, but he did not cry.

One of the two Marine ships beyond the *Gagarin*, a destroyer, darted out toward the approaching vessels. There was no hailing now, and no hesitation. This was combat.

A dozen smaller craft came into view ahead of the *Susco-Foley*, twisting and jumping, releasing ordnance that flared and streaked toward the destroyer. Most of it exploded far away, hit by the ship's defensive lasers, but some got through and exploded close to its hull, sending the Colonial Marine vessel into a spin.

It must have fired in retaliation. Several of the small aggressor's craft bloomed into glaring clouds of gas before fading away.

The *Susco-Foley* was close enough to see clearly now, and as it slowed it released four other craft, bulging ships that rolled across the space between them.

The Marine ship was spinning, spewing atmosphere and leaving a glittering trail of wreckage behind it. If anyone was left alive on board, they must have aimed the ship into a suicide path, but even before it was ten miles from the attackers it blew apart, struck by one of the smaller drones.

The second Marine ship powered up and rocketed toward the *Susco-Foley*, releasing a jagged field of dancing light as its particle beam modulator kicked in. The beam crossed paths with the Fiennes ship.

Nothing happened.

The Marine ship banked below the enemy, and then exploded, smearing across half of their field of vision as its mini-nukes ignited.

"Four down," Ellis said. Everyone else was hushed.

The remaining enemy drones streaked in. McBrain wished he could reach out and grasp them, hold them back, crush them to nothing, but he could only watch as the first of them slammed into the *Gagarin*'s medical ship and exploded.

There were already a dozen lifeboats dropping away as it struck, and the flaming ship expanded to swallow them all.

"Oh, no," a woman said. A man was crying. Others were panicked, asking what they should do, what *could* they do?

"Nothing," McBrain said. It broke his heart. They had always looked to him.

Another drone struck the green dome and turned it into a boiling mass of yellow and red. Two more ships were struck, the drones exploding, ships breaking up and expanding beneath rapidly blooming clouds of super-heated gases and debris. Wreckage spun and collided, several wreckage fields quickly overlapping and causing a chain reaction of destruction between the main body of the *Gagarin* and the drophole.

The two Colonial Marine ships at the drophole swooped in and started firing. They concentrated their efforts on one of the four globular, rolling ships, and it came apart in a hail of mini-nukes, adding to the carnage.

The *Susco-Foley* moved closer—much closer now, swinging into a crude orbit around the battle and opening up with laser arrays and more drones. The two Marine ships swerved and switched direction, working together to cover each other's attacks and retreats.

The command deck shuddered. Debris started smashing against the *Gagarin*'s main control ship. The impacts shivered through the craft, and several faces turned McBrain's way, scared and seeking succor he could not offer.

This was it. They had all been in space for many years,

but none as long as him. Danger was ever-present, and everyone had experienced the terror of dying out here, of being sucked out of a ship and into the cold, airless void. McBrain had officiated at over thirty deep space funerals, always wondering at the amazing journey the dead bodies were about to undertake. Perspective was sometimes difficult to maintain.

"I'm sorry," he said, loudly enough for the crew to hear him.

One of the rolling ships smashed through clouds of debris and came close, hatches opening in its side and dozens of smaller, sleek missiles dropping toward the *Gagarin*. McBrain didn't see them impact, nor did he feel them.

"Clintock?" he asked.

"Airlocks," Clintock said. "All seven have been activated from outside."

"We're being boarded," McBrain said.

"By who?" Ellis asked.

"Visuals," McBrain said. "Show me the lobbies and corridors around those airlocks."

The holo screen folded open again, and a three-dimensional image appeared before him. An empty corridor. Lights flickered. Activation lights glimmered above the double airlock door, and as they hissed and opened a burst of pressurized air billowed out, condensing on the metal walls.

Behind it, a shape emerged. Something dark and spider-like, vicious, nightmarish. It darted along the corridor, and many others followed.

"Xenomorphs," McBrain whispered in disbelief. He'd heard stories about these beasts, but had hoped and prayed never to meet one himself.

His prayers had been ignored.

As the last of their Colonial Marine escorts exploded into atoms, and the first of the screams came over the comms from elsewhere in the ship, McBrain stared through a sea of fire, debris, and death at the drophole.

Wishing his way back home.

*Mistress Maloney:*

Drophole One is in our control.

The battle was quick and easily won. We lost one attack ship containing two hundred soldiers and their handlers, but the enemy lost far more. Six Colonial Marine ships put up some initial opposition, easily overcome. The main constituents of the Titan drophole builder were destroyed. I stand now on the main flight deck of the Titan ship *Gagarin*. The people here are dead, weak flesh rent and torn by our soldiers. The captain is in his seat, stomach opened, skull smashed, brain scattered. None of them appear to have put up a fight. This is going to be easy.

Soon, once some superficial damage to my ship has been repaired, I will prepare our first drop into the Human Sphere. I am paving your way, Mistress Maloney.

I know I am an android, but I feel so… happy.

Your General,
Rommel

# 3

## VICTIMS

*Gamma Quadrant, Various Outer Rim Locations*
*October 2692*

*They're bombing us!*

Private Dan Mann sprinted with his platoon, dashing from the facility toward the beach. The dunes were low, but the sand was loose, and even though his combat suit augmented his strength through successive compression and loosening, he was already tiring. They were told that the atmosphere of Priest's World was perfectly breathable, much cleaner than Earth's and richer in oxygen, but that didn't feel the case right now.

"Incoming!" Sergeant Golden shouted. "Mark your targets!"

"Incoming?" Mann responded. "They're fucking *bombing* us! What is this, the twentieth century?"

"Don't be fooled," Golden said. "Expect the unexpected."

They hit the beach just as the first of the bombs impacted five hundred yards from shore.

*Good*, Mann thought. *Not only are they using outdated*

*weapons, they're also shitty shots.* He and the rest of his platoon from the 13th Spaceborne—the MudSerpents— spread along the beach and took up defensive positions. The ship banked sharply and accelerated up and away, the last of its bombs tumbling from their bay and spiraling down to splash into the white-tipped waves far out from shore.

Crouched down behind a low dune, Mann braced himself for the first of the detonations.

His com-rifle was light and loaded, all systems green and fully fired up. He had six plasma grenades on his belt, full charges for laser and nano-shot, and an old Glock 17 tucked into his right boot. He called that his "Last Chancer." Most marines had a non-tech weapon, backup in case their suit's CSU failed, com-rifle broke, or they ran out of ammo.

Mann felt good, and set against a combat soldier of the twentieth century, he was a nuke compared to a hand grenade.

He was fascinated with military history, and on Priest's World he'd had plenty of times to study. The twenty-first century, still the most destructive of humankind's existence, was his personal area of expertise. This carpet-bombing method was from way back then, over six hundred years ago.

"Where are the explosions?" Mourhanda asked. She crouched to his left, lithe and strong. Always ready for a fight, she glanced his way. "The fuck you looking at?"

Mann grinned and looked back out to sea, just as the second assault ship powered toward them from the horizon.

Priest's World's defense satellites had detected the big ship dropping out of warp just over an hour before. The maneuver had been dangerously close to the planet, and with no visiting craft expected for at least the next three months, the facility's alarms rang long and loud. Especially when the ship had released two smaller craft that had instantly dropped into the atmosphere and headed for Langelli.

The community of Langelli Station served two purposes. First, it comprised a research facility for a colony of Company scientists undertaking a delicate and sensitive study of Priest's World's flora and fauna. This was also the nearest planet to drophole Gamma 34, and as such the staging post for the defensive Marine contingent and tech crews. The drophole had been established for more than three years, the Titan ship that built it even now on its ongoing journey beyond the Outer Rim to the site of the next intended hole, eleven light years distant.

Gamma 34 was a billion miles from Priest's World, the drophole partially supported by a small orbiting station half a million miles distant. Being so close, Priest's World was the most logical and cheapest place to house the bulk of those assigned to protect and maintain the amazing piece of technology.

An orbiting space platform, connected to Priest's World's equatorial region by a space elevator, was the launching point for journeys to and from Gamma 34. Once up to speed, a trip rarely took more than a standard day. A little over nineteen minutes ago, the station had been attacked and all communications lost.

A scout party on the planet's night side had reported seeing a brief flare of destruction just above their southern horizon, and no contact could be made with the space elevator's support teams.

"Heads up!" Sergeant Golden shouted. A gruff bastard, he'd been Mann's sarge for over eight years. He'd passed over selection for the Excursionists, saying that he preferred to keep his feet on rock as much as possible. As such, this posting suited him well. His brother had become an Excursionist a dozen years before, and six months earlier his unit had been one of the first to face combat in the recent Yautja incursion. He'd been injured but survived, and the sarge had displayed an unaccustomed sensitivity when telling the platoon about his brother's exploits.

With the brothers more than fifty light years apart, it must have felt like infinity.

The second ship disgorged its cargo, the falling objects also splashing into the sea hundreds of yards from shore. They looked streamlined and sleek, but not quite uniform.

"What the hell…?" Mann said.

The bombs dropped by the attacking ships resurfaced. They bobbed in the swell, a few of them riding breaking waves. Mann squinted, then instructed his suit to give an enlarged view.

As he took in a breath to swear, the sarge started issuing orders.

"Mark your targets! Xavier, message HQ and tell them what we're seeing here. Those weren't bombs. Repeat, those *were not bombs!*"

"They're changing," Mourhanda said. "I swear some of them are swimming toward us. It's like they're alive."

"They *are* alive," Mann said. "Xenomorphs."

Mourhanda looked at him, shock in her expression. They were friends, close companions, and they had fought together side by side several times, watching each other's backs. But they had never been forced to fight anything like this.

As if at a signal, the fallen objects started surging toward the beach. Sleek shapes became spiked, sharp silhouettes, slashing at the water, churning through it, turning the swells into white, violent waves.

Mann's suit projected a firing grid across his field of

vision, connecting with the rest of his platoon's suits to establish the most efficient firing solution. His own targets flowed red in the grid, and he hefted his rifle and locked on.

"Open up!" the sarge bellowed, and Mann squeezed the trigger.

A barrage of laser fire slashed out from the beach across the waves, impacting the Xenomorphs surging across the water's surface and tearing many of them to pieces. Three of the four creatures in Mann's target grid went down, splashing hard and then seemingly bursting apart in the aggravated surf. The fourth moved more rapidly, zigging and zagging, and he let it have a burst of nano-shot. The explosions starred the air around it and blew it to smithereens.

Many of the creatures were already dead, their toxic insides bubbling across the sea's surface for five hundred yards in both directions along the shore. Steam rose, water boiled and spat, and only a few shapes still moved forward.

Three of them reached the beach and ran at the platoon. Two went down quickly. The third smashed into the side of a sand dune to avoid laser shot, then quickly burst from the other side, lashing out and catching a marine across the chest with its tail. The man went down, and the Xenomorph was on him, pressing him into the sand and smashing into his chest with its extruding teeth.

It hissed a triumphant roar, then it and its victim's corpse were engulfed in a plasma flare. Mann's suit darkened his visor to protect him from the harsh light. He hadn't seen who the victim was, but he must have ignited his belt of plasma grenades during his final moments.

They'd lost a colleague but countered the attack, shooting down the Xenomorphs and emerging triumphant after just a five-minute battle. He'd heard such horror stories about these things, and they were certainly nightmarish to look at, but an overgrown lizard-thing was no match for the concentrated firepower of a MudSerpent's com-rifle.

"Sarge, those ships are coming around again!" Mourhanda shouted.

This time they arrowed toward Langelli Station from inland. Heavy pulse-blasts thumped up from the base, the streaking yellow shot ricocheting from the ships and arcing off across the sea.

"They're shielded!" someone shouted. More pulses powered upward, but the ships drew closer without deviation, rolling like giant thrown balls. The first craft dropped a line of dark shapes that straddled the facility, the sounds of impact clearly audible from several hundred yards away.

"Froggy will take care of them," Mann said, referring to Lieutenant Frogwhich and the other three platoons of Spaceborne housed at the base. Sure enough, the sounds of ordnance discharges and explosions soon drifted across the breeze. Laser glare and plasma flashes lit the dusky sky above the station.

The ship then curved smartly around and dropped another line, and another, each stick of projectiles comprising at least fifty dark shapes.

The second ship closed on them.

Mann raised his rifle and aimed. He selected nano-shot. The craft was too high for rifle fire to have much effect, but when its bay doors opened and a cloud of Xenomorphs tumbled down, he opened up, taking out several of them as they fell.

There were many more than before. They landed in explosions of sand and dirt, quickly forming into lines of twenty creatures or more that closed on the platoon like extending fingers. Take out the first one and the second moved into its place... and so on, and on.

Rifles barked and spat. Xenomorphs went down and burst apart. The air was hazed with the stench of their acidic insides. Sand melted into slicks of fluid glass. Grasses dried by the sun and the sea breeze burst into flames.

The marines began to take casualties. Two went down when a Xenomorph burst through a dune in front of them, its tail lashing out, hands grappling, head slamming down, teeth grinding. Another marine shot a beast with a fan of laser fire, then went in close to finish the job. There was no time to draw breath and shout a warning before the fallen attacker burst apart, showering the marine with a haze of acid. Her suit's protective elements malfunctioned and it melted away, skin and flesh bubbling, her scream cutting through the air.

A laser blast saved her from a wretched end.

"Who the *fuck* is *that*?" Mourhanda shouted, and Mann followed her gaze.

Standing in the hovering ship's open bay door, looking down on the chaos unleashed below, was a man. A human, perhaps, but then maybe not. Humanoid for sure. He raised a hand and moved it left to right.

As he did, the Xenomorphs attacked en masse.

"Fall back!" Sergeant Golden ordered, just as one of the creatures leapt for him, slashing his combat suit across the stomach and spilling his guts in the sand. He fought it off, shooting, punching, and as he retreated the monster stood on his guts and pushed.

"Sarge!" someone screamed.

Fire seared up from Langelli toward the enemy ships, but it was ineffectual. As the two vessels drifted around the base in a slow circle, heavy cannons emerged from their hulls, pouring fire down.

Mann realized the sickening truth.

"There's nowhere to fall back to!" he said, stunned. Behind them, Langelli Station began to burn.

From triumph to disaster, the course of the battle changed in a matter of moments. He and Mourhanda stood back-to-back, rifles blasting and sizzling, lobbing grenades and ducking as the plasma blasts rolled over them. To Mann's left was the sea. It was awash with drifting slicks of bubbling acid from the first wave of attackers they had destroyed. Deadly, toxic, each wave sizzled onto the sand and melted it into sticky molten glass, and he realized that the initial assault had been nothing more than a preparatory run. The acid waters cut off their escape route.

A wave crawled up the beach and he stepped aside, narrowly avoiding the water that washed over his boots. The receding waters deposited something on the smooth, dark sand close to his left boot.

It looked like a portion of a dead creature's hide.

Some letters were stamped on it, and they made little sense. When Mann finally understood what they spelled, they made no sense at all.

*Montgomery*.

To his right the beach was darkened by the spilled blood of his colleagues.

Past the beach, beyond the dunes, a cloud of smoke boiled on pillars of fire as Langelli Station blazed.

One of the enemy ships rolled in to drop another line of Xenomorphs.

"Too many of them!" Mourhanda shouted, panic in her voice.

"We've still got ammo," Mann said. "Let's make it count."

For a while, they did.

* * *

She could not believe her eyes. Maria Grizz was used to flights of fantasy, because she had spent her life looking for the most amazing, outlandish, and bizarre stories from all manner of spacefarers. She had interviewed Colonial Marines and indies, space tug pilots and asteroid miners, settlers on distant worlds and those who had never traveled further than a near-Earth orbit. She had conducted a series of features on the Arcturus settlers, before they renounced humanity entirely.

Perhaps her most celebrated series had been a session of first-contacts, in which she and her production crew traveled to distant worlds to attempt communication with diverse, non-sentient species. Serious scientists had claimed the missions as tasteless and shallow, with no real scientific merit. Her audience had quadrupled over the space of a year.

All of these accounts were gathered and broadcast in the most popular quantum fold in history.

At last count, her fold had received over a trillion visits from around five billion distinct individuals. She might have been one of the most famous and celebrated folders in history, but she rarely let that go to her head. She'd started *Out There* for the purest of reasons, after all. To honor her dead husband.

Garth Grizz had been killed sixteen years before while surfing a sand geyser on a small planet sixty light years from the edge of the Human Sphere. He'd been one of history's greatest adrenalin junkies, traveling light years through a dozen dropholes to experience each new, incredible rush. He'd attempted a thousand mile freefall into a gas giant, ridden the Takogo Rapids that spanned between two dwarf planets, and had even attempted to make contact with the Rheldi Crabs of Glenfoul Prime when he heard that their central community lived in a cave system that led deep into the core of their dead world.

She had loved Garth, and sometimes she had gone with him on his crazy adventures, but Maria had always preferred observing rather than taking part. Garth had lived for the rush, and now that he'd gone, Maria continued to thrive on the knowledge.

Watching now, she was already contacting *Out There* and opening a new room, her eye camera taking images, embedded chip extracting information from the AI of the ship on which she traveled.

Three seconds after seeing the first thing land, she felt a flutter of fear in her stomach.

Ten seconds later, she knew that she would soon be joining her husband.

The Xenomorphs had been fired at them as they approached drophole Gamma 43. Only a dozen light years from the Outer Rim, this was as far from home as Maria had ever been, and something about that thought had made her more uncertain about space travel than ever before. *"We're frontier people,"* the ship's captain had told her, and she knew that he meant it. There were stories about Captain Homme. He viewed the law as something that applied to other people, *"Closer people,"* as he put it—those who lived nearer to home, and closer to the generally accepted idea of how things should be.

Out here, Homme was the law.

They should have fled as soon as they saw the big ship orbiting Gamma 43. All that was left of the space station was a debris field.

The Xenomorphs crossed the void. She was the only passenger, and she and the rest of the crew watched on the flight deck. The shapes glittered and glimmered in starlight, and they must already have been dead.

*Mustn't they?*

Impacting the vessel, the very-much-alive Xenomorphs immediately began to scratch at the hull with their heavily spiked limbs, flexing long fingers into creases between hull plates, scoring solid metal with their tails.

"They should be dead," Homme said. "Nothing lives in space. Nothing!" It was true. In over six hundred years of human exploration, no organism had been found able to withstand the cold vacuum of the airless void, other than certain hardy viruses.

"What's that?" Maria asked. "Homme, get your AI to zoom in on their backs."

The ship's computer heard and did so without the captain's command, apparently as eager as the rest of them to discover what might be happening. It chose a creature clinging to one of the ship's booster sheaths, and moments later they could all see it in shocking, unbelievable detail. There were six silvery globes on its back, each the size of a human fist and fixed using thin, clear straps.

"What are those?" Homme asked. "Are they…?"

"Breathing apparatus," Maria confirmed. She closed her eyes. She didn't want to see any more.

Homme and his crew shouted and argued, refuting what they'd seen, swearing at the ship's AI as it offered opinions, but it was Maria who realized what was going on. Perhaps it was her willingness to believe the unbelievable, or her deeply buried hope that she would one day rejoin Garth—beyond where life ended and death began—to embark on their most incredible adventure of all.

"They want the ship," she said. "Whatever controls them, whoever they are, they want us gone and the ship as intact as possible."

"Captain," one of the crew said. "They've started trying to smash their way inside."

"Impossible," Homme said. "They're animals! Get us out of here."

"Powering up," the ship's navigator said. "We'll be ready to leave in…" She trailed off, and frantically checked her instruments. "I've lost all power to flight control. Computer's down."

"Computer?" Homme shouted.

There was no response.

"Hull breach!" another crew member said. "Deck two. Another on deck four."

The ship vibrated. A roar broke through from outside. From elsewhere, something or someone screamed.

Maria Grizz took a final deep breath and hoped that she would die before the Xenomorphs reached the bridge.

Private Moore watched as the Marine ship ahead of his own was taken into the belly of the beast.

The battle had been short and sharp. The enemy had won, blasting two Colonial Marine frigates to atoms and succeeding in boarding the space station that controlled the drophole. News from the station—before all communication ceased—brought the word that they had all feared.

Xenomorphs.

Soon after that, laser fire from the big ship knocked out their engines. He'd heard someone saying it was a Fiennes ship, though he didn't understand how that could be possible. Immediately they were adrift, floating through the debris fields from the destroyed frigates. Somewhere in that debris were people he had known, marines he had fought with, and the woman he had loved.

*Melinda died quick*, Moore thought. That was his sole comfort. As his own death approached, he only hoped that he would be so blessed.

But he was beginning to doubt that.

"What the fuck are they doing?" Troll asked beside him. He was hunkered down and staring through the same window. They watched the big ship maneuver around so that the other sleek, disabled Marine ship was sucked into its open belly. They were so close that they could see everything that happened.

Steadying arms protruded across the large hold and clasped the attack ship. Dark shapes drifted across the hold to land on the ship, crawling across its hull and spreading themselves, turning the silvery hull black.

"What the hell...?" Moore muttered.

"Xenomorphs," Troll said. "Seen 'em before. Heard about them. This is all them I reckon. They've learned to build ships and fly, and—"

"Don't be an idiot," Moore said, but he had to wonder.

The others were gathered at the windows now, watching, because they were also looking at their own doom. They, too, were drifting, helpless and powerless to resist what might come next. The big ship was coming their way.

By the time its door was blown and its atmosphere vented, they were close enough to see shapes moving inside.

The dark shapes hugging its hull streamed toward the open doorway. Laser blasts burst out, shattering several Xenomorphs, their remains floating aside while others crowded in. More weapons discharged. More creatures died, splitting apart and bursting outward.

Then weight of numbers forced them inside.

Against one of the small viewing ports, something splashed red.

"That's us," Moore said. "Five minutes from now, maybe ten. That's us."

"They want the ships," Troll said. "That's why they

haven't blown us to nothing. Kill us, take the ship—"

"Computer!" Moore asked, but it was still offline. *Everything* was offline, and they were as helpless as a finless fish drifting in front of a shark.

"We'll fight," Troll said. The others agreed.

"To the last," Moore said.

They assessed their weapons, loaded, suited up, and then the cabin grew dark as they were swallowed into the huge enemy ship's open hold.

Less than a hundred yards away from them, the other Marine ship was held in place by fluid-like clamps. Its scars were obvious. Its crew members were dead. Xenomorphs exited and drifted toward them.

"Never go without a fight," Moore said.

"We've got grenades," Troll said.

"Let's wait until they're inside. Take plenty of the bastards with us."

Then Moore turned to face the door. Something scratched outside. *Not everyone dies quick*, he thought, and he instructed his com-rifle to prepare a plasma shot.

He closed his eyes, ready to open them again when the door burst out.

# 4

## ISA PALANT

*LV-1657, Drophole Gamma 116*
*October 2692 AD*

The huge Yautja kneels to come down to her level. Isa can smell him. They all have a scent, like cinnamon and fresh meat, but Kalakta's is richer and deeper, as if age makes it so. Milt McIlveen is behind her, the Company man who has also become a friend. Akoko Halley is there too, the major of the 39th Spaceborne who rescued them all from the ruins of Love Grove Base. Both of these people trusted her before when she insisted that the message of understanding and peace needed to be sent to the Yautja. She needs them to trust her now.

She has never been this close to a living Yautja before. Dead, they are intimidating. Alive he is magnificent, exuding power and strength, and she feels sick to the stomach with terror.

*He's come here for this*, she thinks. *He wants to end it as much as we do. This is not our war. Someone else is waging it against us. Someone using Xenomorphs as weapons.*

Kalakta holds her around the back of the neck and

leans in close, so close that she can feel the heavy moisture of his breath and see the sharpness of his well-used, time-chipped tusks. She gags. To puke into the face of this highest-ranking Yautja elder, just at the moment when an accord is being reached between them, might not be the best idea.

She almost laughs at that thought.

She almost cries.

Kalakta makes a noise. It sounds like motors deep in his body beginning to turn, bones grinding together. She frowns, glancing sidelong at McIlveen to see whether their jointly written program is translating his words. McIlveen is looking at the small datapad in front of him, frowning, and he glances across at her just as Kalakta's laughter begins to grow.

*No*, Isa thinks. *No, not like this, we came here for peace, don't do this to us—don't do this to yourselves!*

"No!" she shouts, but it's too late.

The four Yautja accompanying Kalakta act as if on a silent signal. For ceremonial reasons, and as a sign of trust and respect, they have been allowed to bring their weapons into the vast hold of the *Tracey-Jane*. That was a terrible mistake. They disperse, sweeping their spears around to bear, sighting lasers for their shoulder blasters sending jagged beams dancing across the shadowy space.

"*No!*" Isa Palant screams again. She tries to stand, but Kalakta is holding her tighter now. There's no sign of effort in his eyes—he could crush her neck with one clasp of his hand, and will probably do so soon—but there *is* something else. She cannot tell what it is. Isa has allowed herself to believe that she knows something of the Yautja, but the terrible truth hits home along with the first blasting explosion.

She knows nothing at all.

McIlveen's head erupts in a shower of vaporized brain and skull. He remains standing for a moment, then takes one step back before leaning sideways and hitting the deck.

Halley barks an order and her crew start shooting, trying to track the Yautja across the big chamber, firing, missing, shooting again. Two of the aliens have initiated their invisibility cloaks, and now they are little more than shadows within shadows. The only thing that reveals their positions is the shots from their blasters.

A marine screams as she is lifted aloft on a spear, her blood and trailing guts hanging where it emerges from her back.

One Yautja is taken down by laser fire, its torn parts twitching and writhing as if it's still fighting in death.

Kalakta pulls Isa in close to him, lifting his head and holding her face against his chest so that all she can do is hear.

Shooting, explosions, screams and roars, all of it echoing in the huge hold, the cacophony lessening as there are fewer soldiers left to fight, fewer Yautja to fight back.

Eventually the chaos subsides. Isa feels sick. She can hear something inside Kalakta's chest that might be his heartbeat, but could also be the elder Yautja's continuing laughter at the deception he has sprung.

He eases the pressure on her neck and allows her to see.

Two Yautja are still alive. One of them has lost an arm, green blood spattering from the wound. The second is carrying its heavy battle spear in one hand, and Akoko Halley's head in the other, her eyes half-closed and still glistening behind her shattered visor.

They are already taking trophies.

Kalakta speaks, and it is as if she has the translation program in her mind, ready to filter and recite his words.

His voice is deep, and filled with a promise of more pain to come.

"Foolish to believe you can understand," he says. Then he pulls her close as his mouth opens wider, his sharp tusks scarred with age, his head tilting back as his breath washes over her—

"More nightmares," a voice said, pulling her from a troubled sleep. "They'll stop soon."

Isa gasped and sat up in the cot. Dread and relief washed through her, a strange mix.

"You can cure nightmares?"

The sim-nurse in the holo frame beside her bed smiled. "We can do anything. Now relax, your medicine is on its way. You're on the mend, and you'll be ready for the drophole in two more days. You'll sleep properly then."

"I'm looking forward to it."

The screen went blank. Isa caught her breath, glad for the familiar environment. The Colonial Marine base was everything she'd come to expect of a military installation—efficient, organized, well designed, but gray and sterile. She'd been moved from the medical bay ten days earlier, and her new quarters were small and functional. She had a shower room, a cot, a cupboard.

It was a long way from her complex of labs on Love Grove Base, but that place no longer existed. Svenlap had blown it up, in one of the many acts of sabotage across the Human Sphere that had seemed to precede the Yautja incursion. Despite the presence of an independent security team, many people had died in the explosion and the weeks following, struggling to survive in that inhospitable environment.

The arrival of two Yautja drawn by the explosion had

made matters so much worse. The surviving indies had been itching for a fight.

Akoko Halley and her squad's arrival had brought matters to a head. Sent by Gerard Marshall, one of the Thirteen, specifically to rescue Isa and McIlveen, Halley had arrived just in time. She had also listened when Isa tried to explain why the Yautja were doing this.

They weren't invading the Human Sphere. They were fleeing into it.

Remembering, she sighed and rested back in her bed. An applicator rose from beside the bed and pumped her daily dose of medicines through the skin on her thigh. It tingled, warmed, then faded once more. She'd had many doses now, and every day they were changing where the chemicals were injected. She'd be left with smooth scars in several spots across her skin, but she didn't mind.

Isa might have saved the Human Sphere from war.

McIlveen had mentioned this to her several times, but he lacked the humor and charisma of her old friend Keith Rogers. She'd seen Rogers die when Love Grove Base was blown up, and she missed him now. Sometimes it was his death—and her own personal loss—that helped her comprehend the enormity of what was happening.

Isa stood, dressed, and went to her small cupboard to gather her datapad. It was all that was left from Love Grove Base, and it contained some of her studies. Most of what she had learned over the past few years, however, was kept in her mind, especially now that the labs were gone. Knowledge and experience, postulation, experiment and theorizing—she had built a greater and more complex picture of the Yautja species than anyone else she knew. Isa and Milt McIlveen might have been the two humans most knowledgeable in Yautja habits and behavior.

That she did this for Weyland-Yutani troubled her, but

she would have never come this far without them. Their resources were limitless.

Since her peace conference with Yautja Kalakta of the Elder Clan several weeks ago, she had been on the mend from her injuries. McIlveen had stayed at the base with her, and Halley and her crew had also remained. Halley told Isa that she'd been tasked by Gerard Marshall to protect her at all costs. As one of the Thirteen, the inner council of Weyland-Yutani, Marshall coveted her knowledge, wanting her back in the Sol System as soon as possible. That would necessitate many months of travel and at least thirty drops between dropholes, neither of which she was quite prepared for yet.

Immediately after the peace conference, her head injury had been noticed and diagnosed. She had a bleed on the brain. It was minor, and easily curable, but it meant that any drop might well prove fatal.

A drophole jaunt was risky at the best of times. Because of the almost indecipherable physics that was involved, each traveler had to be held in a suspension pod. Cryo-pods were used for deep space travel, but suspension pods were their smaller cousins, the thick gel contents essentially "freezing" a human's physiology for a short time. Whereas cryo-suspension was like putting someone into a deep, timeless sleep, being immersed in a suspension pod was like holding a breath, or lengthening the period between heartbeats.

If your pod malfunctioned, your journey would feel like forever.

Occasionally after a drop, a faulty pod might be discovered, its inhabitant dead and seeming to have aged decades in the space of just a couple of hours. There were accounts of damaged pods being opened to find wretched corpses floating in rancid gel, mouths open in endless screams, fingernails torn out, finger bones snapped, and the interior of the pod scored with nail marks.

Over the centuries of drophole travel stories had sprung up of people who had decided to remain awake, eager to experience what happened to their consciousness during a drop. Isa didn't believe it, as none of the stories could be proved true. Regardless of their veracity, though, all of the accounts shared a single conclusion. If any of the travelers survived, they were in no state to communicate what they had seen.

The journey had driven them mad.

Isa hated suspension and cryo-pods. A drop felt unnatural, like cheating nature, and in her eyes, a cheat was always found out.

Her own injury was identified after the drop to rendezvous with Kalakta and his peace delegation. Investigating the pain the trip had caused her, the medics informed her that she was lucky to be alive. As a result, she'd been staying at the base on LV-1657 while her injuries healed, and Marshall would have to wait. McIlveen and Halley had remained there with her.

In that time, Isa Palant dwelled upon what might come next.

The life she knew was over. She had made a place for herself at Love Grove Base, and found peace. The planet had been brutal, swept by violent storms whipped up by ongoing terraforming, barren and devoid of life apart from the scientists and indies at the base. She had grown to love it. She'd worked under the banner of Weyland-Yutani, but she was far enough away from them to make the work her own. Her parents had never trusted the Company, and that mistrust had passed down to her. But Weyland-Yutani was so huge that her feelings had never become an issue. The Company did not require people's faith in order to persist. What they *did* need was expertise.

So she lent them hers, while in her own mind she was working for herself. Science was her one true love. Passing at least some of her expanding knowledge on to the Company was a small price to pay for the unlimited resources they could provide.

Those resources were gone now, but others had come into play. Akoko Halley, cool and distant, was one of them, and Milt McIlveen was another. Her instinctive dislike of him as a proven Company man had already been dispelled over their short time together, and what they had been through had surely pulled them closer.

The future had become an uncertain place, and that was why she had welcomed this enforced sojourn on LV-1657. It allowed her the opportunity to take stock.

She didn't belong here, but she knew she would have to grow accustomed to the place. It was a military base, through and through, established simply to police and control the drophole built in orbit around the planet's moon, half a million miles away.

*Not exactly warm and fuzzy*, she mused.

Someone knocked at the door.

"Yeah?" she said.

"It's me." Milt McIlveen. Isa felt a rush of relief at hearing his voice, familiarity among so many unknowns.

"You and…?"

"I've got coffee."

"Then why are you standing out there?"

The door whispered open and McIlveen entered, holding a steaming mug in each hand and a foil bag under his arm.

"I've got breakfast, too," he said, "and some news."

They usually ate together in the canteen, often joined by Halley and some of her crew. LV-1657 was manned by a large contingent of the 5th Terrestrials, nicknamed the BloodManiacs, and Halley and her crew didn't mix well with what they called rock-bound grunts. As such they had been spending much of their time on their ship the *Pixie*, sometimes parked on one of the seven landing pads, often out patrolling the system. Their aloofness had forged an uneasy atmosphere at the base, but it didn't worry Isa too much. She and McIlveen were civilians, after all.

"Hit me with it," Isa said.

"The breakfast?"

"No, fool." It felt good to be sparring with McIlveen. It reminded her of her relationship with Rogers, the brash indie who'd shown his gentle, thoughtful side when in her company.

"Oh, good. Although maybe that's a better use of what they serve here."

"Powdered eggs again?"

He handed her the foil bag. She opened it.

Powdered eggs.

"So, the news?" she asked as she took a coffee mug. It smelled divine and tasted better.

"The Yautja are still in-system."

Isa raised her eyebrows. "You know this how?"

"Heard a couple of the BloodManiacs chatting about it in the canteen. Their ship's been orbiting LV-1657, and its moon and the drophole, maybe a billion miles out. Not hiding, flying sub-warp and just sort of... cruising."

"Good," Isa said. She grinned at him. "It's good, isn't it?"

McIlveen nodded and smiled back. They shared the same fascination with the Yautja, and in the weeks they'd been waylaid here they had continued working together. Their translation program was constantly improving. At the peace conference on board the independent research vessel *Tracey-Jane*, she'd interacted directly with Kalakta of the Elder Clan, recording their exchange so that it could be analyzed later. Even by then she had known enough to be able to hold a reasonable conversation with him, and from that came a ceasefire between their species.

Since then, she and McIlveen had taken several significant steps in their understanding of the Yautja language. First, they'd realized that it wasn't one language at all, but several variations of a similar form. It went beyond being simple dialects, differing as much as English deviated from French, with some similar root words and others that were completely different.

Second, Yautja was a constantly evolving language. In their meeting Kalakta had spoken of having interacted with humans before, and in some of his phraseology they'd encountered a hint of human speech—not so much in the words as in their order and usage. Just as it was believed that the Yautja gathered or captured technology from other races or civilizations across the galaxy, so it seemed as if they also adopted and incorporated languages and speech patterns.

"Damn, I wish we could meet them again," she said. She sipped more coffee, contemplating the bland but nutritious breakfast in the bag. Weren't Marines supposed to be well supplied and well fed? Didn't they pride themselves on having great food and support, wherever it was they were based?

Then again, perhaps they considered *this* good food. If so, she'd hate to be present on a Marine ship or base cursed with bad cooking.

"Maybe we will," McIlveen said. "They must be hanging around for a reason."

"It's difficult to try and second-guess the Yautja," Isa

said. Her dream returned to her. With it peace turned to war, triumph to bloodshed.

"Maybe that's where Snow Dog and her crew go, too."

"Don't let Halley hear you calling her that."

McIlveen shrugged.

"So you think they're out there tracking the Yautja?" Isa asked.

"Like you say, can't second-guess them. There might be a ceasefire, even peace, but the Marines won't just be letting them fly around the system without keeping tabs on them."

Isa nodded her agreement. "I wonder if Kalakta's stayed with them," she said, blinking slowly, seeing his mouth open and his tusks ready to impale her face and rip it from her skull. She shivered.

"He got to you, didn't he," McIlveen said quietly, but it was obvious that the elder had got to both of them.

"It's his age," Isa said. "I was so close I could smell his breath, see into his eyes. The only other humans who have ever been that close to him…"

"He's probably got their skulls in a trophy cabinet."

Isa stared into her coffee. "He might be a thousand years old. Might have traveled across the galaxy. We're exploring, pushing further every year. Our tech's advancing too, new ship drives coming online. One day a Titan ship will arrive somewhere to build a drophole, and there'll already be a human colony there."

"That's progress," McIlveen said.

"What *we* think of as progress," she countered. "To the Yautja, we're barely crawling. Sometimes I think we're like deer and they're the lions, coming into the Sphere from time to time just to play." She blew onto her coffee, watching the small ripples and the drifting steam. "The things they've seen."

"So how are you feeling?" McIlveen asked.

"Good. Ready to get off this rock."

"Even if that means starting for home?"

"Home?" Isa asked. The idea surprised her. She'd never really thought of any place as home, because she was most comfortable wherever her studies were, and for more than a decade that had been Love Grove Base. Perhaps it was time for a rethink.

"You know Marshall's not the bad guy here, right?" McIlveen asked.

"Says you."

"I know him. He's one of the Thirteen, sure, but that doesn't make him a bad man."

"The Thirteen, who possess the tech to send instant sub-space comms but don't share it? Think what that could do for people, Milt."

"I don't know anything about that." This was a loaded conversation, strained because it was rare the two of them talked about McIlveen's origins and intentions. Isa believed that he was a good man, and honest. But when on occasion they discussed Gerard Marshall, McIlveen stank of the Company, with all its shady ethics.

"He wants me near because of what I know about the Yautja," she said.

"He wants you *safe*," McIlveen protested. "Who knows what's coming? And you said yourself, we just can't second-guess them. This temporary peace they've agreed to might just be part of a bigger plan."

"You don't believe that."

"No," McIlveen said after a shrug. "Guess not. But you've forgotten more about them than I'll ever know, and that makes you important."

"I swore I'd never return to Earth."

"Things have changed," McIlveen said.

They left her room and walked together across the

base, approaching the recreation block where they spent most of their time. There were comfortable chairs there, decent coffee, and table games they could play when they were turning over differing ideas in their research. Sometimes they walked outside, but LV-1657—though a calmer planet than the one they had left behind—still held its dangers. Terraforming had made the air in this sector breathable, and thousands of square miles of forestry was becoming home to many species of insects and small lizards. Though they were all known and imported, some were very quickly adapting to the environment. Mutations were commonplace, their frequency propelling this new evolution all the faster.

A few species had become hunters. There had already been several deaths from innocent-looking bites, delivered by previously harmless insects that had developed poison glands in their rise to the top of the food chain. It was feared that vermin from visiting supply ships had escaped into the wild, and there was no telling how they were adapting.

Sometimes Isa wondered just what humanity was doing. Exploring was one thing, but in forcing a place to be something it wasn't, maybe they were stamping humankind's poisonous influence across the galaxy.

Perhaps one day, someone or something would object.


Akoko Halley and her DevilDogs were in the recreation block. They were a welcome sight. There was still a distance between them, but she and they had shared experiences at Love Grove Base, and more than one of them had told her that she had saved many lives. Because she was not a Marine, friendship between them would be difficult, yet they held her in visible respect.

Sometimes the politics of human nature confused her.

That was why she loved studying the Yautja so much.

Halley was a cool customer, and one of her crew, Private Bestwick, had told Isa that Halley's nickname was Snow Dog. Bestwick was a small woman, wiry and strong, and she'd smiled as she spoke the name.

"Sometimes cold as they come, but I'd follow her into hell," she'd said.

But Isa liked Halley. As a major in the 39th Spaceborne, this was a strange posting for her, commanding a small ship and an even smaller crew. She was used to having thousands of marines under her command, not five. Yet without Halley there, the broadcast Isa had sent out to all Yautja forces likely never would have been sent. A lieutenant might not have had the gumption to make the call. Halley had everything to lose, but she had made the right decision.

"They say I'll be ready to use the drophole soon," Isa told the marines. "Couple of days."

"Thank fuck for that!" Nassise exclaimed. He and Gove were playing table tennis, and they'd both become pretty good at it. Nassise was a weird character, harsh and distant. He seemed to resent having the time to become good at anything other than being a Marine. "I hate this rock," he added. "Can't wait to get back out there."

"We've been prepping for the trip," Halley said, lounging back on a seat. She was reading an old-fashioned book, and Isa wondered where she'd found it. "I considered using a bigger ship, but the *Pixie* is the fastest vessel available to us right now. It'll still be almost six months, with dozens of drops." She tented the book on her chest. "You sure you're up to this?"

"Up to traveling, or being hauled back to Gerard Marshall?"

Halley glanced away. Isa had seen the same reaction from the Major every time Marshall was mentioned. She disliked him as much as Isa did, and Isa found that comforting. Even unspoken, it seemed to put them on the same side.

"Orders," Halley said. "I mean the journey."

"Yeah, I'm up to it. We could have gone days ago if it had been my decision."

Halley stood and stretched, approached Isa, touched her forehead. "Don't want to damage this precious thing, do we?" Someone chuckled and Isa glanced around. Sprenkel was looking her up and down. She'd never liked the big man, had hardly heard him string more than a few words together. He always seemed animated, even when still—as if filled with something eager to be released. Some Marines were just born for a fight.

"Sprenkel," Halley said, and the big man looked away.

"It's going to be cramped on the *Pixie*," Halley said. "You and your boyfriend can bunk up."

"We're not together," McIlveen said. "It's not like that…"

Halley did not reply. She crossed the room toward the refreshments area, and silence fell, the only sound coming from the regular, hollow impact of the table tennis ball.

Back and forth, back and forth.

"Come on," Isa said, grabbing McIlveen's arm. "Work to do."

"Hey, Palant," Bestwick said. She was sitting in a holo chair, headset on and absorbed in some unseen scenario. "Don't let us get to you. We've been here too long, and we're just twitchy."

"Yeah, thanks," Isa said. "No worries." Gove gave her a smile while returning a curving shot from Nassise. Huyck, Halley's sergeant major, lifted his cap and winked at her, then went back to sleep. Even Halley offered a smile, though it did little to lighten her expression.

Sprenkel examined his fingernails.

"Still, can't wait to get the fuck away from *here*," Nassise said, emphasizing his last word with a vicious shot that bounced way across the room. "Yes! You lose, Gove. Shithead."

Isa and McIlveen left the room without the coffee they'd sought. Isa steered them toward the media room. They could continue their studies there.

"Marines," McIlveen said, quietly.

"Yeah."


The day passed slowly. It was uneventful. They established another variation in Yautja speech patterns, and Isa caught a hint of something intriguing, a verb structure that resembled some forms of an old Celt tongue vanished for almost sixteen centuries, last spoken in one of the old Welsh kingdoms.

She and McIlveen tested the new idea, trying to be objective about it. Isa knew well that she was often too close to her studies, and too passionate about them. Sometimes she feared that she forced ideas to fit the shape she wanted, rather than allowing them to form their own dimensions.

Later that afternoon she went for her usual daily check-up. The medic skipped through the familiar tests, then finished with a holo scan of her brain.

"Looking good," he said. "Give it two more days."

Isa felt nervous. There was such a long journey ahead, with only the Marines and McIlveen for company, and she wasn't sure how she would manage. She was used to her own company in comfortable surroundings. Though she knew the marines respected her and what she'd done, she already felt like an outsider in their midst. She hoped it was just in her head.

And McIlveen? She liked him, but…

That evening the two of them left the base to watch the sunset. The facility was built on a wide plateau above an ancient glaciated valley. Sheltered from harsh easterly winds by a range of snowcapped mountains, the plateau was green and lush, criss-crossed by a network of streams that tipped over the cliffs in a dozen places. A haze of mist often hung above the waterfalls that plummeted into the valley below, and this often produced stunning sunsets. Today was no exception.

The far horizon was smeared orange, streaks of high clouds painted pink by the sinking sun. Closer, rainbow shades shimmered and flowed above the cliff edge, waving and dancing like giant multicolored gossamer wings.

To the south Isa could just make out the pyramidal shapes of the atmosphere processors. They were still working, though where previously they had accounted for most of the oxygen output, they were now far down the list. The vast swathes of new forests had become the lungs of the planet.

The place hadn't even been named, other than the traditional number, LV-1657. Isa found that sad, yet also somehow appropriate. It was as if the planet was still free. Once humans stamped it with a name it would become a destination, and then everything here would change even more than it already had.

"Beautiful," McIlveen said.

"Yeah, and we're leaving it behind."

McIlveen didn't reply. It wasn't his fault that Marshall had called them back to Sol.

Once again she was struck by the idea that she could simply refuse to go. It had taken root some days ago, and she'd wondered why she had never considered it before.

Halley and her DevilDogs had saved their lives, that was true, but she was not beholden to them. She was a civilian, not military. They couldn't order her to go.

But they *could* take her by force. That was what she feared, that she would become a prisoner instead of a passenger. She had no other means to get away from here, nowhere else to go, and no one else alive who might offer her help. She was lonely and lost, and the fact that Milt McIlveen was her only friend spoke volumes.

Sighing, watching rainbows, and dreaming of freedom, she jumped when the siren sounded from the base behind them.

She and McIlveen turned as Bestwick ran toward them through the long grass. She looked agitated.

"Come on," she said. "Back to the base."

"Why?" Isa asked. "What's happening?"

"A ship's dropped out of warp, unexpected and unregistered. It's come from the Outer Rim, and we're getting reports of attacks on several dropholes across the Rim."

*It's beginning.*

Isa's heart started beating faster. The danger the Yautja had been fleeing was here.

"What else?" McIlveen asked.

Bestwick, panting, shook her head. "Something weird," she said. "The ship's very old. Base computer's telling us it's a Fiennes ship called the *Susco-Foley*."

# 5

## GERARD MARSHALL

*Charon Station, Sol System*
*October 2692 AD*

"It's begun," General Paul Bassett said. "It seems as if your Yautja friends might have been telling the truth, after all."

"They're no friends of mine," Gerard Marshall said. As usual in the General's company he felt as if he was being talked down to. Bassett treated him like a child, not one of the Thirteen. He tried not to bristle. Tried not to let Bassett get to him, yet as usual, he rose to the bait.

"I thought it was the Thirteen who made peace with them."

"It was the woman your troops were sent to rescue."

"Well," Bassett said. He mocked without smiling, and looked down on Marshall without saying anything overt. Marshall used to think it was how the General spoke to everyone, a result of his position, or perhaps the way he'd made it that far up the hierarchy. But he didn't think that anymore. Now, he believed it was personal.

Bassett commanded the most powerful military

humanity had ever seen, and he didn't like the fact that the Thirteen were still his superiors.

"So what are we looking at?" Marshall asked. He'd been summoned to the General's command center by a battle droid once again, a second-hand message rather than a personal call. Just one more way of trying to put Marshall in his place.

They stood on a raised walkway above the Colonial Marines' main control globe, the place from which the General controlled his army and, by implication, Weyland-Yutani maintained its control over the whole of the Human Sphere. The Marines had been in its exclusive employ for many decades, a privatized military the only way to grow to its current size and maintain stability. When a company became so large and powerful that it threatened nations and planets, it naturally became the ruling power.

The room was large, fifty yards across, and bustling once again. During the Yautja incursion it had been a hive of activity, and now that same buzz was present. Holo frames floated and glowed, stellar maps zoomed in and enlarged, terminal points drifted back and forth along with their controllers. A non-stop hubbub of subdued voices filled the room, most of them communicating in a language Marshall barely understood.

On one curved wall was a grid of images, flickering as users scrolled through various caches of information contained in the holo files. There were at least thirty blocks in the grid. At present, each file contained an image of a ship of a class and style he did not recognize.

"Fiennes ships," Bassett said.

"Really?" Marshall responded. "From centuries ago? What's your interest in them?"

"Some of them are coming back, and we think

they're carrying an army the likes of which we've never seen before."

"Xenomorphs?" Marshall asked. "Just like the Yautja hinted?" He stared at the changing images. Could it really be true? He tried to sort through the implications—that these ships had been captured, and were being used by some unknown enemy. It made terrible, dreadful sense.

"Yes, the warnings were there, from the Yautja," Bassett said. "I don't trust those bastards for an instant, but we've received a broadcast from an Excursionist unit beyond the Outer Rim. They picked up two survivors from another unit that crash-landed on a Yautja habitat. They've been there for some weeks, hiding from the Yautja. They lost most of their unit, but toward the end of their time there they boarded a ship of unknown origins, docked at the habitat, and found something… strange.

"Come on, I'll show you." He gestured for Marshall to follow him, and they left the control hub together, heading through into Bassett's own huge office and quarters.

Marshall had been here several times over the past couple of months. The most memorable visit had been just after Bassett's pilot son had been killed in one of the rash of sabotage attacks that had appeared to accompany the Yautja incursion. The General had seemed perfectly normal, and then just for a moment his guard had slipped, and Marshall had seen his human side. He still couldn't help feeling sorry for him now, even though Bassett was back to his soldier persona.

Perhaps that was *why* he felt sorry. The man wouldn't even allow himself the time and space to grieve.

They both took seats before a large holo screen and Bassett waved at the controller. An image flickered into view—a man pinned to a wall by a long spear, the bodies of Yautja and Xenomorphs arrayed at his feet.

No, not a man. Not quite.

"I haven't seen an android like that for quite some time," Marshall said.

"This is what Lieutenant Mains found aboard that habitat, in the unknown ship," Bassett said. "He claims the android was controlling the Xenomorphs attacking them, called itself Patton, and that all of the creatures had that name stamped on their hides."

"Controlling them how?"

"Mains doesn't know."

Marshall gazed at the image until Bassett changed it, bringing up a view of deep space.

"Just before they were rescued, Mains and another Excursionist discovered how to use some of the strange ship's controls. Some of them were of human origin. The private accessed some deep space scanners and found evidence of Fiennes ships moving straight toward the Human Sphere, at speeds far greater than they were ever built to achieve."

"I guess it's true what they say," Marshall said. "You reap what you sow."

"And who's sown this?" Bassett demanded. "Do you know anything about this?"

"Me?"

"Don't act surprised. It won't work with me." Bassett seemed tense, alert.

"What's happening out there, Paul?"

"Ships have been dropping out of warp close to dropholes, launching blistering assaults from air and ground, taking control," Bassett said. He sighed and slumped back in his chair. "It's happening all across Gamma quadrant of the Outer Rim. Some of those ships attacking larger outposts are the massive Fiennes ships, heavily armed and adapted for war. Others are less familiar vessels, but they're all loaded with weaponized Xenomorphs."

"My God," Marshall muttered. "Only in Gamma quadrant?"

"No attacks reported so far in the other seven quadrants."

"But where the attacks are taking place, you have Marine units there, don't you?" Marshall asked. "Ever since the Yautja situation?"

"In some places, yes. Other task forces are still en route, leaving some of the dropholes defended only by indies. But it's made little difference."

"So whoever the enemy is, they're winning?"

Bassett stood and strode over to his desk. He picked up a glass and swigged its contents. He did not offer Marshall a drink.

"I'm telling you that we're putting up a fierce resistance," he said, trying to keep his voice even. "But, yes, some dropholes have fallen."

Marshall stood up in shock. "The Human Sphere is under attack."

"And we don't know by whom." Bassett poured himself another drink from a bottle, hesitated, then waved it Marshall's way.

"Drinking on duty?" Marshall asked.

"It's apple juice."

"So what are you doing to counter this?"

"Everything we can," Bassett said. "All of our reserves have been mobilized, across the Sphere. Drophole defensive units will be boosted as best we can, all Colonial Marine units have been made aware, and are on high alert."

"And the Fiennes ships?"

"Breeding grounds, as best we can tell," Bassett said. "Nurseries for the weaponized Xenomorphs. Whoever's attacking us isn't unknown to us—their use of an android is proof of that. They must have gathered the Fiennes ships from across many light years of space, adapted them, and now they're entering the Sphere, causing chaos and many casualties."

"War always leaves casualties, General," Marshall said, "and it always has a winner. Your job is to ensure that winning side is ours."

"I've issued orders to destroy any Fiennes ship on sight," Bassett said. Even he seemed shocked by what he'd said. He looked into his glass, swirled it around, and Marshall wondered just how much he wished it was whiskey. Bassett was far too professional to drink while on duty.

And he was *always* on duty.

"How many people?" Marshall asked.

"The smaller, earlier ships carried around seven thousand in cryo-suspension. As time went on their size and capacity increased. The fifth generation Fiennes ships, the last ones that were sent out around four hundred years ago, carried around forty thousand passengers."

"You can't just wipe them out," Marshall said. "That's—"

"War... and war has casualties." Bassett nodded at the holo screen. "We had a brief burst of confused broadcasts from Langelli Station, a Company facility on Priest's World. They were attacked by the Fiennes ship *Susco-Foley*. Hundreds of Xenomorphs were dropped, and soon after we lost all contact with them. They were guarding and controlling Gamma 34. There have been other attacks, and some battles are ongoing. It looks like a concerted effort by whoever's behind this to take control of dropholes, and that can only mean one thing."

"They want to come deeper," Marshall said.

"Into the Sphere."

The two men stood silently for a moment, both looking into some private, nightmarish distance.

"We can shut them down," Marshall said.

"Are you fucking insane?"

Marshall blinked. He'd never heard Bassett even come close to losing control.

"You can't start shutting down dropholes," Bassett pressed.

"But we have the ability to do so," Marshall said. "If necessary."

"Of course you do," Bassett said, "and only you Thirteen know about it. But if you shut down a hole, you'll leave everyone on the far end trapped there, light years from anywhere. One hole, that's not so bad, but if you shut down a range or network of them... you could be condemning people to die a lonely death in deep space. Without drophole capability, even an Arrow ship would take over thirty years to travel here from the Outer Rim."

"So the Colonial Marines need to do their job," Marshall said.

"And they will," Bassett responded, reasserting his composure. "I was simply apprising you and the Company of the situation."

"Consider me apprised." Marshall stood to leave, expecting with every step toward the door to be summoned to return. But Bassett remained silent. Marshall didn't give him the satisfaction of looking back.


Marshall had never trusted Isa Palant's communications with the Yautja. She had brought the conflict with them to a close, true, or at least, she had slowed it down. There was still news of intermittent attacks by Yautja elements. It seemed they were like humans in one respect at least—they didn't all follow one leader, and some chose not to follow any leader at all.

According to Kalakta, Yautja had always hunted Xenomorphs, not fled from them in a blind, cowardly panic. But this... tale of weaponized Xenomorphs, conducting controlled attacks, showing strategic awareness, and acting as units rather than individual creatures...

It was crazy, and terrifying.

It was wonderful.

Marshall was the director of ArmoTech, and a Xenomorph under human control was his dream prize. Weyland-Yutani had been trying for centuries to incorporate the Xenomorphs into their bag of tricks. They had experimented on every sample they could acquire, attempting control using a variety of methods— electrical, mechanical, nano, even more eldritch means such as psychic control. They had only ever found limited success, and their experiments on these creatures always seemed doomed to failure.

Sometimes fatal failure. On the few occasions when they'd acquired a queen, then genetically engineered and modified her offspring, the results had been catastrophic.

Now, someone or something else had succeeded where Weyland-Yutani had perpetually failed.

Marshall made his way back to his own suite, swallowing down the faint sickness that always assailed him when he was moving around Charon Station. He hated space. Once in his rooms, he wasn't surprised to see a contact request from James Barclay, notional leader of the Thirteen. He would speak with Barclay soon and reveal to him the full details of what was happening. After that he would contact Isa Palant. She and McIlveen had been sitting around recuperating for too long, and

Major Akoko Halley and her unit had to be itching to be on the move.

He had a mission for them all.

For the moment, however, he sat down and took a real drink, and imagined how his life was about to change.

# 6

## BEATRIX MALONEY

*Rage Ship* Macbeth, *beyond Outer Rim*
*October 2692 AD*

Beatrix Maloney was a very old woman, but today she was feeling young. And today more than ever she felt rage.

"…but the trail is far from cold, and I *will* catch Liliya," Alexander said. He was one of her greatest generals. His image balanced before her, twitching and flickering with sub-space distortions. Maloney used to think such interference was the movements of God, but she had long since stopped believing, as science had fueled the Rage and wonders rose from that science. Now the distortions were imperfections in their communication systems. Glitches in their broadcasts. They were far from perfect, but they were getting there.

The communication ended and Maloney signaled that she wished to reply. Recording systems whispered into action.

"Alexander, I need not tell you that Liliya is our greatest threat," she said. Her platform floated gently in its suspension field, and her gel containment suit's temperature was perfect for her body, limbs and torso held comfortably in place. It had been a long time since she had felt air on her skin anywhere other than her face. She looked older than was possible, more wrinkled than mere aging would allow, but Maloney resisted full submersion. The gel compound they had found on that distant alien world was amazing, but she still grasped onto shreds of her humanity.

"She knows our plans and strength," Maloney continued. "She understands our ships and their capabilities, our intentions, our targets and aims. Most of all, she carries the secret to our armies, and if she falls into the right human hands, she might initiate an effective resistance. I want her alive. I *so* want her alive, that I can make her suffer for all she's done. But if necessary, I'll have her dead." She paused, then smiled, feeling the parchment skin of her face creasing even more.

"Don't return until you have her."

She nodded, the recording ceased, and she indicated that it should be sent. Then she sighed. A tendril-thin metallic limb rose from her suspension platform and tended to a split in the skin beside her mouth, a result of her smile. Her face wasn't used to such an expression.

*But it'll have to get used to it again*, she thought. *Because we're close.*

The assault had begun. Her generals were marching to war with her armies, paving the way for her arrival and the Rage's triumphant return. She was old, yes, and sometimes she was very tired, but she had never been so excited.

The *Macbeth* was still skimming through hyperspace, closing on the outer reaches of the Human Sphere and preparing to slow down. Activity on board was at its height as reports were received from the generals. Most of them were fulfilling their missions perfectly, hardly a surprise with the advanced weaponry and Xenomorph armies they carried with them. Some were yet to enter into combat, some were still fighting, a few had failed and been defeated. Maloney did not like that, but it was war. She had calculated on taking losses.

Even though they were approaching the culmination of decades of planning and preparation, she still liked to undergo her daily routine. Once the message was sent to Alexander—and his mission preyed on her mind, Liliya and her betrayal burning and flaming like a recent wound—she called on her helpers.

Dana and Kareth were always close by, and they were beside her within seconds.

"Mistress," Kareth said.

"You know where."

Dana and Kareth nodded and each took hold of one side of her platform. She was perfectly capable of guiding it through the ship. She knew the *Macbeth* as well as she knew herself, every space and solid component, every hidden shadow and forgotten secret. She flowed through its corridors and hallways like blood moved through her own veins, visiting every part of it, giving the ship life and similarly taking life from it. Theirs was a symbiotic relationship. On occasion she enjoyed seeing the engine room, marveling at what it had become.

The creature they had found when they arrived on *Midsummer*—they called it the Faze—had made the *Macbeth*'s engine room its home. Sometimes it still chose to move around the ship, building, bettering, remolding parts of the vessel to its own mysterious design, extruding new materials and controls from its various appendages. But the engine room was the ship's muscle, and the creature wandered those vast spaces, continuing to build the *Macbeth*'s strength.

They had never succeeded in making any meaningful contact with the entity. For a long time that had troubled Maloney. She never allowed any experiments upon it, fearing that it might take exception to such aggression and unmake all the wonderful creations it had given them. It wasn't even clear whether it was fully a creature as humans understood the concept, or some sort of machine that had been left behind on *Midsummer* by its ancient builders and inhabitants, to continue building, growing, and bettering.

Over time such worries faded away. The *Macbeth* grew better and faster, the Faze seemed never to tire, and Maloney started to believe that fate had brought them together.

Today, however, she was not visiting the Faze. Today, her destination was the hold.

Kareth and Dana were quiet, and in their silence she sensed unease about what was to come. They were shipborn after all, and to them the Human Sphere was something they were told about as children, an almost mythical place that over time formed part of something they regarded as the Promise. A promise to return, a promise to regain, a promise to avenge being driven out into the depths of space in the first place.

Even the shipborn grew up feeling adrift, and focused on the concept of Home.

"Don't worry," Maloney said to them. "The war's begun, and everything will turn out fine."

"But what is it really like there?" Dana asked. "We've heard the stories and legends, seen the holos. What's it really like in the Sphere, Mistress?"

"It might have changed in the centuries I've been away," Maloney said. "But we've grown strong. Once we triumph in war, the peace that follows will allow us to make of the Sphere exactly what we desire. We'll have taken control, and time will be on our side—but for now, the hold. Quickly. I want to see her."

And there she was.

The queen sat secured in the center of the large hold. Her great head and body were held in place by a network of carbon-filament bindings, gentle yet strong, dark lines sweeping across the chamber like scratches on reality. Her mighty egg sac, half the length of the hold, was suspended by material extruded from her own body, a hardened substance that looked like saliva made solid. The sac bulged and flexed constantly, a subtle movement that to Maloney was almost hypnotic. Many times she had found herself sitting in this observation pod for hours on end, just staring. So wonderful. So terrifying. Here was the source of the Rage's vast army, still doing what nature drove her to do even after so many decades in captivity.

They had found the queen on a mission out from the artificial habitat they called *Midsummer*. They had been actively seeking Xenomorphs by then, and it had taken them over twenty years to find them. More than five hundred unmanned drones had been sent out into the void, and when one of them found a nest, it had sent back excited chatter, like a bee leading its hive to a new patch of flowers. The recovery mission had been risky, and costly, but by then the Faze was working on the *Macbeth*, and *Midsummer*'s technology was incorporated into their own.

As Maloney watched, another egg was laid. The pulsing end of the queen's egg sac drooped down to the floor, dribbling thick fluid that hazed the air. The egg was squeezed out, placed gently, secured in place by more of the hardening secretion, and then the sac was delicately lifted away.

The queen gasped. Steam formed around her head, settling on her wide chitinous collar and condensing into water.

For decades no human had been inside the hold, and survived. Instead, Xenomorph soldiers under Rage control performed tasks instructed by the scientists. Groups of them huddled around the edges of the room, dark shapes like shadows waiting to leap. Every now and then a pair would break away from their waiting place, skitter across the floor, grab an egg that might have been laid weeks or months before, and make their way toward the exit.

Every single time this happened the queen watched, seemingly bereft. She tried to lure them back with their precious cargo, but these Xenomorphs were no longer hers to control.

None of them were.

Maloney had once tried counting the eggs in the hold, but she had stopped at two hundred. They were everywhere. The queen laid between forty and fifty eggs per day.

The hold's atmosphere was warm and damp, intensely humid, and sometimes skeins of moisture formed small clouds that drifted back and forth according to her breath. The viewing pod's outer glass was cleared by wafts of warm, dry air. Otherwise Maloney wouldn't have been able to see anything. There were other pods around the hold at various heights along the walls, and she could just make out the pale shapes of Rage scientists in one or two of them. Some would be making observations and taking readings, ensuring that the environment was stable and that the queen was still safe and secure. Others would simply be watching.

Always, people watched.

"You're old, just like me," Maloney said. She often talked to the queen, even though she knew the creature could not hear. In a way the beast had become her most trusted confidante. Maloney could tell her anything. "Old and tired, but still we go on, because instinct drives us. Your instinct to lay eggs and perpetuate your species, and mine to find my way back home. To take what is ours." She tapped the glass. "What is *mine*." The hold was huge, the queen probably two hundred yards away at the center, but still her head seemed to shift, just a little. Steam drove from her mouth as she exhaled, or growled.

Maloney glanced left and right at Dana and Kareth.

"When did she last feed?"

Kareth consulted a datapad on the wall beside the viewing window.

"Seven days ago."

"She'll be hungry," Maloney said. "Contact Wilder. Tell her to feed our queen. And tell her I'm watching."

"Mistress," Kareth said. He dashed away, leaving Maloney alone with Dana.

"Will you watch with me?" Maloney asked.

"Of course! It's a beautiful thing to see."

"It truly is," Maloney said.

They observed in silence. The queen laid another egg. Mist drifted across the hold. Several minutes later Kareth returned.

"Three are being sent in," he said.

"Good. Good." Maloney drifted closer until her platform nudged the viewing window, and below her and to the left she saw movement.

Three Xenomorphs entered, each of them carrying a human being. The humans were naked, thin, pale, and weak from their centuries-long hibernation. Several hundred cryo-pods were kept in a separate hold, liberated from one of the Fiennes ships before it was sent on its way with thousands more of its subjects already impregnated. These few hundred were not impregnated. Instead, they were kept for an even more important purpose than birthing a soldier of the Rage.

They were awake.

The first barely moved as he was laid before the queen. Only his expression changed, to one of sheer horror, as she eased her huge head down and her mouth extended, inner teeth lashing out and smashing the man's head apart. One leg spasmed. The queen ate.

"Be strong," Maloney said.

"She'll want more," Dana said.

"Of course. She has to build her energy."

When there was little left of the man but blood and shreds of skin, the second man was presented to her. He had time to raise a hand before her teeth smashed into his chest, and she lifted her head and brought him with her, giving one massive shake that split him in two. His upper part thudded to the floor as she ate his lower torso and legs.

The third human, the woman, had seen what was happening. She might have been screaming, although Maloney could not hear, but she was certainly thrashing, striking out at the monster holding her, weak ineffectual impacts that the Xenomorph ignored.

Just for a moment Maloney empathized with the woman. There was something quite amazing about her, too—she had last been awake centuries ago. Everything she knew was gone, everyone she had ever known either dead or light years away with a Xenomorph in their chest, just waiting to be birthed.

She had volunteered for a Fiennes mission, expecting to be awakened when a potentially habitable planet was reached. It might have been hundreds of years before they reached anywhere suitable, they had all been told. It might have been thousands.

Instead, she had woken to this.

It might be a kindness, Maloney supposed, if the woman believed herself to be having a nightmare.

But the heat on her skin. The slickness of the Xenomorph's carapace. The sound of the queen hissing and growling as her head snapped down and then bit off the dead man's head.

No nightmare could ever be so real.

When the Xenomorph dropped her she tried to stand and run, but she was too weak. Maloney saw her mouth open in a scream of terror moments before the queen crushed her to the floor and ripped out her guts.

"More?" Dana said.

"No. Not for a while. We want her strong enough to keep giving birth, but not *too* strong. Keep her hungry. That way she'll always be ours. Now, accompany me to the bridge. It's time to start taking stock."

Challar was on the bridge. Another of the original Founders who had become Rage, he was older than Beatrix Maloney by a few years, but those years had not been as kind. Both legs had been amputated thirty years before, and one arm, and now Challar's other arm was starting to wither and die.

Yet his mind was still strong. Completely submerged in the life-giving gel, what was left of Challar floated in a large crystal globe. The gel gave him oxygen and sustenance, maintaining life long past the time when it should have withered along with his limbs. He communicated via an artificial voice box attached directly into his larynx, giving his words a mechanical lilt. What he said, however, was all human.

"Fucking fantastic!"

"Eloquent as ever, Challar," Maloney said.

"We're almost there. It's happening, Beatrix. After so long!"

"Did you ever doubt?"

"Well, no… yes, I don't know." He hovered his own platform close to one of several viewing screens on the bridge, analyzing data that came through. "We lost Patton," he said.

"I know. Unfortunate. He was one of our better generals."

"And to the Yautja, too. They were supposed to be a test for our armies, not destroyers."

"If you look at the data more carefully, I think you'll note that there were Excursionists present on the habitat, too."

"Doesn't matter," Challar said. His mouth still moved when he spoke, in a mockery of talking. His gel was mostly clear, although Maloney could see specks of skin floating in it, and streaks of body fluid. It didn't disgust her—she'd known him too long for that—but she did make a mental note to suggest that he change his gel.

"What *does* matter is that we've still not heard from *Othello*," she said. "Any contact?"

"No, Mistress Maloney," a shipborn controller said. "We've tried on all channels we know, sub-space and quantum fold, even traditional radio. There's nothing."

"Hmm." Maloney frowned and scanned the screens, taking in all the data that had reached them so far from their advance armies. Successes were far in the majority.

Things were going well, but the *Othello* still should have been in touch.

The *Othello* was their sister ship. They had parted company many years ago, on the same mission and general course, but approaching the Sphere via two different routes. That way, Maloney hoped, if something happened to one vessel, the other would still make it through. Until recently there had been periodic contact, so she knew that the *Othello* had fulfilled its mission as well as the *Macbeth*, up to a point.

They had hunted down and taken control of the old Fiennes ships, nurtured huge stores of Xenomorph eggs in order to impregnate the sleepers and give birth to armies. Then, at a pre-arranged time, they had turned their attention back toward the Human Sphere.

Beyond that, she knew nothing of the *Othello*. It was possible that the ship had met a bad end, just as the *Hamlet* had on the Founders' original journey away from the Sphere, three centuries before. Space was filled with dangers, and traveling at such immense speeds held its own unique and mysterious hazards.

She cared, but not too much. Even without the *Othello* they would triumph. Her own true plan, constructed long ago and nurtured over time, involved only her ship.

Soon, her time would come.

# 7

---

# JIANGO TANN

*Space Station Hell*
*October 2692 AD*

Jiango Tann was growing old, and Hell was his little slice of Heaven.

The origin of the station's name had always amused Tann, not least because there were at least a dozen different stories about how the name had come to be. The one he believed—the tale generally accepted and most supported by solid and anecdotal evidence—concerned a woman named Maxella Murian May. Her name was outlandish, her story even more so.

She harked back to the past, when reputation had been important and exploration was still seen as a subjective, adventurous pastime for anyone with the hunger for discovery and the means to indulge that hunger. They were still around, these explorers, but as he'd grown older, Tann had come to see Weyland-Yutani's growing and strengthening influence as a dampener of adventure. Exploration became a corporate endeavor, more concerned with monetary profit than a growth in knowledge. Adventure became a thing of the past.

His own story had a lot to do with that opinion, but Maxella Murian May's tale began long before Tann was born.

Fifteen decades ago, Hell had gone by its original name of WayStation 14, a staging post for mining expeditions into the Scafell Minor system. Consisting of seven planets and more than forty moons, the only one officially named was LV-301. No life had been found in the system, and LV-301 itself was a barren rock notable for one thing—a large deposit of trimonite. This discovery had led Weyland-Yutani to launch several huge mining missions, and it had built and commissioned WayStation 14 in an orbit between Scafell's third and fourth planets.

Crewed by over a hundred, the station had been vast—large enough to provide docking facilities for dozens of ships and storage for huge amounts of mining equipment and supplies. For over thirty years of industrialized mining on LV-301, it might have been one of the busiest places in the galaxy.

WayStation 14 had quickly adapted to the needs of miners. Though on Company missions funded by Company money, the miners were a tough, rough bunch, and very demanding. Spending up to a year at a time on and beneath the planet meant that their infrequent rest and recreation journeys to WayStation 14 were boisterous affairs. Gyms were converted to drinking dens, storage hangars became gambling centers and combat arenas, and male and female prostitution on board was rife. Though mining crews were always mixed, while on their infrequent rest periods they preferred to mix it up sexually with people not scarred by rock falls or grown pale through prolonged periods underground.

Weyland-Yutani still funded the station, but they had quickly lost control. WayStation 14 became its own beast.

While the trimonite continued to flow the Company did not care, but after the last few tons were extracted and the mining operations began to wind down, a group of miners made an offer to the Company to administer the space station.

W-Y agreed. To decommission or move it would cost too much, and usually in cases like this they would either abandon the station or set it on a degrading orbit into the system's sun. The deal set a precedent that over the following century saw many more space stations and ships falling into private hands. By then the Scafell Minor system had a decent-sized population on four worlds and a dozen moons. Where there were enough people, there was a call for what these ex-miners wanted to provide.

Maxella Murian May was one of the miners. Nicknamed MayDay—allegedly due to her voracious appetites for drink, food, and sex that left many exhausted and despairing people in her wake—she also had a sharp mind, and had always embraced the privateer's outlook. She'd worked for the Company on LV-301 for two years, always knowing that the trimonite was running out and that the station would be up for grabs.

Three months after she and a consortium of other individuals took ownership, she unwittingly changed its name during the first of their broadcasts. Back then they were calling themselves the Private Club, but that name was destined to change.

"Come to see us, we're always private at the Private Club," the broadcast went. "Formerly a Weyland-Yutani mining post in the Scafell Minor System, we're now a *fun* place to be. Forget the Company, come *here* for company like you've never had before. Everything you want, everything you need, everything you desire… all the good things they do in hell, without the eternal damnation."

Seventeen days later the first indie ship arrived.

The crew spent a week on the station, and by the time they left it had been renamed Hell. The name stuck, but Hell quickly became something else. Not only a credit-spinning enterprise for May and her fellow ex-miners, it started to attract others who had become cynical about working for the Company. Indies, pirates, independent salvage crews, private mining enterprises, rich spacefarers on voyages of exploration, the lost and dispossessed found their way to Hell, and many ended up staying.

The original crew of a hundred, all long dead, would never have recognized their station which was now home to over two thousand people, with anywhere up to a thousand extra visitors at any given time. A rough place, it also maintained a sense of community that kept trouble mostly at bay. Hell was no longer simply a playground for those looking for illegal drugs, drink, and illicit sex— although of course, those were still to be found.

For many, Hell had become a safe haven, a destination rather than a waystation. Some had come to call it home.

Jiango Tann and his wife Yvette were two of those people. They had arrived five years earlier, after fleeing halfway across the Sphere, and it was a long time since they had felt so at peace.


"There's more today," Jiango said. Yvette groaned something from beside him, rolling over and opening one eye. "Morning," he said.

"Is it?"

"According to the clock." He was sitting up in bed with an old datapad on his lap. They had owned it for almost as long as they'd lived on Hell, and over that time Yvette had adapted and upgraded it so that it was probably now up to military standard. Quite brilliant. Quite illegal. That pretty much summed up their whole existence.

"Wake me for breakfast," Yvette said.

"Your turn to cook it."

"Oh, really?"

"Yeah. I bought bacon yesterday. Four rashers, bread roll, rat sauce for me, please." Rat sauce tasted exquisite. No one knew what was in it, apart from the man who made it, Marx Kellant, and it had taken on some random name because, for all anyone knew, it was made of space rat.

"Ugh."

"And coffee." Jiango worked the datapad, sweeping pages aside, accessing quantum folds that should have been secure. Yvette had written a protocol that took him in under a different identity every single time, kicking his location around so that even if his hack was noted, its source would be untraceable. So she said. He trusted her. The station had yet to be taken out by a Marine nuke.

Not that it wouldn't happen... eventually.

"I'm so comfortable."

"Hmm." And then there was another one. Just a shred of communication—three errant words plucked from a secure quantum fold... *"morphs dropped from"*...

"Go on, make breakfast."

"Hmm," Jiango said again. He zeroed in on the message source, refined its frequency and depth, expanded the search grid on either side from seconds to a minute. It would take a few moments to analyze such a wide data range. He tapped the screen, impatient.

A hand crept across his thigh.

"I'll give you a hand job," Yvette said lazily, stretching beneath the covers.

He looked at her, raised an eyebrow, considered.

The datapad chimed... and what he saw caused him to

sit up straight, knocking Yvette's hand aside and startling her properly awake.

"Look at this," he said, offering her the pad. "Look!" It was the most complete transmission he'd yet found, and it confirmed to him that something important was happening.

```
down from the ship disgorging a wave of
Xenomorphs before peeling away and
```

"What the hell does that mean?" Yvette asked.

"I'm not sure, but it follows on from the increased activity over the past few days, and those snippets of transmissions I've managed to pull."

"Meaning what?"

"Meaning I think the Colonial Marines are at war with someone, or something."

"Xenomorphs?"

The word chilled them both. Jiango actually felt goose bumps, even though they kept their suite warm. Yvette sat up and moved closer to him, her familiar warmth and smell comforting.

"How far away is this?" Yvette whispered, voicing a natural concern. Even in the depths of space, a little less than a light year from the nearest drophole and twenty light years from the Outer Rim, danger could be close.

"Not far from the Outer Rim," Jiango said. "Where anything can happen." It was a saying they used a lot, a familiar part of their marital language that others might not understand. They had been in space for a long time. They had seen a lot, suffered so much. "Anything" had happened to them.

Their son had been dead for over ten years.

Their only child, Christopher Tann had fulfilled his childhood ambition of becoming a pilot by the age of twenty, and achieved a commission into the Colonial Marines at twenty-three. Eight years later he was a lieutenant, and that was when he grew far more secretive about what he was doing. They saw him every couple of years, having based themselves on an asteroid community a light year from Addison Prime, one of the major Colonial Marine bases in the sector. While he made a name for himself as a pilot in the 6th Spaceborne, Yvette and Jiango pursued their interest in alien intelligences.

In particular, they studied the Xenomorph. There were many who considered the beasts as little more than animals, but the Tanns believed that they possessed a complexity of thought and behavior that research had barely touched. Just because they did not resemble humans in societal structure and dexterous intelligence didn't mean that they weren't on an equal level. The Tanns frequently accessed old research into a species long-since extinct on Earth, the dolphin. It had possessed an ability to communicate, the gift of empathy, and an intelligence close to that of a human, and they could draw many parallels between dolphins and Xenomorphs.

True, there were no accounts of dolphins pursuing and slaughtering humans wherever and whenever the species drew close, but there was an irony inherent to their comparisons—dolphins had also been used by the military.

Because the species fascinated them, and they had possessed limited resources, the Tanns' fascination required proper funding.

As a result, they worked for a company that worked for the Company.

A great, expansive tree of organizations began with Weyland-Yutani as the main trunk, branched into a network of sub-companies with ever more nebulous relationships, and finally their small concern was a green shoot on one of the outer limbs. Nevertheless, funding found its way through, and they believed that their organization's directors somehow reported directly to Weyland-Yutani. Yet while they divulged some of their research, easily as much again was kept to themselves. By mutual agreement, from the beginning of the Tanns' employ the husband and wife team had been using the oldest storage media known to mankind.

Their brains.

While they pursued their interests, Jiango performed more covert research into his son's unit, postings, and what missions he embarked upon. With Yvette's technical expertise he could go deep, and they were fastidious about covering their tracks.

When he realized that Chris was working for ArmoTech, the bottom fell out of their world.

Jiango and Yvette were explorers. They traveled, but most of their exploring was in the realm of knowledge. Space was a wondrous place to them. There were dangers out there for sure, but while most people saw species such as the Xenomorph and Yautja as terrors to be avoided, the Tanns wanted to know them better.

Chris was seeking to make weapons out of such wonderful discoveries.

Devastated, distraught, wondering how they had gone so wrong and their son had come to work for such an organization, they'd had to keep their discoveries quiet. If they confronted him, he would ask how they knew. ArmoTech was extremely covert, and knowing that he worked for them would prove that his parents had been snooping into Weyland-Yutani and Colonial Marine matters.

They had no wish to end up in prison, or worse. But way beyond this, they had a duty to their son. They decided that the next time they had contact with him, they would reveal that they knew.

They never saw him again.

Seven months later they received news from a somber but impersonal Marine major, telling them that their son had been killed on active service. That he was brave and dedicated, he had died doing what he loved, and the Colonial Marines would forever be in their debt. They would receive compensation in the form of his pension lump sum, please provide preferred account details...

The grief had been crippling. Yet almost instantly, so had the need to know. Day and night they had searched, and eventually they'd discovered that Chris had been killed on a mission to hunt and gather Xenomorph samples from a derelict ship that had been discovered adrift in a remote star system half the sphere away. A whole Marine contingent had been sent, along with advisors and so-called experts, and every one of them had died. The Marine craft was destroyed, the derelict still adrift, and perhaps somewhere on board the body of their son lay rotting.

Yvette wanted to leave it alone, let it lie. Their son was dead and now they only had each other. If they pursued the matter and revealed what they knew, they'd be charged with espionage and imprisoned separately, and she could not imagine her and Jiango being torn apart. They might never see each other again. After losing so much, she told Jiango, she couldn't bear that idea.

It was ironic, then, that it was Yvette who eventually broke and tried to make the news public. Planning a widespread release of the information, she demanded transparency in the Company's Xenomorph program, suggesting that their experiments were putting humanity at risk, and that their covert projects and development of alien-inspired weaponry needed to be made public.

She named one of the Thirteen, Gerard Marshall, as the perpetrator of these crimes, suggesting that as director of ArmoTech he had to take responsibility. His orders had resulted directly in the death of her son, as well as dozens of other Colonial Marines.

For a while they became notorious.

The people standing up to the Company.

The radicals.

Then came the attempt on their lives. A ship venting to space, a catastrophic depressurization, six dead and dozens injured. The source had been a drive shaft close to their cabin on the passenger craft on which they were traveling. They had only survived because they'd gone to the mess for an unusually late meal.

It was an accident, of course.

That was how it was reported, and in more innocent circumstances they might have believed the same. But the Company had already been breathing down their necks, suggesting that they were paranoid and misinformed, then becoming threatening when they asked how the Tanns had come into ownership of classified information.

They had gone on the run and ended up, eventually, in Hell.

"It doesn't matter," Yvette said, standing from their bed and tugging on some clothes. "Whatever's happening, it's a long way away from us. It doesn't matter."

The more she claimed that it did not matter, the more it did.

The Tanns lived on one of Hell's larger docking arms, their cabin a collection of small rooms that provided a comfortable place to retreat to while being away from the hubbub of the station's central core. It was a half-hour walk down the arm to the core, or a three-minute elevator ride. They usually chose to walk. Well into their seventies, the Tanns were fit and healthy, and looking forward to another four decades of life at least.

What they would do with those years was often the subject of discussion. They had been on Hell for almost a decade, and both knew they could not remain there forever.

In the vestibule at the base of the docking arm, they paused at one of the big holo screens that showed a 24/7 status of Hell and its occupants. There were the semi-permanent occupants like them, given resident status by Hell's station council and allowed to travel to most areas of the vast structure. Then there were the visitors, who were invariably welcomed with open arms, but monitored for the duration of their stay. The holo screens provided information concerning new arrivals and those who had departed, and they were always an interesting read.

Today, Jiango read the screen with greater focus than usual.

"Autonomous Exploratory Salvagers," Yvette said. "Four crew."

"Indies or pirates," Jiango said.

"Yeah." Yvette waved at the screen and images of the crew appeared close to them. "They even have a uniform."

Jiango grunted, but he was looking elsewhere, scanning the other arrivals from the eight days since the last time they had been down here. There were six. Four of them were from in-system, the other two having journeyed from the nearby drophole over the last couple of months. One was the pirate ship, the other an independent mining expedition planning to search for precious minerals on one of the system's many moons.

No one to concern them. Yet he was still concerned.

"Come on," Yvette said. "Since you wouldn't cook me breakfast, even though I offered you a hand job, you can at least buy it for me."

He relented and they headed through the vestibule and into the station's core. As ever the place was abuzz, the wide plazas awash with people, musicians playing for credits, a varied soup of humanity ebbing and flowing and sometimes simply sitting to observe. They went to their favorite cafe and ordered food and coffee, then sat and watched in companionable silence. It was only after their order came and Jiango poured his coffee, that he said what was on his mind.

"I think we should move on."

"That's a bit out of the blue." Yvette paused with her coffee mug raised halfway to her mouth. The sound of a hundred voices washed over them, but for a while a heavy silence seemed to hem them in.

"It might be dangerous," he said.

"Because of what you saw? That's a long way away, and we have no idea what it really is." She put her mug down. "We should stop snooping. No good can come of it."

"We've talked about leaving before," Jiango persisted, trying to justify his fears.

"A hundred times… but aren't we happy here?" Her eyes clouded a little, because they both knew the truth, and Jiango did not need to reply. They could never be truly happy ever again.

"Just a thought," he said, relaxing against the back of his chair. "It's got me…" He waved his hand. *It's got me agitated*, he thought. *I know it's never over, not with them. Other sons and daughters are being sent to die at the Company's behest.*

He fucking hated them. But the hate of one man meant nothing.

They spent the day swimming, walking in Hell's green dome that had been added only a couple of decades before, and watching a holo in one of the several theaters. They bumped into a few people they knew and chatted for a while, and also talked with a couple they didn't know, rich travelers undertaking a forty-year journey out from Sol to the Outer Rim.

It was while they were wandering the core hub, considering where to have a meal, that a familiar sound sang in. A ship was approaching Hell, and the chiming meant that it was as yet unidentified. Regular visitors were issued with beacons. This ship was unknown.

Jiango and Yvette made their way to one of the holo screens and joined a small crowd watching for news. It was curiosity more than anything, the thought of new visitors causing ripples of excitement.

None of them seemed afraid.

The chiming ended. The pause was comfortable, the hubbub of conversation good-humored. Jiango heard a child laughing. A man coughed. In front of him a woman whispered into a man's ear, and he turned to her and smiled.

Then a more frantic buzzing began, and a red glow burst out from the holo screen's surround.

"Oh, no," Yvette said as the whole image was replaced with a long-range scan of the approaching ship. It was sleek and sharp, spiked with weaponry, heavy at the rear, and it possessed the familiar blister-skin of a cloaking shield. "Yautja."

People started running. Some were heading for home, a few sprinting for the walkways and elevators leading to various docks.

Jiango and Yvette hurried toward their own docking arm, a fifteen-minute walk away. They passed a small group of indies marshalling close to one of the hub's main plazas, and some voluntary militia dashed by, looking around as if they were searching for someone to give them orders. Hell's defenses consisted of an indie unit of thirty troops on retainer and some militia, most of whom were more used to dealing with internal squabbles than threats from outside.

"What the hell is a Yautja ship doing here?" Yvette asked. "I thought there was a ceasefire. It was all so far away."

"See?" Jiango said as they entered the docking arm. They queued for the elevator to their suite. "Dangerous."

# 8

## LILIYA

*Approaching Space Station Hell*
*October 2692 AD*

After fifty-one days traveling with Hashori of the
Widow Clan, Yautja warrior and perpetrator of torture,
Liliya might have expected to know her better. But it
had been a long, quiet, exasperating seven weeks.

The Yautja ship was very small, with hardly any room
to move about. Hashori, all nine feet of her—Liliya could
still only assume the Yautja's sex—remained strapped in
her flight seat for the bulk of their journey, not sleeping
and only eating on rare occasions. She did not wear her
helmet or armor, but kept her battle spear close at hand.
She seemed immune to boredom. Liliya knew that some
Yautja were far, far older even than her, and perhaps with
age came a more sedate appreciation of the passage of time.

For long periods, Liliya retreated to a small cubby
close to the engine pod. There, the android did her best to
treat her own wounds.

Hashori had tortured her, recognizing her as of the
same group responsible for shattering attacks upon

Yautja interests across this sector of space. The torture had been imaginative and unrelenting, until their ship the *Zeere Za* was attacked by the Rage general Alexander and his forces, in pursuit of Liliya. At that moment, Liliya knew that her continued existence was balanced between life and death. But Hashori had chosen to believe her, and they had escaped only an hour before the *Zeere Za* had been destroyed.

In her veins, Liliya carried the same tech that enabled the Rage to control their Xenomorph army. In her mind, she bore the truth of the Rage's intentions, their plans, their capabilities and numbers. That was the only reason Hashori had allowed her to live—the chance for revenge.

At the beginning of their journey the Yautja had seemed willing to communicate. Liliya sat beside her on the small flight deck, a place obviously designed for one, not two, and they conversed using Liliya's basic grasp of the Yautja language.

She learned that the Rage attack had come as a surprise, destroying Yautja habitats and ships, assaulting some of their worlds, and wiping out many strands of their species' history. The Yautja placed no value on possessions, places, or objects. They carried their stories deep inside, and their heritage was in memory and recollection, tales of journeys undertaken and ancient hunts. With every Yautja death part of that history was snuffed out, and this had been the most damaging assault on their species in living memory.

Over several days Liliya listened to Hashori's sporadic descriptions of new atrocities she had heard about. Liliya never detected any broadcasts, never saw any sign of communications between this small ship and any other, but Hashori would occasionally mumble to herself, then sit up straight as if listening.

One of the last pieces of information she passed on was that Yautja and humans had entered into an uneasy peace. Initially the Yautja had fled into the Human Sphere. As was their wont, they launched opportunistic hunts as they went. Now something of the truth seemed to have dawned on the panicked humanity—and perhaps, too, the Yautja had seen sense.

*It's just what Beatrix and the Rage wanted,* Liliya thought. *Test her armies on the Yautja. Spread panic. Confuse the Human Sphere before launching their main assault.*

Soon after this, Hashori fell silent.

Liliya continued to attempt communication, but as time went on the alien grew more and more distant. She went through various procedures—checks on the ship, course assessment, a silent communication between her and whatever powered and controlled the vessel. At the same time, she started acting as if Liliya was not even present.

On a larger ship that might not have been a problem, but this vessel was barely more than a bridge, an engine pod, and little else. Liliya assumed there were weapons arrays, a life support unit, some sort of fuel source, and other equipment spaces that she could not see, but it was so different from any of the Rage ships—or anything she had ever seen centuries before she became part of the Founders and the Rage—that she found it difficult to understand.

Hashori's control panel was a smooth, silvery mass, and whenever she reached for some instrument it coalesced up out of the panel and formed for her hand. There were no communication devices to be seen. Her seat was molded with the floor, fluid and flowing, and the smaller seat she had conjured for Liliya sank down whenever the android moved away. The ship seemed to be more a part of Hashori, than apart from her.

That idea made Liliya feel even more like an invader.

For most of the trip, she kept out of sight.

Liliya spent some time attempting to heal and repair her wounds. Back on the *Zeere Za*, Hashori had tortured her, using tools, chains, and an insectile creature that laid eggs inside her. Those eggs were hatched and dead now, but the damage they had left behind still remained.

Soon after she had been created and commissioned, Liliya had chosen pain. All androids were given the choice, and she had decided that to be as close to human as possible, she should be able to suffer as a human did.

Huddled in that small room in Hashori's ship, held down by a makeshift harness because of the zero gravity, she wondered whether she had endured more than any human alive. Perhaps more than anyone *could* endure before giving in to madness. She repaired physical damage where she could, either signaling her flesh and blood systems to concentrate more healing cells to particular parts of her body or, in a few cases, performing impromptu procedures on the most severe wounds. She used strands of hair to stitch, a shred of one of her nails as a needle. It took a long time, but time was something she had in abundance.

The days passed by, marked only by her internal calendar. She had spent long periods of her existence on her own. This was nothing compared to the decades drifting before the Founders had picked her up, centuries earlier and deep in the Human Sphere. But now, as these days passed, there was an urgency to her existence. A frustration.

From time to time she tried to impress this upon Hashori, but the Yautja remained impassive. She would glance at Liliya and then away again, as if she was not there.

Liliya did not understand, but then, the Yautja were not a species easy to comprehend. They followed no human laws or protocols, and their vaguely humanoid shape and build—two arms, a torso, two legs—was about as near to *Homo sapiens* as they came. Beyond that similarity in shape lay only mystery.

On day fifty-two of their journey, Liliya was lying in her small space when Hashori's shadow fell across her.

"Your people have found us."

"Alexander," Liliya said. She stood and floated behind the tall Yautja, back onto the bridge, where the small seat had already emerged from the floor. They sat together at the smooth control panel, and Hashori passed her hand across a raised metallic globe.

The viewing screen darkened, and moments later a three-dimensional map appeared.

There were several glowing points.

"What's that?" Liliya asked.

"Us," Hashori said, pointing. She shifted, her seat flowing across the floor, and indicated a small speckle of lights. "Them."

"How far away?"

"Five billion miles."

"They know we're here," Liliya said. Of course they knew. Being so close could not be coincidence. "You said your ship's cloaking ability would hide you from anything."

Hashori hissed softly. Liliya couldn't translate, and she was not even sure the sounds were words. Perhaps it was a whisper of anger at her ship and talents being questioned.

"How did they find us?" Liliya asked, exasperated. "I don't understand. It shouldn't be this hard to hide."

"Nevertheless, they've started to close on us," Hashori said.

"What's that?" Liliya asked. There was another shape

on the wide display, a glowing blue circle an equal distance from their ship in the opposite direction.

"Our destination, and now our only chance," Hashori said. "A human drophole."

"We're close to the Outer Rim?" Suddenly Liliya felt excitement, and a sense of fear. She had departed the Human Sphere almost three centuries ago, with the Founders, seeking a better existence elsewhere. She was returning at the forefront of a war. Arriving here wasn't the end of anything, but the beginning of what might be the most painful part of her life, and the most destructive conflict humanity had ever faced.

Guilt bit in deep. She had never felt so human.

"It's one of the outermost dropholes."

"Can we beat them there?" Liliya asked.

That hissing again, as if Hashori was offended that Liliya had cast doubt on the abilities of her ship.

"We'll have to communicate with the drophole's control center," Liliya said. "I know some codes. We can probably even operate it remotely, if your ship has the correct broadcast configuration."

"Here." Hashori stretched past Liliya and touched the smooth silver control panel. Mounds formed, then sharper edges, and in moments an array of controls and display screens manifested in front of Liliya.

She looked at Hashori.

The Yautja offered what might have been a shrug. "I'm flying."

Liliya turned her fluid seat toward the controls and grinned. It felt strange on her face, stretching skin unused to stretching. She could not remember last time she'd had cause to smile.

Glancing up at the big display, she realized that the cluster of Rage ships was already significantly closer.

Alexander had found her, somehow, and he and his army of monsters were coming for her. Alive or dead, they would not let her escape without a fight.

The drophole drew nearer, but it already seemed as if they would be intercepted before reaching that point.

"Hashori—"

"Silence," the Yautja said. Her hands danced across the controls, the desk flexing, forming, flattening again beneath her touch as controls rose to her command. "You have your task. Leave me to mine." The ship vibrated, but it was the gentlest of movements.

"What was that?" Liliya asked.

Hashori did not reply.

So Liliya set to her task, attempting to bypass the drophole control base and access the advanced computers controlling the hole itself. She had a sinking feeling in her gut, knowing that she was leading the attacking force toward those who were protecting the drophole. She might be dooming them, but buried beneath that was the hope that Alexander and his army might even be stopped, repelled, or defeated, especially if the Colonial Marines were now protecting these Outer Rim dropholes, following the Yautja assaults.

The codes and information she possessed didn't work, and seemed obsolete. She tried again. Still there was no response.

For years, Liliya had been gathering information about the drophole expansion. Even so far away from the Human Sphere, she had hacked into quantum folds and collected any errant transmissions concerning drophole access, use, and initiation. She had built a fractured picture of how their design was advancing and changing, and how the holes worked. It had been something of a personal project of hers. She had been quite open about her research, and

Beatrix Maloney had considered it valuable.

Liliya now knew why.

But before fleeing Maloney and the Rage, she had retained far more information than she had ever shared. As her suspicions about Maloney's aims had grown, so had the ever-more-human part of her mind that allowed deception and secrecy. The structure of her brain—the network of her mind—was similar to a human being's, except that she could retrieve any information stored in there, accessing it at any time. She was an android, after all.

She tried a different set of codes, at the same time attempting to identify the drophole.

"Where's your navigation?" she asked. Distracted and concentrating, Hashori waved a hand and brought up a complex set of screens.

Liliya looked at the big display again and saw one less Rage ship closing on them.

"Oh, sorry," she said. "I didn't realize we were in a space battle."

The ship shuddered again. She hoped the Yautja was shooting, and not being shot.

She tried to access the navigational computer, and succeeded. Once online, it was surprisingly easy to use. She quickly established which sector of the Outer Rim they were in, and which drophole they were approaching. It was Gamma 23. She consulted her own deep memory and brought up what she needed. Completed four years ago, Gamma 23 had been built between the sixth and seventh planets of a star system, its control base on the sixth planet's moon a million miles from the hole. There were also several orbiting stations closer to the hole, some home to independent space farers, one a base for a Colonial Marine Spaceborne unit.

She listened for chatter. Anyone on the moon or

stations would have detected the ships now—theirs and the Rage's—but she heard nothing.

"Strange," she said.

"Can we use the drophole?" Hashori asked, a surprising edge of urgency to her voice.

"I hope so," Liliya said. She sent command codes to the moon base, expecting an instant response from flight control. There was nothing, not even an automated response. If the codes she was using were outdated or had recently been changed, they would have been queried.

"We need to drop," Hashori said.

"Can you do that?" Liliya asked. Humans required suspension pods to use a drophole, their minds and physiologies unable to cope with the dimension-twisting aspects of the physics involved. She could survive a drop, even remain awake, and had done so before. But even for an android it was an unsettling experience.

"You know nothing about Yautja," Hashori said.

"Don't slow down," Liliya said. "I'll have the drophole ready. How long until we hit?"

"At this speed, seventy seconds."

Liliya got to work. With no response from the control base, it was still possible to initiate the drophole herself. It all depended on whether the complex network of codes she attempted to use were still current. If she sent a wrong code, it might result in the hole being closed down pending rebooting from the base. She wouldn't know whether or not she had the correct code until she sent it.

After a few seconds preparing the brief transmission, she sent some more exploratory messages toward the base and orbiting stations. Still no response. She scanned frequencies, touching a local quantum fold, as well, and that was where she found the split-second message. It was on a cycle, repeated every three seconds, and less than half a second long.

But it was enough.

Liliya absorbed the transmission and slowed it down, seeing the pain and destruction, hearing the desperate voice that had no time to do anything but scream.

"They've been here already," she said. "The control base has been taken. I think the stations are destroyed. If there is anyone left alive, they'll be hiding."

"So we can't use the drophole," Hashori said. She steeled herself, bringing up a whole new array of controls that Liliya thought must have been weapons.

"I didn't say that," she said. "How long?"

"Twenty-five seconds."

"Don't slow down."

"If the drophole is not open—"

"It will be." Liliya knew the implications of striking the drophole at speed if it was still locked. At least neither of them would feel anything.

She checked the code she had entered one more time, paused for a second, then sent it.

For an agonizing few seconds nothing happened. There was no acknowledgement, and no automated response denying access.

A glowing mass the size of her fist lifted from the control panel, and Hashori sighed heavily.

"It's open," she said. "Six seconds."

Liliya entered a random code and prepared another transmission, timing it to send the instant they passed into the drophole. If her timing was accurate, the hole would receive the new, incorrect transmission and immediately deactivate. It might give them a head start, at least. But she knew that Alexander and his army would eventually follow her through. The Rage had already taken the control base on the moon. They would not have been stupid enough to destroy it.

"Two seconds," Hashori said. Liliya saw her lean back in her seat, the structure flexing with her body and cupping around her to keep her still. She gripped the armrests, her long-clawed hands clasping tight. She even heard the Yautja take in a deep breath... and then let it out slowly, like a final exhalation before death.

In the viewing screen, the drophole structure appeared before them. It grew rapidly in size as they approached. It had been a long, long time since Liliya had been through one of these, and she had a second to marvel at its size, complexity, and beauty.

Then she, too, prepared. Smashing through a hole, awake and at this speed would destroy a human mind, drive the person mad with the twisted slew of dimensional disturbance and deep time. For the first time in a long while she tried not to think of herself as human.

A second later, she could not think at all.

Wake up.

The voice might have been inside her mind. It had the sound of an echo, perhaps drifting in from hundreds of years ago. They captured the lifeboat, opened it up, pulled her out and tried to wake her. Decades alone and she had fallen into a strange fugue, deeper than sleep, not quite death.

*Wake up.*

Wordsworth had been there when she eventually came around. Reality came into focus, slowly finding its way through the other hallucinations. It took her a while to make out which was which. Though she didn't know it then, a time would come when she would wish they had never found her at all.

*Wake up, human.*

Liliya opened her eyes.

Beside her, the Yautja slumped in her chair. Her face was splattered with blood. She was breathing heavily, releasing a labored sound.

Before them, the wider viewing screen displayed star systems she did not recognize.

"We're through," Liliya said breathlessly. Hashori did not reply, and she took that as confirmation.

Liliya stood from her seat, drifting to a side wall, holding on and stretching, hearing joints click and feeling muscles stretch. It felt as if she'd been prone in that chair for a long time, but it couldn't have been more than a few seconds.

"And them?" she asked.

"No sign that they followed," Hashori said. She pointed at the control panel, indicating that Liliya should check. It was she who'd activated the drophole, after all.

She pushed off and landed in her seat, and it took only moments to confirm what she had hoped was true. Her random transmission at the instant of dropping had been timed perfectly, causing the drophole to close behind them.

"How long do we have?" Hashori asked.

Liliya thought it through. Every Rage ship—from *Macbeth* and *Othello*, to the captured Fiennes ships, to those battle vessels built specifically for war—was equipped with drophole intelligence, but her knowledge about drophole tech had been expanding faster than she had shared it with Maloney and the Rage. Even back then she'd known that something terrible was looming.

"Probably not long," she admitted. "The hole will have closed when wrong info was sent, but once Alexander and his crew filter out the correct codes..." She shrugged. She didn't know, and with the control base already taken out, all it would require was a visit to the moon.

"We'll be long gone," Hashori said.

"How far did we jump?"

"Seven light years."

"I wish that felt far enough," Liliya said.

"I have something," Hashori said. She was sitting up straighter now, and if she was in pain the Yautja did not show it.

*How long did it seem to her?* Liliya wondered, but Hashori was right—in truth, she knew little about the Yautja.

Hashori pointed toward the control board and an image rose on the screen, accompanied with a haze of information written in Yautja.

Liliya tried to translate. It was harder than trying to speak Yautja, but after a couple of minutes she thought she'd absorbed enough. A remote space station in an unimportant system, with only tenuous Company links. A waystation where a stranger might be welcome.

"Hell is people," she said.

"What?"

"An old android saying," she replied. "Yes, that looks good." *Maybe we can hide there for a while*, Liliya thought. *Maybe there'll be someone there who understands that I can help.*

Hashori waved her hand and established their route.

# 9

## AKOKO HALLEY

*LV-1657, Drophole Gamma 116*
*October 2692 AD*

Major Akoko Halley and her crew were readying for action—suiting up, checking the weapons they kept close at all times. The major was ready first, and by the time Gove came online seven seconds later, she'd already connected with the *Pixie*'s computer and the base commander, Major Reece of the 5th Terrestrials, BloodManiacs.

While Halley's suit ran a rapid diagnostic check, she sent the *Pixie* an order to prep all systems.

"Major Reece, what's happening?" she asked.

"They're coming in from the west," Reece said. "Three ships approaching rapidly."

"The base has air defenses?"

"Of course, but they've misfired. The intruders must have some sort of advanced decoy system."

Halley saw no need to express her doubt or surprise. It had already happened.

"Tell us how we can help."

"I thought your first order was to protect those two civvies?" Reece said, his voice dripping with disdain. Halley had hoped that the recent conflict with the Yautja might have brought Marine units closer together, but it seemed that the historical antagonism between Spaceborne and Terrestrials was as strong as ever.

Anyway, he was right. Palant and McIlveen were her prime concern. If he'd been a decent tactician, he would have seen how this inspired her question.

"Defending this base is the best way of keeping them safe," she said. "You *can* defend this base, can't you, Major?"

"Of course," Reece said.

A pause. Halley saw the images from the base's outer defenses, blurred action relayed to her suit's visor via its central CSU. She looked around at her crew. They'd all seen it too. Three ships flitting and rolling in toward the base, bay doors open, hundreds of shapes huddled inside. Like huge pregnant insects, the ships were about to give birth.

"You know what we're facing here, Reece?"

"I've seen the same reports you have," he said. "East Quarter. You'll be defending the external access there with a platoon of the 5th."

"Thank you, Major."

Reece signed off before Halley could.

"You all heard?" she asked, looking around.

"Let's get busy," Sprenkel said.

"Private Bestwick, where are you?" Halley said into her comms unit. She led her crew out of the rec room and across a lobby, heading for the East Quarter. Information assailed her, relayed both from the base's central command and the *Pixie*'s computer. Her suit filtered it down and passed on what was important, storing the rest.

"East door," Bestwick said.

"You've got Palant and McIlveen?"

"They're both with me."

"Wait inside, we're on our way."

They rushed through the East Quarter, and behind them from the west they heard the first explosions. Her suit showed her what was happening—dark shapes dropping from the ships and landing on the plateau, bouncing through the tall grass, unfurling, standing, and then running at the marines who defended that sector of the base's inner perimeter. Laser fire flickered back and forth, plasma grenades bloomed across the ground, nano-shot exploded in great destructive swathes.

The Xenomorphs kept on coming.

This was warfare through strength of numbers. It had been tried before, the Company's scientists creating armies of androids that they could send to be killed without a moment's hesitation and, more importantly, without public outcry. That had proved too expensive, and ironically creating an android dumb enough to willingly sacrifice itself meant that it was too dumb to understand tactics, take orders, and become a quality soldier.

The Xenomorphs obviously didn't "think" like that.

As Halley and her crew ran, she kept one eye on her visor display, and the scores of Xenomorphs being cut down beneath withering fire from the BloodManiacs. As they fell they seemed to self-destruct, blasting apart and melting across the ground. Grasses burned, sending plumes of dark smoke across the plateau.

"They're just stupid animals," Gove said.

"You've never been up against them," Sprenkel said. "I have. They're not stupid."

"They're throwing themselves in front of those lasers," Nassise said.

"Testing our firepower," Halley said, "and someone or something's controlling them."

They reached the end of the East Quarter and the main door, which stood open, and outside the daylight flared and glowed with reflected explosions from the west. Marines hunkered down inside and outside the doors, ready to repel any attackers.

Bestwick stood inside with Palant and McIlveen.

"Get suited up," Halley said to Bestwick, and Gove lobbed a bag at her. "You two okay?"

"Fine," Isa said. "What's the plan?"

Halley walked past her, Huyck by her side, and stepped outside. The doors opened onto a wide concreted area, beyond which was the grassy plain leading to the edge of the plateau. To the west, the battle raged.

The Xenomorphs were dark specks at this distance, darting left and right through smoke and fire. Closer to the building the BloodManiacs formed defensive lines, cutting down attackers with heavy fire. Above the battle hovered several robot drones, relaying information to the base's central computers and from there to the marines' combat suits. They showed a wide plain of grass, fire, and melted aliens. As yet there appeared to be no Marine Corps casualties.

"Major Reece, tell your troops not to get too confident," Halley said. "Those ships are still out there."

"Of course," Reece replied. "We've sent a swarm of drone missiles after the ships—no strikes yet, but they can't evade them all."

"Maybe, maybe not."

"Major!" Nassise said. "Company!"

Half a mile away, a ship was rising above the plateau's lip, its bay doors open and Xenomorphs dropping like seeds on the breeze. The ship powered toward the base, continuing to shed the creatures as it came. Some of them landed and bounced, then uncurled and ran at the base's eastern door. Others were already running as they landed.

As the BloodManiacs guarding the doors opened fire, the Xenomorphs started to fall.

*Too easy*, Halley thought. *Something's not right. Something—*

The enemy ship rolled to its left, laser blasts skipping from its hull, nano explosions starring around it but being repelled by an invisible shield. The vessel rocketed vertically for half a mile directly above the base, shrugging off all attempts to bring it down.

Then it paused, hung motionless…

…and started falling again.

"Cover!" Halley shouted. The ship was no longer a ship. It had become a bomb.

She dived for Palant, but she and McIlveen were already huddled down inside the wide open doors, protecting each other.

The impact was huge, the subsequent detonation even greater. The ground shook and the air pulsed, smacking the wind from Halley's lungs, shoving her sideways against the wall.

*Out!* she signaled, but her crew already understood the danger and were rushing for the open air. Halley grabbed Palant and hauled her up. Bestwick dragged McIlveen.

Outside, they turned aside from the open doors and ran.

The explosion tore through the base. The structure cracked like an egg, walls and roof ripped apart and thrown upward on a rapidly expanding plume of fire and smoke, spinning, roaring, burning. Flames boiled along corridors, following lines of least resistance moments before the shockwave tore the buildings open behind them. They blasted through the exterior doors with an agonized screech, as if the base was screaming its last.

Half a dozen marines were incinerated in the conflagration's path, and five more fell immediately as the Xenomorphs reached the concrete area, ignoring the dancing flames and leaping on unfortunate soldiers knocked off their feet by the explosion.

Stunned, feeling as if she'd been punched by a planet yet still on her feet, Halley took aim and opened fire. She cut one Xenomorph in two as it prepared to bite into the throat of its BloodManiac victim. Its head toppled and fell, then exploded, taking the top half of the marine with it.

There was no time to mourn. She switched her aim and fired again, again, backing from the burning base and ensuring that Palant and McIlveen were protected.

"Sound off," she muttered, and every one of her squad confirmed that they had survived.

The BloodManiacs had not been so lucky. Those who had not been injured or killed in the massive explosions were facing the full onslaught of Xenomorphs. Halley and her DevilDogs did what they could to help, laying down defensive fire while Nassise and Sprenkel dashed across to aid those fallen. A few got to their feet and carried on fighting. A few more were too badly injured.

Nassise grabbed one by the arms and started pulling, but a Xenomorph leapt at him. Sprenkel cut it down with a nano burst, the creature impacting the ground and self-destructing, spattering a hail of acid blood across the two men. Their suits smoked and spat, resistant to the acid for now, but the combat suits could only take so much.

"To me!" Halley shouted. "Form up! We fight off this wave, then we can help. Major Reece?" No answer. Glancing behind her, Halley realized why. The central core of the base was gone, destroyed in the ship's suicidal attack. The control center had been located there. "Reece?"

"Another ship, northeast," Bestwick said. The ship powered in from above the mountains, descending so rapidly that Halley thought this one was going to impact the base as well. If it took out the landing pads where the *Pixie* was parked...

But this ship hadn't yet finished unloading its cargo.

The Xenomorphs dropped in lines, bouncing and rolling, uncoiling while still moving, and running at the base.

Directly at Halley and her crew.

Her combat suit marked targets, CSU merging with the others' suits so that they each concentrated firepower on different targets. The first wave of aliens went down. Halley glanced behind her at Palant and McIlveen, ensuring that they were safe. They both looked helpless, and she wondered whether she should hand them some sidearms.

The assault on their senses was brutal—explosions, screams, the shrieks of the Xenomorphs as they attacked and died, the stench of ozone as lasers scorched the air, the heat of plasma explosions playing across their skin, the stink of blood and shit and burning flesh as the dead mounted, and the assault continued unabated. Halley had her suit to mask some of the effects, at least. Palant and McIlveen were naked to the onslaught, and they were terrified.

"Major!" Sprenkel shouted. "The ship!"

After dropping its cargo, the enemy vessel roared overhead and descended quickly to the ground, close to the cliff's edge. Its propulsion system was not visible, but rocks and soil were blasted aside, clouds of smoke rising as it bumped to a rest.

Its rear doors were already open, and a man appeared there. He was watching the chaos.

Halley magnified the image.

He was smiling.

"Android," she said.

"He's the one controlling them," Palant said.

Halley's crew needed little more encouragement. They all concentrated their fire on the ship and the android now standing beside it, but laser skimmed aside and nano-shot exploded far from the craft.

"Still got that weird defensive screen," Halley said. "Never seen anything like that."

"Major, I've got a sit-rep from the BloodManiacs' lieutenant," Huyck said.

"Let's see it." While her crew continued shooting, setting themselves in a protective half-circle with the base's East Quarter and its burning hub at their backs, Halley assessed the situation that appeared on her visor screen.

It wasn't good.

"We need to get to the *Pixie*," she said.

"We're running?" Nassise asked.

She speared him with a look. "You ever known me to run?"

They stopped firing on the protected ship and made for the landing pads, half a mile across the plateau from the main base. There were signs of combat where they were heading, and Halley knew that the four pads were protected by a Marine contingent, but from what she'd seen on her screen, the BloodManiacs were fighting a losing battle against the invading force.

For every Xenomorph killed, three more took its place. The bastard controlling them was watching, protected behind some sort of blast shield. It was only a matter of time.

They ran, Huyck and Bestwick taking point, Nassise and Sprenkel either side of Palant and McIlveen. Halley and Gove took the rear, using their suits' sensors to keep watch on their backs.

Halley felt the familiar coolness that descended around her during a fight. They called her Snow Dog, but there was respect in the name, because she was always able to view a combat situation dispassionately. Her strategies were flawless, her decisions fed by the demands of battle, not the heat of fear or doubt. She sometimes hated that in herself. She'd seen people die because of her decisions, when sacrificing a few could save many more.

That's where the dispassion made her feel less than human. Some people thought she made those decisions lightly, but those who really knew and respected her— her real family, the DevilDogs—understood the pain that coldness caused.

Now, she was trying to find balance between two priorities. First, her mission to protect Palant and McIlveen. Second, her duty to fight these attackers and protect what was left of the base. If she could make these considerations work together, all the better.

Closer to the landing pads, she saw the destruction that had been wrought. Two BloodManiac ships were smoking ruins, and the third was swarming with Xenomorphs. Some of the attackers seemed to voluntarily lie down while others bit into their chests, smashing them apart, dashing aside as their brethren self-destructed and splashed smears of molecular acid across the besieged ships. Junctions between surfaces melted, acid ate inside. A fire began.

The *Pixie* was surrounded by Xenomorphs. As they tried to launch themselves onto the ship to disable it, the *Pixie*'s computer took them out. Weapons arrays were deployed, and heavy laser blasts had already laid waste to a score of aliens. Halley had never been so grateful to have an AI as a ship's computer.

As the DevilDogs approached, the attacking

Xenomorphs turned—as one—and redirected their assault.

"Two teams!" Halley shouted. They knew the drill. Huyck, Bestwick, and Nassise went left with McIlveen, while Halley, Sprenkel, and Gove veered right, Palant between them. The Xenomorphs charged. The shooting began.

With the combat suits running target acquisition, all the troops had to do was point and shoot. They cut down Xenomorphs left and right, and as the dead or dying creatures burst apart, the marines huddled around the unsuited civilians to protect them from sprays of acid blood. Halley tried to keep one eye on the progress of the overall battle, but the BloodManiacs' lieutenant must have fallen or gone offline.

One glance back toward the base was enough to tell the story.

The burning buildings and their surroundings were almost completely overrun. Laser fire flashed right to left, and the dark, darting shapes of Xenomorphs streamed left to right, slinking low through high grasses, charging positions in ordered lines, leaping fallen brethren and slashing, biting, thrashing when they reached Marines lines. Plasma grenades exploded, white-hot plumes billowing outward. Nano-shot speckled hundreds of smaller explosions across the battlefield. Xenomorphs crawled across the roof of the burning base and dropped behind defensive lines, emerging from the flames smoking but uncowed. More humans fell.

The *Pixie* was their only hope.

Halley drove forward, com-rifle warm in her hands as it unleashed its crippling firepower upon the attacking force, but the Xenomorphs were many, they were fast and silent, and they were utterly without fear.

To her left, a creature jumped into their group. Nassise shoved McIlveen aside and went down beneath the beast.

Bestwick leapt on the alien and fired her rifle directly into its head, blasting a portion aside, but it didn't die. It bent forward and its inner jaw lashed out, smashing into Nassise's visor, shattering it, taking his head apart.

"Bastard!" Bestwick shouted. She kicked the Xenomorph from her friend's body and rammed a plasma grenade into its ruptured head. Gloved hand smoking with deadly acid, she and Huyck shoved McIlveen aside and fell on him as the grenade exploded.

Halley's visor darkened against the blast and she looked away. Nassise was gone. He'd been one of her soldiers for a decade, and they had fought side by side. Wiped out in the blink of an eye.

Snow Dog took control, shoving aside sentimentality or regret.

"Billy, we're coming in!"

"I see you," Billy said. The *Pixie*'s computer had been assigned no name when they'd been given the ship, but Halley and her crew had quickly called it Billy. It was much easier than talking to a nameless entity.

"Get ready to open the aft hatch. On my order."

"Ready. Watch out, to your right."

Halley spun just as a burst of laser fire from the *Pixie* took down two Xenomorphs.

*That's what we need*, Halley thought. *Proper firepower*.

They closed on the ship, reforming with McIlveen and the two DevilDogs guarding him. Bestwick was wide-eyed with shock. Halley tapped her around the head and she blinked, looked at Halley, nodded.

"Protective perimeter," Halley said. "Billy, now!"

The aft hatch powered down, the ramp flexing into steps. McIlveen and Palant went first, then Sprenkel and Huyck to prep the ship for flight. Bestwick fired off three more nano rounds, gritting her teeth, swearing under her breath, before Halley shoved her toward the ramp.

"Gove!" Halley said.

Gove ran for the ramp.

The Xenomorphs appeared from behind the ship, hidden by the dropped ramp until the last moment. Two went for Halley, two for Gove.

Halley's com-rifle was knocked from her hands. The first creature shoved her off the ramp and down onto the landing pad. It hissed, dribbling onto her visor and obscuring her view. Another shape reared behind it. The second Xenomorph.

Halley drew the combat knife from her boot and slammed it into the side of the first creature's head.

It screeched and thrashed, limbs and tail whipping at the air and knocking the second monster from its feet. Halley shoved it aside and withdrew the blade, but the metal was already melting. She dropped the smoking knife and dived toward where she'd seen her com-rifle fall.

A bright light erupted around her, suit hardening against the blast. She was blinded by the glare, her visor smeared with a Xenomorph's blood and innards, unable to react.

"Halley!" someone shouted, and she stood and ran toward the voice, colliding with the ramp and being hauled aboard by Bestwick. Tripping on a step, she fell and turned onto her back, wiping her visor so she could see.

Gove was crawling toward them, screaming. A Xenomorph was slumped across his legs, half of its torso blown away, and Gove knew what was about to happen.

The dead creature exploded. Its head came apart, toxic insides slumping down across Gove's back and head, blood splashing down around him and across the *Pixie*'s ramp. He screamed again as the gel-like insides ate away at his suit. Perhaps if it had been whole he might have survived, but the dead Xenomorph must have slashed at him before he killed it.

Acid blood found its way inside, eating at the damage in the suit and melting its way deeper. Flesh bubbled, boiled, blood steamed and spewed from the slashes in his suit, and his body began to liquefy from the inside out. As Gove began to burn, Halley pulled her sidearm and put a laser shot through his head.

"Here," Bestwick said. She held out her hand and Halley took it, hauled inside just as the smoking ramp began to close.

Inside the ship, combat suits were being shed as acid steamed, sizzled, and made the atmosphere acrid and rank. Billy turned life support to maximum and there was a breeze as air was cycled.

"Get us up," Halley said.

"Already moving," Sprenkel said.

"Gove?" Huyck asked.

Halley shook her head. She looked at Palant and McIlveen, checking them over for injuries. They seemed fine. "There are two spare seats," she said.

Halley and her crew took their seats, Sprenkel piloting and Huyck at the weapons point.

"All weapons online," Huyck said, "but Major, the *Pixie*'s designed for space combat. Anything other than the lasers on low charge will be like—"

"Let's worry about that when we're airborne," Halley said. "Billy, let's have a schematic of the battle, as accurate as you can."

The ship's computer formed a grid of information in holo screens before each of them, combining all transmissions from combat suits on the ground and anything left working in the base to form a picture of how the battle was going. It made for sobering viewing.

The defending BloodManiacs had been driven back against the burning base. Xenomorphs were still charging, and others continued dropping onto them from the base's roof, rushing through flames that would have killed anything less hardy.

"Lasers, half charge," Halley said. Huyck glanced back at her but said nothing. "And keep an eye on that bastard android's ship."

Sprenkel guided the *Pixie* toward the base, drifting sideways so they were always nose-on.

"Do it," Halley said.

Huyck opened fire. Lasers streamed out from the Arrow-class ship, smashing through lines of Xenomorphs and scorching half-mile trenches in the ground, blazing furrows filled with the torn and melting remnants of a hundred enemies. Even from this far away, they could see the marines retreating, huddling against the base's walls and protecting themselves as much as they could from the lasers' sparkling emissions.

"Hold," Halley said. Smoke and fire obscured the battlefield.

"Third ship's coming in again," Bestwick said.

"How far out?"

"Two miles and closing."

"Nuke 'em." Halley knew it was overkill. But no one questioned her, and none of them really knew just how effective the enemy's shields were.

But before they could fire the nukes, the enemy ship exploded above the forests, and a few seconds later massive shockwaves shoved the *Pixie* sideways over the base and into the billowing column of smoke and fire.

Sprenkel guided them out, lowering them over the besieged marines. In the air out beyond the cliffs the explosion expanded, dropping debris and fire into the forests below, trees flattened, the fresh new landscape altered forever by conflict.

"What the hell—?" Halley said. She couldn't hide the fact that she was shaken, Snow Dog or not.

"Another ship," Billy said. "On screen now." A ship appeared, magnified many times and flying in delicate, diversionary patterns.

"Yautja!" Palant said.

"Come to help," McIlveen said.

"Let's not jump to conclusions," Halley said, struggling to damp down the awe she felt, in spite of herself. "Guys, keep an eye on that ship. This isn't over yet."

With sensors keeping watch on the Yautja ship as it orbited the site of the raging battle, Halley and her crew turned their attention to the landed craft, and the humanoid figure that still watched from beside it. A score of Xenomorphs stood around him, hunched and ready to defend him against attack.

"Open every channel," Halley said.

"Open," Bestwick confirmed.

"Stand down or be taken down," Halley said.

"Who are you?" a voice said. Deep, emotionless. From this distance they could not see his mouth working, but Halley heard the hollowness of an android.

"Major Akoko Halley of the 39th Spaceborne," Halley said. "I'll take your surrender or your head."

"Oh, boss, you make me hard," Sprenkel muttered.

Halley cracked a smile. The crew were together, solid, and the loss of Nassise and Gove would only hit home after this was over. She and Huyck really had picked the best for this mission.

For a while, the android did not respond. Then he spoke.

"I am General Rommel of the Rage," he said, "and the Rage never surrender."

At Rommel's silent signal, the remaining Xenomorphs across the plateau launched a final attack against the regrouped marines. A surge of laser and nano fire erupted, lighting up the sky.

"Huyck."

At Halley's command, the Arrow's laser cannon pummeled the ship. Rommel fell sideways, then disappeared in a haze of smoke and deflected laser blasts. Huyck kept firing, and after a few more hits the ship's shield collapsed and blasted apart, exploding across the plateau and wiping out the android's guard.

"You got this?" Halley asked, opening a channel to the BloodManiacs. In her holo screen she saw marines advancing across the grassy plains, executing the few remaining Xenomorphs as they charged, working in small groups against the faster, more brutal enemy.

"We've got this," a voice said. "Just make sure you've got *him*."

"That's my plan. Sprenkel?"

The *Pixie* purred across the plateau and circled the burning ship, weapons at the ready. There was no sign of the android, and Sprenkel moved out so that Billy could scan the cliffs.

"There!" Palant said, pointing at her holo screen. "Something moving, bottom of the cliff."

"That's a hundred-yard drop!" Sprenkel said.

"He's an android," Halley said. "Take us down. We need him."

"Few Xenos went with him," Bestwick commented as they drew closer.

"We've got a bigger gun," Halley said. "Put us down."

As they dropped toward the android Rommel and the remains of his Xenomorph army, they saw him scurrying across shale slopes at the base of the cliffs. The creatures remained close to him, forming a protective shield. He didn't even appear to be limping.

Halley considered her next move. It would be easy to kill him, but he was valuable to them. If they caught him, accessed his core, maybe they could discover so much more about this new enemy that was attacking them. The Xenomorphs were just weapons, but this was their master. To know the identity of *his* master might give them the upper hand.

"We could go down there," Bestwick said. Sprenkel drifted the *Pixie* sideways, slowly shadowing Rommel's movement along the cliff's base. The android glanced at them now and then, and did not appear to be in a hurry.

"I'd want to take out those Xenos first," Halley said. "Huyck, can you be that accurate?"

"I wouldn't be confident of not hitting him," he said. "The ship's weapons are designed for maximum effect, not pinpoint accuracy."

"Shit!" McIlveen said. "Don't you see where he's heading?" He pointed at his screen, and Halley only saw the cave at the last minute.

Then Rommel was inside, closely followed by his Xenomorph guards. One of them paused just inside the narrow cave entrance, sun shimmering from its dark carapace. Waiting.

"Damn it!" Halley said. "Billy, can you scan that cave, see how big it is?"

"Give me a minute," the ship's computer said.

"You two okay?" Halley asked Palant and McIlveen. Palant seemed to be shaking a little, head back in her chair.

"I got splashed," she said, revealing her forearm. On

it was a bubbled, bloody mess the size of her thumb. "It's nothing."

"Nassise will…" Halley said, voice drifting away.

"I've got it," Bestwick said. She stood and grabbed a small first aid box from beneath the seat, then squatted beside Palant.

"Really, it's nothing," Palant said.

"Chill," Bestwick said. "None of this is your fault."

Halley felt a swelling of pride. Bestwick, hard as nails and twice as sharp, had read Palant's concerns and tried to put them down.

"The cave system is extensive," Billy said. "The entrance is narrow, but it soon opens up into several tunnels and caverns, some going quite deep. There's evidence of volcanic activity further in, but past that my sensors can't reach."

"We'll have to go in there," Halley said.

"Yeah," McIlveen said. Halley and the other marines looked at him. He withered beneath their glare. "I… I mean… that android's important. We need to…"

"They know what they need to do," Palant said.

"Sprenkel, find somewhere for us to—" Halley said no more.

Then the world exploded.

The ship rolled and spun. Something struck Halley's head and darkness fell, accompanied by the sounds of screaming.

# 1 0

---

## J O H N N Y   M A I N S

*Outer Rim*
*November 2692 AD*

Patton grins at him. It's unnatural, because an android like this was never meant to grin. He is not one of the more graceful creations built to look, act, smell, taste, and exist like a real person. He is more functional than that, more targeted in his design and purpose.

Patton is built for war.

Johnny Mains tries to back away, but his dead crew are piled around him. Faulkner, arm melted and bone showing through. Cotronis, her features bloodied and frozen in terror. Snowden, her body whole, face caved in by a Xenomorph's teeth. Behind them stand the aliens, the android's army hissing, dribbling, and waiting for his orders. Patton's name is stamped on their hides. They might as well be machines, droids to the android, and perhaps beneath their hard, reflective skins there exists a metallic skeleton, carbon-filament organs. Acid for blood.

He reaches for a sidearm, but all his weapons are gone. His combat suit is malfunctioning, torn in several places and letting in the monsters' toxic body fluids. He can feel himself beginning to burn.

Even behind his grin, Patton is still damaged, searching for something inside his wounded chest. His smile falters a little, his hands delving deeper into his wound. Pinned to the wall, still he has full motion, and the heavy Yautja spear does not seem to concern him.

His left hand pushes fully inside his chest, fluids spurting, blood hissing as it strikes the Yautja corpses at his feet. It's as if he and the Xenomorphs are actually of the same species.

Mains searches around for a weapon of any kind. There's nothing. His dead crew stare at him, lifeless, loveless. He is there now only as a witness, one man left alive among so much death and destruction. He wishes himself dead. He wishes he could be part of his crew again.

Patton screams.

It's a scream of triumph. Startled, Mains looks back to the android and sees what he has done.

His wounded chest has been wrenched open around the spear. The weapon has passed close to his spine, splitting ribs and destroying internal organs, but that's not what captures his attention. His whole focus, for those last few seconds, is taken by what Patton holds in his hands.

The heart is a mechanical wonder, still pumping and dripping white fluid as if dispensing the seed of life, but Mains knows from Patton's expression that life is not his wish.

The android grasps his beating heart in both hands, squeezes, and—

Mains snapped awake, panting in the darkness and confused at his weightlessness. Perhaps the explosion had blasted him out into space. Maybe he was dead, shattered and burnt to atoms by Patton's self-immolation, and his memory was only now catching up with that knowledge.

"Fuck me!" he said. Then he felt a hand on his chest and lips against his ear, and the cabin's light glowed softly. Lieder sat up beside him and reached for a drink, holding onto the bed straps to prevent herself from floating across the cabin. She passed him the water pouch. He nodded his thanks.

"Same dream?" she asked.

"Yeah."

"Crew hears your screaming, they'll wonder what I'm doing to you in here."

"I screamed?"

Lieder shrugged. Smiled. "More of a loud grunt."

"Thanks for making me feel even worse."

"Hey, you're awake and here with me. How bad can you feel?"

She had a point, but the humor masked her own lingering depression, and a grief that they both knew would never fully fade. They were a lieutenant and a private without a ship or crew, adrift in an uncaring universe. That they had each other, Mains thought, was probably all that prevented them both from going insane.

"I wish Durante would initiate gravity," Lieder muttered.

"His reason's a good one," Mains replied. Durante had filled them in about the Yautja incursion, and the *Navarro* was still on a war footing. Forcing the crew to operate in zero gravity prepared them for conditions should they enter into combat. Mains had forgotten how much Durante liked to run things by the book.

"Yeah, it is," she admitted. "I like him, and his crew, and I still can't quite believe they got to us in time."

"One day we'll find someone who can be fucked to calculate the odds." Mains took a drink and looked Lieder up and down. They slept in their underwear, like any good Marine, always ready to slip on their combat suits in a matter of moments.

"About what I said when I woke up," he said.

"About dreaming?"

"No, the other thing."

"Is that an order, L-T?"

Mains signaled for the light to dim down, and the darkness that welcomed them was warm and sweet.

In an Arrow ship built for eight, ten people did not make for comfort. But the *Navarro*'s crew welcomed Mains and Lieder, and Lieutenant Durante ensured they had a small cabin to themselves. He hadn't even asked if the two of them were comfortable sleeping together. Mains wondered if it was so obvious.

It had been almost thirty days since they'd been rescued from the ship docked at UMF 12, and Mains and Lieder were trying to be as useful as possible. It was difficult. The *Navarro* flew itself, heading back toward the Outer Rim at top speed and under orders to patrol the area around drophole Beta 37, now only two days away. The crew went through routine maintenance briefs and diagnostics, but spent much of the time working out, eating, and filling their time with holos, reading, and sleeping.

Mains was well used to the boredom that could set in on a long journey.

He found Durante on the flight deck, sitting in a seat that must have been specially built for his big frame, feet up on his control panel, reading from a datapad and sipping coffee. Three of his crew members were there, the others either in the rec room or sleeping.

"Eddie," Mains said.

"Johnny." Durante stuck the datapad to his chair and sat up straight. Even seated he looked huge. He hardly had the build for space travel, especially in a cramped ship, but he oozed charisma and was a natural leader.

"What're you reading?"

"*Combat Tales from the Twenty-Second Century.*"

"Always took you for a Stephen King kinda guy."

"I scare easily," Durante said, and they both laughed.

"Any more contact from Tyszka Star?"

"Nothing new," Durante said. "Three drophole attacks confirmed in Gamma sector, and contact has been lost with five more, two of them deeper into the Sphere."

"So why send us to the Beta quadrant?"

"Insurance," Durante said, shrugging. "Can't guarantee whichever bastards are doing this will confine their attack to just four-hundred-thousand square light years of space, can we?"

News of the attacks had continued to arrive, proving what Mains and Lieder had said, but he'd rather have been wrong. It was still unclear who was behind the attacks—human agencies, Yautja, or some other alien species—and the involvement of the Fiennes ships only confused the situation more.

If Mains and Lieder had hoped for a rest following their traumatic time on board UMF 12, they were destined to be disappointed.

"We're still heading for Beta 37?" Mains asked.

"That's our destination. We're in constant contact with the control base there—it's on a platform five million miles from the drophole. They've upped their defenses, got a squadron of indies under their employ with five ships and a battle station."

"How many troops?" Mains asked.

"Two hundred. They're led by an ex-Colonial Marine, a sergeant retired from the 3rd Terrestrials, so they should know what they're doing."

"But we'll be the first Marines there."

"Yeah," Durante said. "Let's see how that sits with the indies, eh?"

"They'll have no choice." Mains drifted across the flight deck to the nav computer, making himself busy checking their route, velocity, and other data. It was strange being on an Arrow's flight deck and not in command. During the first few days on board he'd thought he would get used to it, but every time he stepped onto the deck he felt a pang of loss. His ship was gone, his crew was dead, and Lieder was all he had left. He couldn't help feeling like a failure, no matter how much Lieder and Durante told him that wasn't the case.

They'd fought long and hard on the Yautja habitat UMF 12, and Durante even suggested their story should make it into the *Annals of the Colonial Marines*. He was an authority on combat tales, always had been. Theirs was a hell of a story, he claimed.

But Mains wasn't interested in telling their story, or becoming famous, or dwelling on how amazing and unlikely their survival really was. He thought of his crew and friends, and the grief their distant families would feel at their loss. An Excursionist often left family behind forever, but even across mind-boggling distances contact was made, messages sent. Three hundred light years of space didn't mean that someone was lost to you. Death was the ultimate distance.

"Hey, Johnny," Durante said. "Got something weird here. Moran, bring this up for me."

A holo screen formed at the front of the flight deck, its

frame soon enclosing a view of space. As Moran entered information into his control unit, several points of light appeared within the frame.

"That's us, and that's Beta 37," Moran said, pointing with a laser pen.

"What's that blue light?" Mains asked.

"That's the something weird," Moran said. "It's a ship of some kind, although I can't pick up any recognizable trace."

"Heading for the drophole?" Durante asked.

"Looks like it, boss." Moran swept the air in front of him, performing calculations. "Spike, can you confirm this?"

Spike was their ship's computer. Durante had named it after his pet dog from when he was a kid in New Paris. It was fond of impersonating the crew's voices, which often caused mirth, but in serious moments it reverted to its programmed voice.

"Confirmed, Moran. I agree with your assessment. At current speeds, mystery ship will reach the drophole approximately three days after us."

"Fiennes ship?" Mains asked.

"Not one that is recognized in any of my records," Spike said.

"Lieder had access to Company quantum folds she shouldn't have," Mains said. "That's how she recognized some of the signs as Fiennes ships when we first saw them."

"I know," Moran said. "She and I have spent some time downloading information from the fold, Spike has it all now. Whatever this is, it's not showing any of those old ship's traces."

"But it can't be a coincidence," Mains said.

"Damn right," Durante said. "Don't believe in 'em. Moran, prep a message to the control base at Beta 37. Tell them what we see, give them an ETA. We might have a fight on our hands as soon as we get there."

"I've got a better idea," Mains said.

Durante raised an eyebrow, perhaps resenting someone questioning one of his orders on his ship.

"Why not take the fight to them?" Mains asked.

The big man smiled.

Two days later, they were closing on the mystery ship. Spike still had found no identifying trace from the ship's drive or warp wave, but it had managed to gather some other, shocking information about the mystery vessel.

The ship was more than three miles long, and powered by a drive that Spike could not identify. If it was human, it was like nothing any of them had ever seen before.

The *Navarro* was on full combat footing. It had been gently suggested that Mains and Lieder remain in their cabin, but one look at Mains's expression had convinced Durante to find room for them on the flight deck. Two seats from the rec room had been welded in place against the rear bulkhead, and now Lieder and Mains sat together just behind Durante's command chair. They had a decent view of the *Navarro*'s crew, and they were dressed in spare combat suits, bearing standard Excursionist weapons.

It felt good to be weaponed up again, although Mains still missed his shotgun.

"One thousand miles," Spike said. "There's some debris around the ship's stern. It looks like the remains of several ships."

"Maybe it's been attacked," Moran said.

"Or escorted," Durante said.

"Any sign of course deviation?" Mains asked.

"No," Spike said. Mains frowned. Had the computer really sounded brusque with him? Maybe it didn't like talking to someone who wasn't crew.

"We're going in assuming it's not friendly," Durante said. "All weapons hot. Spike, take whatever readings you can, scan that bitch so it's cooked from the inside out, but at the first sign of aggression we're blasting it to hell."

A few moments later the ship appeared on their screen. Matching warp speeds meant that background starlight was visible as smears across space—an echo of time—creating a disconcerting effect that Mains had never really got used to. Even at these speeds, movement was all relative, and the *Navarro*'s pilot guided them in toward the vast vessel with consummate skill.

"Moran?" Durante asked.

"No sign we've been noticed," Moran said. "No weapons arrays coming online, no change in attitude or velocity."

"Anyone seen anything like that before?"

"It's weird," Lieder said. "Some of it looks almost human, I'd say centuries old."

"Fiennes ship?" Mains asked.

"No, not that old, but a lot looks like it's been… changed."

"Like someone flew it through a sun," Durante said. "Weird and melted."

"It's a hugely efficient ship," Spike said. "There's barely any trace at all, even this close. No radiation leakage, no warp drive echoes. I've never heard of a ship so clean."

"And it's fucking huge," Hari said. An Indian woman, she was the only crew member who'd not made Mains and Lieder feel particularly welcome.

"Life readings?" Durante asked.

"Yeah, and that's another weird thing," Hari said. "Gimme a minute."

They circled the ship. Spike took control of the *Navarro*, dodging some of the debris still moving along with the vessel.

"I can identify some of the wreckage now," Spike said. "It's not from the main ship, but is of a similar construction. And I'm able to get a look at the inner structures. Very peculiar. Mostly metallic, but there is some biological material, as well. Almost like they were grown instead of built."

"It gets better and better," Lieder muttered.

"Somewhere we can dock?" Durante asked.

"I've already identified six different docking ports," Spike said. "Five are closed, but one has open doors, and the hangar is large enough for the *Navarro*. It also appears empty."

"Convenient," Durante observed.

"We're docking on that thing?" Moran asked. "Seriously?"

"No other way to get on board," Durante said, "and I *do* want to get on board. If this has something to do with the attacks on the Gamma sector dropholes, there's plenty we could learn."

"Yeah, like, oh fuck I'm being chased by Xenomorphs."

"Don't think so," Hari said quietly.

"Hari, got those life readings for me?"

"I've got some sort of reading. It's huge. Massive. Odd. I can't find anything moving, but it's like the whole ship's filled with some sort of low-level plant life. It's hazy, like the hull is confusing the signal."

"Maybe," Durante said. Mains saw him biting his lip, contemplating what to do. It would be easy enough to blow the ship apart, but as yet they had no reason to. It had made no threatening moves. They weren't about to declare war on someone, or something, without good cause.

Durante glanced at Mains, eyebrow raised. Mains felt a rush of gratitude to the man for acknowledging that he had another experienced lieutenant on board.

"Could be stuff on there we need to know," Mains said. "Go in fast, have Spike keep the *Navarro*'s weapons hot."

"That's what I'm thinking," Durante agreed. "Moran, take us into that open hangar. Fly aggressive."

"Got it," Moran said.

"Okay, gang," Durante said. "Start your motors. Let's party."

With all external viewing sources open, the *Navarro* fell into shadow as it entered the belly of the beast. It was taken in and smothered with darkness, like a reverse birth, and Mains felt a sinking in his stomach.

*I'm never getting out of here alive*, he thought. It was a strange idea, and he wasn't used to such irrational fears. Perhaps his time on UMF 12 had affected him more than he believed.

"We survived that," Lieder said, almost as if she could read his mind. "We can survive this."

Spike kept the ship afloat in the huge hangar for a time, pivoting slightly left and right like a dog sniffing at something new. The crew's eyes were fixed to their viewing screens, while Hari watched for any changes in life readings.

"Looks weird," Moran said.

"Yeah, like it's grown," Mains said, echoing what had been said earlier. Weird was the right word. The hangar's walls and ceiling were bulbous, smooth in places and rough in others, twisted and curled like a confused intestine. The *Navarro*'s lights shone around the large space, glinting off pinks and reds and only increasing the impression of being inside something once alive.

Or perhaps *still* alive.

"Remember that old flat-movie?" Durante asked. "Can't remember the name. They landed in an asteroid, but flew into the mouth of some giant worm-thing."

"Thanks for that," Mains said.

"It's all structure," Hari said. "Not living material. Not quite sure what some of it is, but it's not living."

"Let's put a shot in it, just to make sure," Moran suggested.

"We only shoot if we have to," Durante said. "We're going off-ship. Me, Moran, Lieder, Hari, Mains. The rest of you stay here, keep watch, keep channels open at all times. Any changes in velocity, life readings… any changes at all, and you scream. Got it?"

"Yes, boss," came the chorus.

"And at my order you get the fuck out of here, and blow the ship to hell."

No response.

"Got it?" Durante demanded. He stood, magnetic boots holding him to the floor, head almost brushing the ceiling. The alien ship seemed to have no artificial gravity. They were all used to working in zero-G, but it sometimes made sudden movements and reaction times more difficult.

"Got it, boss," someone said, and the reply was echoed by the others.

"I don't plan on losing it here," he said, "but these are interesting times, and it might be that no one gives a damn what my plans are."

The five of them congregated at the doors leading from the flight deck, checking each other's suits and weaponry, and Lieder and Mains stood close. They were the last of the VoidLarks, potentially going into battle one more time. Perhaps one *last* time.

"It can't be worse than the habitat," Lieder said.

"Can't be," Mains agreed.


They held their com-rifles in one hand, using the other to guide themselves, push, hold, and steer. Moving in zero gravity was a true talent, and these marines had been in space for long enough to make it second nature.

The hangar was also open to space, placing them in a vacuum, so their suits fed them a suitable breathing atmosphere. Ventings froze into drifting clouds of ice shards. They shoved off from the *Navarro's* ramp and drifted across the hangar, aiming for where sensors indicated a doorway led into the ship's interior.

Mains was pleased to discover that their magnetic boots found purchase, even though much of the material used in the construction didn't seem metallic. It was gray and smooth, slick in appearance, looking as if it had been poured rather than molded. He almost expected it to flex underfoot, but the floor was solid.

They moved across the vast hangar, and he wondered what ships it might once have held. It could be that the wreckage drifting along with this huge ship was the remnants of what had docked in this and other hangars.

They reached the end wall and an entry portal. A simple swipe on a control and it spiraled open, and all five marines aimed their com-rifles, ready to unleash hell on anything that came at them.

But the hallway beyond the portal was cold, dark, and silent.

Their visors switched to infrared, giving them a hazily tinged view of their surroundings. As the doors closed behind them Mains heard a hissing sound. It grew in volume until his suit indicated that there was an atmosphere. After a quick analysis, the sensor confirmed that it was perfectly breathable.

Designed for humans, or something similar.

"Why the hell wasn't there decompression?" Moran asked. No one had an answer.

The hallway was straight, wide and low with several corridors leading off to the sides. The walls and ceilings were smooth and even, more what they were used to, and here and there were what might have been control points for doorways, or communication points. Hari examined one, then shrugged.

They moved off to the left, heading for the front of the ship. Drifting quietly, trying to avoid contact with surfaces, they went uninterrupted. No signs of movement anywhere, no indication that their intrusion had been noticed by ship or occupants, and Mains found that disconcerting. He felt observed, as if a silent, mysterious presence followed them like a shadow, not breathing, not even alive. Several times he glanced over his shoulder at Lieder, and he knew she was thinking the same thing. She carried her com-rifle tight across her chest, ready to bring it to bear at a moment's notice.

It was Hari who stopped them. She was being fed constant sensor information from the *Navarro*, and she shoved past Mains and Lieder to converse with her lieutenant.

"Hold up," Durante said. He and Hari whispered, then she touched his chest and pushed to turn herself around, then shoved off to the corridor wall.

"Through there?" he asked.

"Yes," Hari said. She seemed haunted.

"Keeping us in the dark?" Lieder asked.

"Weird life readings," Hari said. "Through this wall, not far away."

"So we take a look," Mains said.

They searched until they found a door. Its controls looked similar to those leading from the hangar, and it was Durante who reached for them.

"Ready?" he asked, hand paused.

"No," Mains said.

Durante stroked the control, and the door whispered open.

The hold beyond was vast. Mains wasn't sure he'd ever seen such a huge enclosed space, not even inside UMF 12. It was so wide that the far side was out of sight, even using infrared. Mist seemed to drift across, sparkling clouds that shimmered in their enhanced vision. The hold stretched left and right, end walls also beyond their view.

Huge—mind-blowingly so—but far from empty.

At first Mains thought they were trees, massive growths bearing a rich, strange fruit. Then he realized that trees wouldn't be rooted at both ends. These structures rose from floor to high ceiling, stretched horizontally between thick trunks were branches, and the fruit on their long, twisting limbs was like nothing he had ever seen before—nor ever hoped to see.

Each seed-shaped pod contained a human being. Those close by were in plain view, naked bodies suspended in a thick, clear fluid. There seemed to be no skin to the pods, simply a globe of gel held together by its own surface tension. They were connected to the solid branches by sturdy red stems, and some of these stems seemed to pulse. Sending nutrients to the bodies, perhaps, or maybe drawing something from them.

"Holy fuck," Lieder said. "It *is* a Fiennes ship."

"No," Moran said. "These aren't traditional suspension pods. I've never seen anything like them. Nothing human made this."

"But where did all these people come from?" Mains asked.

"Taken from Fiennes ships and brought here, maybe," Durante said. He was the first to push through the doorway and into the hold, drifting close to a branch thick with pods. Mains went with him.

Leaning in close to one grotesque fruit, he could clearly make out the naked man within. Long hair, thin limbs, a strong body, his eyes closed and a serene expression on his face. If he dreamed, he dreamed happy thoughts. Mains had spent years of his life in suspension, but it was weird to think how old this man might be.

If he truly was from one of the Fiennes ships, he would have been born long before Mains's great-great-great-grandparents. He'd know nothing of the Human Sphere, their intrepid expansion out into the galaxy, the discoveries that had been made. He might never have heard of the dreaded Xenomorphs, or the brutal Yautja, Arcturians, or any other alien species encountered or discovered. The burgeoning drophole technologies would be a mystery to him, as would the planets and moons colonized, and new worlds terraformed and inhabited by brave explorers.

Everyone he had ever known and loved would be long dead, and he would have gone down expecting to be woken only if his ship found a habitable planet. He was the bravest of the brave, and Mains could only look at him in awe.

"What's that?" Durante asked. He was pointing below the man at a shriveled, wrinkled mass beneath his body. It was like shed skin.

"Don't know," Mains said. "Can't quite…" He moved to another pod, this one containing a woman, young and looking fit despite her probable age. She also shared the pod with a shriveled object. He looked closer.

"Oh my God," he whispered.

"Xenomorphs," Lieder said from behind Mains. "That's a Xeno egg layer. She's been impregnated."

"Check the others," Durante said, but Mains already had a sick feeling in his chest.

"Nurseries," he said.

"These too, boss," Moran said, drifting from pod to pod and pushing himself higher up the branch. "And these."

"And look up there," Mains said. "Up on the thicker trunks." Xenomorph eggs. He could see them now, hunched shapes, all of them empty and slumped down over time.

"Get back down here," Durante said.

"How many are there?" Mains asked. "There must be thousands."

"I can't see the end of them," Lieder said. She was close to Mains but looking into the distance, and he could see her visor deflecting slightly as she instructed it to magnify. "It's unbelievable."

"Spike's done a quick sensor sweep," Hari said. "He estimates forty thousand pods in this hold."

Mains swallowed.

"*This* hold?" Durante asked.

"There are five others in the ship," Hari said.

"We've got to get out of here," Lieder said. "If this is a nursery, where are the nurses?"

"We can't just leave them," Hari said.

"We can't do anything for them," Lieder said.

"We can't just—"

"They're finished!"

"There is something we can do for them," Durante said, and the coolness to his voice froze them all.

"Boss," Moran said. "Movement behind us, coming closer. Six readings."

"Get ready," Mains said. He held his com-rifle and stroked the trigger, eager to see the Xenomorphs, keen to blast them apart and watch their acid splash the walls. He wanted to kill them, just as they and their masters had assuredly killed these tens of thousands of people.

No human had ever been saved after being impregnated by a Xenomorph.

"Form up," Durante said. "This side of the entrance, we'll take them in the doorway."

Mains and Lieder drifted back a little, resting against one of the structures with pods to either side.

"Bekovich, we've got incoming," Durante said, talking to one of the ship's crew. "Keep an eye on life sign movement for us."

"We got it, boss. See you, six bogies moving toward you, that's it for now."

They waited, eyes on the doorway and their visor displays, ready to open fire. Mains feared that once the shooting began, a lot more Xenomorphs would make themselves known, and somewhere on this massive, monstrous ship he was sure they'd find one of those bastard androids. He wondered what name he or she would have been given.

"Five yards," Moran said.

A shadow fell across the doorway.

Mains touched the trigger, a plasma pulse programmed to melt the doorway around their ears.

"Hold!" Hari shouted.

Mains almost fired in shock, then he saw the woman in the doorway. Short, terrified, she was dressed in a torn space suit of a design he'd never seen, and carrying a long metal bar. Even the gravity boots she wore were worn and tattered. A couple more faces appeared behind her, one man with burns across one side of his head and face, a woman behind him with no hair and one arm amputated at the elbow.

The burned man pushed past her and aimed a laser pistol at the marines. His hand was shaking, but he had defiance in his eyes.

Then confusion.

"Who are you?" he asked.

"Seems to me we should be asking questions and *you* should be answering," Durante said. "This your ship?"

"Of course," the man said. "Who… who are you?"

"Colonial Marines," Mains said.

The man's eyes went wider, and perhaps he even smiled.

"You come from *outside*? From *beyond*?"

"Is this a Fiennes ship?" Lieder asked.

"No. No. *No.*"

The man lowered his gun. The woman stepped forward and held him, and Mains was shocked to see that he had started to cry.

"We're shipborn," the woman said. "We were once of the Rage."

"What the hell *is* this?" Durante asked.

"This is the *Othello*," the woman said, "and we are Founders once again."

The one-armed woman behind her started to cry.

"Hurry. *Hurry!* They're coming!"

# 1 1

## LILIYA

*Space Station Hell*
*November 2692 AD*

"I think maybe you need to hide," Liliya said. The Yautja language still felt strange in her mouth, and she wondered how quickly she could adapt again to the standard tongue. Hashori had never shown any eagerness to learn or speak anything other than Yautja.

"Yautja don't hide," Hashori said. "Weaklings hide. Criminals and cowards hide. I am a warrior, and I—"

"Just for a while!" Liliya shouted. "Seriously, do you want to march out there and start killing again?"

"I hadn't intended that," Hashori said.

"Well, that's what will happen. Look. They're already here." She nodded at the viewing screen that had emerged from the control panel, and contained within was a 360-degree view of their surroundings. They had docked at one of the space station's more remote docking bays, and already there were soldiers swarming around the hangar, drifting across the wide space and bringing a range of weaponry to bear on the Yautja craft. There were many hand weapons, but also a few heavier-looking laser cannons magnetically affixed to floor, walls, and ceilings.

"If they open fire my ship will—"

"*Please*, Hashori. Try to think about this not as another battle, but as a potential place of peace."

"They appear eager to start a fight," the Yautja said.

"No, no. They're being cautious. They probably recognize the ship as Yautja—and what does that tell you?"

"That they respect our warrior prowess."

Liliya sighed and closed her eyes. *I can't have come this far to be blown to pieces here and now.*

"Please, let me go out first," she said.

"I will not hide," Hashori said, and Liliya tried to understand the situation from her point of view. The Yautja was a proud beast, still troubled at fleeing from the *Zeere Za* even though the ship's fate had been sealed. They had run from Alexander and his army instead of remaining behind to fight, and that must have burned, too.

The Yautja did not flee a fight, and Hashori was right—they certainly did not hide.

"I understand," Liliya said. "Really, I do, but if you step out there before me, they won't ask questions first. Right now, I'm the best chance anyone has of turning this war around."

Hashori considered for a while, and Liliya could almost *feel* her internal conflict. Her people had been decimated, losing ships, habitats, and even a couple of planets to the Rage. All she wanted to do was to fight, but sometimes a good fight needed a long preparation.

"You can leave the ship first," Hashori said finally.

"Thank you." Liliya felt exhausted, but also a tingle of excitement at exiting this confined space she had shared with Hashori for so long. She had fled the Rage, been taken by the Yautja, and then run from them again, this time with

Hashori. They already had a history together, but so long spent so close together had left Liliya's nerves frayed.

Sometimes, she had to remind herself that she was an android, and that helped, but she was also very, very old, and in many ways she considered herself more human than many of the Rage. With them, age had hardened them, stripping away empathy and concentrating the twisted desire for some sort of revenge against the humanity who had apparently persecuted them, and the Founders before them. With her, age had made her more human than she could have ever hoped. It was an irony that she held onto, and the main reason she had finally left them.

"You will explain why we're here together?" Hashori asked.

*Because I went to you for help*, Liliya thought. *Because you tortured me, keeping me on the edge of death for so long*. But that was in the past, and Hashori had not been obliged to save her. Liliya saw past the bad to the good, and she knew that she would not have survived if it were not for this proud, furious Yautja.

"I will," Liliya said, "and then you can leave the ship, too."

She hoped.

Liliya readied herself. While Hashori made a show of taking the ship's weapons offline, the android stood close to the airlock, trying to make herself presentable. There was no need for a space suit—the docking bay doors had closed behind them, trapping them inside, and sensors indicated that atmosphere had been leveled. There was no artificial gravity, though. Perhaps that was reserved for the station's central core, not these outlying docking bays.

This was it. Her first contact in centuries with the humanity that Liliya had returned to save. It should have been a great moment, but this space station was called

Hell. It seemed run down in places, and the soldiers outside were not wearing matching uniforms. They certainly were not Colonial Marines, at least not as she remembered them from almost three centuries ago.

She had to make the best of things. But as the hull became fluid and an outer door appeared, she could not help thinking that she had made a huge mistake.

"Hold it right there!" The woman's voice was strong, but also worried. Liliya could hardly blame her—a Yautja ship had landed on her space station.

Liliya held up her hands in the universal gesture of supplication and compliance.

"That's a Yautja ship!" the woman said. She stood at the controls of a laser cannon.

"It is," Liliya said, "but we have not come here for a fight. I've returned with something that—"

"You're flying it? You've stolen it?"

"No."

"Is there a Yautja inside?"

"There is," Liliya said. All around the bay, soldiers hunkered down closer to their weapons, and the air almost sparkled with violent potential.

"Step away," the soldier said.

"First will you hear me?"

"Step away from the ship!"

"No!" Liliya said. She looked from face to face. They all wore combat suits of some sort, but many did not match. Neither did their weapons. These were mercenaries. That did not make them any more or less dangerous than Colonial Marines, but it did mean that their orders could be diverse. They might run Hell as a military council, or perhaps they were merely employed to protect it.

Either way, Liliya could not let this meeting descend into violence. She had come all this way to *end* the violence. This was an important, loaded moment, and so much depended on how it played out.

She only wished she could convey that importance to them.

"Let me tell you who I am," she said, looking directly at the soldier who seemed to be in charge. The woman stared back along the barrel of the heavy cannon. She could end Liliya's long life without her even knowing, send her into darkness at the speed of light. The idea of such oblivion had never worried Liliya, but now she found it terrifying. So many lives might depend on her staying alive.

"Please."

"Who are you?" the woman demanded.

"My name is Liliya. I've come in peace, accompanied by a Yautja who has suffered terribly at the hands of the Rage."

"What's the Rage?"

"You've heard of the attacks across the Outer Rim?"

"We keep to ourselves here, but yes, we've heard."

"The Rage is the group committing those attacks. I've come from them, I know their plans and capabilities, and I've stolen something that might help the Human Sphere defend itself."

"Right," the woman said. "Step aside."

"No," Liliya said. "You have to let me—"

"Step aside, or I'll shoot *through* you!"

"Do that and you doom yourselves to die." Liliya sensed a ripple pass through the bay, and she suspected the mercenaries were communicating. What happened in the next few moments would indicate what was being said.

"Why choose here?" the soldier asked.

"We're being chased by a Rage army," Liliya said.

"They know the threat I present to them, and they want me captured or destroyed."

"So you're leading them to us?"

"No. We've shaken them." Liliya's lie was hard, but she saw no benefit in admitting the truth. She had to move past this stalemate and onward, seeking help, exposing herself to someone other than these soldiers who only had violence on their minds. In a way, perhaps it *would* benefit her if Hashori and they entered into combat— but she had seen too much death already. She had come bearing a message of hope, and she had to reflect that message in her actions.

"We want to see the Yautja," the soldier said. "Tell it to come to the doorway."

"I can't tell Hashori to do anything," Liliya said. She hoped that giving the Yautja a name might personalize it in these soldiers' minds.

Then she sensed Hashori behind her, just out of sight. She could smell her, musky and warm, and she wondered whether that smell had always been present in the ship. Or it could have been a natural smell of excitement, as Hashori readied for a fight.

"The fate of the Human Sphere and its peace with your people rests here," Liliya whispered to Hashori. Then she stepped from the ship and floated aside.

Hashori stood in the doorway. Resplendent and threatening in her warrior's garb, shoulder blaster drooped and inactive, blades on her belt, her heavy trident in one hand, helmet held beneath her other arm, she remained tall and proud as several laser sights played across her chest and face. Part of Liliya wished she had worn her helmet and mask, but then to reveal herself like this showed that she was an individual being, not merely a creature of war.

Hashori spoke, and Liliya translated.

"She says… your space station smells of fear."

The mercenary woman bristled, but then stood from behind her laser cannon. She took three steps forward, shoes clomping softly as they attached themselves to the deck. She seemed uncertain, glancing around at her troops as if to gauge their mood.

"Tell her, welcome to Hell," the woman said.

Liliya translated. Hashori chuckled. The tension in the air wasn't totally defused, but she noticed some of the soldiers relaxing, and the woman walked closer. She seemed fascinated with Hashori.

"I need to speak to someone in charge," Liliya said. "Is this a Weyland-Yutani vessel?"

"Not at all," the mercenary said, not taking her eyes from the Yautja. "We're independent."

"But you have a way to contact the Company?"

She frowned, looked at Liliya, and the mistrust in her gaze was palpable.

"Just who the fuck are you?"

Liliya smiled. Human curse words had not changed over three centuries and a thousand light years.

"I've already told you."

"Well, you can tell me again—but not here. Come with me." She glanced around, and at some silent signal most of the mercenaries lowered their weapons. Most, but not all. "We can't stand around pointing guns at each other all day. I expect you've come a long way."

"You have no idea," Liliya said.

The mercenary led the way, and Liliya and Hashori followed. Accompanied by ten other mercenaries, she took them from the docking bay and down in an elevator toward the main body of the space station. It was huge, and the closer they got to the main section, the more people they saw. The reaction to having a Yautja with them was one of fear, and shock, and Liliya was hardly surprised. But people were also fascinated, and soon they gathered a small crowd behind them.

The mercenaries formed a security ring around Liliya and Hashori, two deep and still heavily armed, and when they reached the vast main open space, artificial gravity asserted itself. Liliya's stomach dropped and she slumped a little, but Hashori only grunted and stood straight. She looked around at the soldiers and dozens of people following them, and no human could hold the Yautja's gaze. Even without overt antagonism, still Hashori exuded aggression. Hers was not a visage evolved for peace.

Liliya began to wonder whether they had come to the right place.

The Rage's knowledge of the Human Sphere since leaving almost three centuries before was sparse. Liliya had gathered intelligence on the dropholes, but much of that had been from chatter and broadcasts across the Outer Rim between Titan ships and their escorts. Events deeper inside the Sphere, up to five hundred light years from the Outer Rim, remained more mysterious, more unknown.

They knew that Weyland-Yutani were still a power to be reckoned with, a corporate ruling entity that spread its influence across human space and beyond. Whether or not they had taken control of the Colonial Marines was uncertain, but it seemed likely that the Company acted more as a governmental power than simply a business enterprise. An organization so huge saw beyond profit and loss, and control became a greater motivator.

Liliya had long suspected that to ensure what she carried in her blood, and the knowledge she bore, got to the correct people to use it, she would have to submit herself to the Company. Now, in this first interaction with humanity within the Human Sphere, it seemed she was as far away as ever.

Still she felt as if she had taken a huge step. Leaving the Rage in the first place had been easy, especially after Beatrix Maloney's admission that their return would be a horrifically violent one. Submitting herself to the Yautja had been a mistake, but one which might yet prove to be a blessing. And now landing on Hell might be the first large step toward making contact with the people who mattered.

Liliya only had to persuade the station's controllers that she was here for benevolent reasons.

They escorted them to a cell. It was to be expected, but it still took Liliya some time to persuade Hashori that it was for the best. Hell's defenders were simply being cautious.

The cell was more of a contained room, well appointed and larger than the interior of Hashori's ship. Liliya paced back and forth from wall to wall, enjoying the sense of space. Hashori stood in one corner, staring at her without any apparent expression. They'd let the Yautja retain her weapons. Liliya liked the implied trust in this, but she also knew that they could probably both be killed in an instant. The room was comfortable, but she suspected it had systems and defenses necessary to preserve the station's integrity and safety.

A man brought them some food and drink, wide-eyed and staring only at Hashori. He seemed more excited than scared. Hashori glared at him until he looked away.

Liliya did not require sustenance, but she ate for the sake of appearances. She had yet to reveal that she was an android.

As she was picking at the food, the door slid open again, and an older man walked in. He assessed them both briefly before signaling that the door should be closed behind him. Then he sat opposite Liliya, took out a datapad, and leaned back in his chair.

"They've asked me to come and talk to you," he said.

"You're the leader here?"

"Hell has no leader. We've got a ruling council, which has a chairperson, but all decisions are democratic, voted on by that council. Business takings are split, but our internal monetary system is very simple. We're self-sustaining, and only take payments from visitors. We don't trust anyone." He looked her up and down, eyes narrowing slightly. He seemed wise. "So, no, I'm not the leader. My name's Jiango Tann, and they've asked me to speak to you because I've had dealings with the Company."

"My name is Liliya," she said, extending her hand. He took it, shook, then tilted his head.

"You're an artificial."

"Yes." She was surprised that he'd picked up on that. "But I've chosen as many human aspects as I can, and I do consider myself… a person."

"Then so will I." He smiled for the first time and Liliya relaxed, feeling the same sense of peace that she'd once enjoyed with Wordsworth. With him it had been wisdom and benevolence. She hoped the feeling this man inspired in her was the same.

"So they've told you why I'm here?" she asked.

"Yes, although I'll admit, we don't know an awful lot about what's been going on at the Outer Rim. I've picked up some transmissions myself. Broken messages. They seem to involve Xenomorphs."

Liliya saw a shadow cross his face and thought to herself, *He has some history with them.* But now was not the time for sensitivity.

So she told him the basics of her story. She began with

the awful truth about her time aboard the *Evelyn-Tew* almost three centuries before, and ended with her arrival at Hell with Hashori.

Tann sat back and listened, not once interceding with a question, though she knew he had many. When she'd finished he regarded her for a while, tapping the datapad he had not once used and seemingly staring through her to something far away.

"You were on the *Evelyn-Tew*?"

Liliya nodded. "I'm surprised you've heard of the ship."

"Lots about me might surprise you," Tann said. "But really? Weaponized Xenomorphs?"

Liliya nodded. She spoke to Hashori, who also nodded at Tann. It was a peculiarly human gesture from the Yautja.

"I hoped the day would never come." Tann sounded sad, and scared. "The Company will do anything it can, and everything possible, to get its hands on them. It's spent centuries trying to do so, and many people have died in its quest. They have advanced nukes, particle modulators, and certainly other weapons we know nothing about, but the Xenomorph is the ultimate—a soldier crossed with a biological weapon. And you have in your blood the means to give them that?"

Liliya nodded.

"Exactly what *is* it that you carry?"

"A combination of advanced human science and alien technology that's almost mystical. The human science is something… I stole. On board the *Evelyn-Tew*, they had Xenomorph samples, including a queen, and they were experimenting with control mechanisms using nanotechnology. It was rudimentary, but they were encountering some decent results. I caused a catastrophe. Stole the research. Fled."

Tann was now using his datapad furiously. He would

be checking on her story, she knew. She felt shame, but this was beyond personal feelings. Complete honesty was the only way to gain this man's trust, and she sensed that he was someone who could help her, if he chose to do so.

She only hoped her instincts were sound.

"I was adrift for decades until the Founders picked me up. The research I carried was intended as insurance. Wordsworth knew that there were great dangers out beyond the Human Sphere, the Xenomorph perhaps the least of them. But an ability to control that beast—perhaps to control *any* alien species we might come across—might protect the Founders from devastation. Wordsworth didn't just want to survive, he wanted to thrive.

"What I carried was cutting edge research, but when we landed on *Midsummer*, and it was combined with the ancient technology we discovered there, it became remarkable. We found traces of a dog-like species, long dead, but with incredible science, way beyond what we had ever seen before, or even imagined. Among other things, there was the Faze. A being—creature, creation, or perhaps something indefinable—that literally rebuilt our ships from the inside out. It grew mechanical parts, extruded materials, and bettered everything it touched. No one ever truly understood it, and no communication or contact was ever achieved. Nevertheless, we gave the two Faze we found free rein on our ships, *Macbeth* and *Othello*. It was as if they advanced our science a hundred times faster than was destined, and we were happy to let them."

"So what did combining the stolen Company tech and alien technology produce?"

"I'm sure you know plenty about nanotechnology."

Tann nodded without looking up from the datapad.

"Not like this," she continued. "Combining the alien tech with the stolen research, the technology the

Founders developed was far beyond the mere physical. Controlling the Xenomorphs, psychically attuning them to one particular general, that's only part of it. They can be programmed. They're set to destruct if they're fatally wounded or killed, destroying any trace of the artificial elements in their blood. We can also promote the construction of controlling elements in a biological being from light years away."

Tann looked up at this.

"Nanotech built from a body's own elements, prompted by sub-space transmissions at a certain wavelength," Liliya said. "It's… a word you might use is arcane. It's almost beyond science, and I'm not sure anyone really understands it."

"You're playing God," Tann said.

"God?" Liliya was surprised this man would even mention such an ephemeral deity.

"A manner of speaking," Tann said, but she wasn't sure. He had a scientist's mind, but she knew that some scientists could retain a spiritual side. Wordsworth had been proof of that.

"I'm filled with regrets," Liliya whispered.

Tann seemed not to hear.

"You carry this incredible technology in your blood. Something that has become so destructive, in the wrong hands, and you want us to help you get that to the Company?"

"Understanding it might be the Human Sphere's only chance," Liliya said. "You heard what I told you about Beatrix Maloney. Her hatred. Her determination. Even I don't know her ultimate plan for the Sphere, but trust me when I tell you that it's nothing good."

"My own son died working for the Company, trying to get them Xenomorphs."

"I'm sorry," Liliya said, "but it's not only what's in my

blood that might help. I know Maloney, and the Rage. I've been with them from the beginning. I understand some of her thinking, and the strategies she might employ. I know some of her plans."

"That's why she wants you dead."

"Of course."

Tann stood and walked to the door. Then he glanced back at Hashori and Liliya.

"I never thought I'd see the day when Yautja and human stand together."

Liliya smiled at his reference to her as human. He was a learned man, a wise man, but troubled, and probably correct in his fears. He'd confirmed to her that Weyland-Yutani controlled the Colonial Marines, so now they were faced with a heavy dilemma.

Give the Company the power it had sought for generations to truly control the dreaded Xenomorph?

Or withhold what she carried, and take the risk?

"I need to talk with the Council," Tann said.

"Of course," she said. "But Jiango... we may not have much time."

"You said you'd shaken Alexander and his army sent to find you."

"We did," she said, "but they have ways and means, and he's tracked me down once before."

# 1 2

## B E A T R I X   M A L O N E Y

*Outer Rim*
*November 2692 AD*

She was almost home. The end of the beginning of her grand plan was close at hand—but still her greatest threat, Liliya, was at large. Beatrix's greatest general had yet to capture her.

"...and we should be able to drop through before long," Alexander said. "However she managed to close the drophole behind her, we'll find the solution at the control base. But General Parks made a mess of the place when he attacked eleven days ago, and we're forced to sift through the wreckage. Trust me, mistress, that Liliya will be in my hands very soon. You have my word."

Maloney wished she could shout and rage at Alexander now, face to face, instead of listening to his message with fury simmering within her, and nowhere to vent it. Dana and Kareth stood at the room's extremes, uncomfortable but knowing that she would never take out her frustration on them. Never.

In her mind, Maloney saw blood flowing across the

floor, and she did not care where it came from.

Eyes closed, breathing hard, feeling her gel massaging and renewing her muscles and limbs and skin, she resisted the temptation to record an instant response. She should not doubt him. He was the best of her generals—that was why she sent him and his army after the deserter, the traitor—and he was aware that he was on the most important of missions.

He would succeed, given time, but at almost three centuries old, time was something Maloney did not have.

"Mistress, your bio levels are raised," Dana said.

"Of course they're raised!" Maloney shouted. When she did so, pain thrummed through her head, her hover platform dipped and moved to the left, and then Kareth was there, holding her steady as she struggled to maintain balance. Kareth was *always* there. Shipborn, he was as dedicated to her as anyone had ever been. Her rock. He and Dana deserved only the best, and losing her temper with them was unforgivable.

"I apologize," she said, voice harsh nevertheless.

"There's no need," Kareth said. "It's what we're here for."

"No!" Maloney said, but this time she reined in any loss of temper. "No, you and Dana are here for my well-being, not to be the target of my anger. Anger is weakness. I should have learned that long ago. I am sorry."

"It's frustration," Kareth said. "Everything is going so well, but Liliya…" He trailed off.

"Liliya could ruin everything," Maloney said. The words hung heavy, their import a weight on the air. "Take me to it."

Kareth and Dana guided her through into the next room. The Watcher was here. Maloney could think of no better name for it. Extruded from the Faze that now spent most of its time huddled against the *Macbeth*'s core drive, the Watcher was still a part of that being in some way, though its purpose was not in creating and rebuilding. Upon Liliya's violent departure from the *Macbeth*, the Faze had produced the Watcher, unprompted and unasked, and this new being had mysteriously begun tracking her.

It had an identical sibling aboard Alexander's ship, both creatures somehow following Liliya's journey toward and into the Human Sphere.

The alien they had brought up from the dark depths of *Midsummer* was one of the few things that still frightened Beatrix Maloney. The Faze moved and worked independently, most of the time appearing as unaware of the humans around it as the sea is of life within. Its actions and creations were slow, yet everything it touched, extruded, formed, or remade was an improvement on the original. Its decades-long work on the *Macbeth*—and its cousin's efforts on the *Othello*, before contact was lost with that ship—had made the vessel significantly stronger and much, much faster than ever before.

Its origins were lost in the faded history of the dog-like aliens, now long gone, who had once called *Midsummer* home. Some shipborn even regarded the Faze as some kind of god. But to Maloney it was a tool, and so long as it served her purpose, she was happy to leave it alone to continue its work.

Its strange, unknowable sentience, and its apparent knowledge of the Rage's intentions, was shown in many ways. One of the most startling had been its ability to track Liliya. Maloney suspected it had to do with the amazing nanotech the android had stolen from the Rage, and injected into herself to take to the Human Sphere. Part of that tech had been developed by Weyland-Yutani, the results of in-depth studies of Xenomorph samples and captives.

Liliya herself had stolen that for the original Founders. Weyland-Yutani hadn't yet succeeded, but their research had been given a new, remarkable edge on *Midsummer*. Now, this incredible creature could somehow sense its own bio-tech, and track it over many light years.

Maloney no longer questioned the how and why. There had still been no successful communication with the Faze. She simply accepted what it did, and how it benefited the Rage.

Kareth and Dana backed away and left her alone in the room. The Watcher was small—no larger than a human head—but even being in its presence made Maloney's mind thrum with energy. As usual, it seemed instinctively to know what she desired. A star image was projected onto the room's far wall, and a small blue blur indicated Liliya's presence in the vastness of space.

She was now within the Human Sphere. Alexander was light years away, but then the creature folded the image to show how close he and his army could jump once they established control of the drophole.

Maloney frowned and tried to look closer, and the creature enlarged the image.

It appeared as if Liliya was no longer moving.

"If you don't catch her this time…" she whispered, but she decided that such pleas, or threats, should not carry across space.

General Alexander had already made his promise.

# 1 3

## GERARD MARSHALL

*Charon Station, Sol System*
*November 2692 AD*

The dream of real-time communication across trillions of miles of empty space had only been realized very recently. It took mind-bogglingly huge energy expenditures, involved equipment that had cost billions of credits, and used ultra-rare resources, which was why Weyland-Yutani—and specifically, the Thirteen—still held the technology close to its chest.

The time would come when they would benefit from releasing it to the wider Sphere, but for the moment, such groundbreaking tech gave them an advantage, and the Company always sought an edge.

Gerard Marshall had always believed that real-time communications would make space feel smaller, but he'd found the opposite to be true. Sitting in this holo suite with General Bassett, talking with projections of James Barclay and the rest of the Thirteen, it only made him contemplate the staggering, belittling scope of the universe.

*I'm seeing them as they are at this exact moment*, he

thought, yet concepts such as "moment" fell apart over such distances. If he could truly look across space and time, and see one of the Thirteen, he would be viewing her as she'd been seventeen years ago. Not as she appeared to be now, berating General Bassett, flickering slightly as unknown sub-space quirks skewed her image, making her appear thirty years old and then sixty again in the blink of an eye.

No one knew why this odd flickering occurred. This was a new technology, and though disturbing, Marshall liked the idea that there were still more things to discover.

Some of those things had teeth.

"I don't want to hear the word 'sketchy' again!" the woman said. "General Bassett, we are the Thirteen, and we deal in facts. The fact is—"

"The fact is, I know more about what's happening than all of you put together," General Bassett replied. Marshall could almost feel the heat of his anger, and he couldn't help respecting the General's attitude. It wasn't every day that someone—even the commander of the Colonial Marines—sat facing every member of the Thirteen, let alone interrupting one.

Most people would be scared silent, but Bassett was an old soldier through and through. Anyone non-military had to work very, very hard to gain his respect, and complete trust was always reserved for fellow soldiers. Nothing scared him.

Marshall was glad to have him on their side.

"Please, if I may," Marshall said, holding up his hand.

James Barclay, the Thirteen's notional leader, nodded at Marshall, a signal for him to proceed.

"Thank you," Marshall continued. "Perhaps General Bassett's use of the word 'sketchy' was inappropriate, but the fact remains that contact with Colonial Marine contingents in the Outer Rim's Gamma quadrant has been intermittent and troublesome at best. What contact we have received only goes to confirm what we've known for some time—that we are under a sustained and concerted attack. You've all read the report, I know, but I think it's important that the General outlines the most essential facts himself."

"Given those reports, why bother?" someone asked. "This broadcast is costing more credits per second than you make in a year, General."

"Why bother? Because I'm a Marine," Bassett said, "and in these matters, what I know is more important than your damned credits."

"I agree," Barclay said. "Please proceed, General."

Bassett gathered himself, and continued.

"We know that whoever they are, they're attacking drophole locations, taking out control bases, and securing the dropholes for their own use. They flip out of warp very close to these installations, then launch lightning attacks. Surprise has been their main weapon, but even when we're prepared, our forces have been largely usurped. Some of those dropholes taken by the enemy have been used, and they've commenced further movement into the Sphere.

"That is a great cause for concern, because although our systems can remotely indicate those holes that have been used, the codes the enemy is using are somehow masking their targets. For each drop, there are up to four potential emergence sites, often up to twenty light years apart. They're disappearing… presumably until they attack somewhere else.

"They shouldn't even have access to the drop codes, but that's for our intelligence agencies to figure out as they're trying to discover the identity of the attackers. My main concern is the immediate conflict. If we can shed more light on who they are, and what their aims may be, there may be some way to exploit that information."

"We're losing every battle?" another of the Thirteen asked, an edge of fear in his voice.

"Not *every* drophole that's been attacked has ended up being taken, but they're assaulting with overwhelming and brutal force." He paused, then added, "We simply weren't prepared."

"Are they more advanced even than the Colonial Marines?"

"First indications confirm that, yes, they are," Bassett admitted. "The larger ships they're using are some of the old Fiennes ships. They've been radically upgraded, with deep warp drives and weapons systems beyond our own, both in range and payload. There are also escort ships of unknown design. Not human or Yautja, but something we haven't seen before. All of their ships are protected by advanced shields beyond anything we've ever been able to construct."

"Any first-hand sightings?" another woman asked. "One-on-one contacts? Are there any images available of the bastards who are doing this?"

"Their close-quarter assaults are carried out by weaponized Xenomorphs."

At that Marshall sat up straighter.

"You'll have seen my report concerning this," he said. "It looks as if the Xenomorph battalions are under the control of androids."

"We've read all this in the report," Barclay said, "and it makes for grim reading, indeed, General. However, you have yet to tell us anything new. What are these insights you tout so highly?"

Bassett frowned at that, and when he spoke, his tone was crisp.

"I do have some new information," he said. "A Marine squadron has located a Fiennes ship emerging from drophole Gamma 77. It was accompanied by four escort vessels. The squadron was orbiting Gamma 77's control station at the time, and within the hour they were in full combat with the attacking force. We lost three frigates and an Arrow-class ship, but the Fiennes vessel and its escorts were destroyed."

"Which Fiennes ship was it?" one of the Thirteen asked.

"Initial indications suggest it was a ship called the *Harmes-Cox*." The General paused, then added, "It was launched over four hundred years ago. Nineteen thousand souls were aboard."

"It's obscene," the woman said, although Marshall suspected she was referring to the fact that Weyland-Yutani was being attacked, and not the loss of life. "Who's doing this? Did the encounter with the *Harmes-Cox* yield any clues?"

"None," Marshall said, "but if you'll let the General continue…"

The other twelve faces flickered and faded in and out of focus, ripples in sub-space giving them animated expressions. He saw Barclay as a twenty-year-old man, and an aged, wasted scarecrow. A lifetime of possibilities, or perhaps a timeless collection of truths.

"The ship and crew involved in the recent Yautja peace initiative were also at a base that came under attack," Bassett said. "They were crewing my own Arrow-class vessel, the *Pixie*. Isa Palant sustained injuries before she made peace with the Yautja Elder Kalakta, and she has been recuperating on LV-1657, a Colonial Marine base close to drophole Gamma 116, around seven light years from the Outer Rim.

The Fiennes ship *Susco-Foley* dropped in-system and immediately attacked. Thanks to the actions of Major Akoko Halley and her DevilDogs, the *Pixie* was able to take off and destroy most of the attackers. At first the android controlling the attack was believed to be killed, but then he was seen fleeing into a cave system, protected by a few remaining Xenomorphs."

"So we have them trapped," Barclay said, becoming excited. "Do we have a Xenomorph sample?"

"No," Bassett said. "Two things were made clear by this attack. First, the Xenomorphs have something in their system that causes a complete meltdown the moment they're fatally injured or killed. Occasionally some of their hide survives, but no whole samples remain, and no retrievable samples of their blood."

"And the android?" Barclay asked.

"It also self-destructed," Bassett replied, "but with much more force. At least two megatons."

Barclay's face dropped. Other members of the Thirteen faded in and out, as if to transmit their disappointment.

"And the *Susco-Foley*?" Barclay asked.

"Several minutes after the android self-destructed, the old Fiennes ship executed a dive into LV-1657's atmosphere. It came apart and burned up. Nothing was left."

"It's a loss, but we've also gained important intelligence," Marshall said.

"How about the crew of the *Pixie*?" Barclay asked. "Palant and McIlveen? Did they survive the explosion?"

"They survived," Marshall said.

"Good," the leader of the Thirteen said. "Then you know what orders to issue to your forces, General. They've let an android give them the slip once already, but they can correct that error. If they can gather us a sample of these weaponized Xenomorphs, good, but their priority has to be to take one of the androids prisoner."

"They've been fighting for their lives, Barclay," Marshall said. He heard a grunt from Bassett, and hoped it was approval.

"As are we all," Barclay responded. "Make it happen, Gerard, General. Knowing the enemy is defeating them."

Marshall nodded, but the holo images had already started flickering to nothing. Moments later they were gone.

"Fucking idiots," Bassett said.

"Careful, General," Marshall said. "I'm one of those fucking idiots."

Bassett's mouth twitched into the semblance of a smile, but not for long.

"I'll contact Major Halley," Marshall said. "I can speak to Palant at the same time. You have plenty on your plate, as well."

"Just fighting for the future of the Human Sphere," Bassett said. He stood and gestured at the door. "We should leave."

Of course. It was his holo suite, after all.

"We're on the same side, Paul," Marshall said.

"Yes… Gerard." The General waited for him to leave before following him out.

*Never turn your back on an enemy*, Marshall mused.

"Major Halley," Marshall said. "I hope you're well." He was transmitting from his office now, via a holo frame, but still using the Company's instantaneous tech. The situation was evolving too quickly for him to send a recorded message.

"Marshall," Halley said brusquely. Her image shimmered, but her voice was clear. He only wished her hatred for him wouldn't taint every conversation they had. He knew of her history as a phrail addict, but that didn't mean he didn't respect her as a soldier, and a person. Why couldn't she understand that?

"Really, Akoko," he said, "how are you and the crew?"

"We lost Nassise and Gove," she said.

"My commiserations," he said, "but I'm afraid we don't have time to dwell on that."

"You have new orders for me?"

"I'm afraid so. These are terrible times," Marshall said. He meant it, and wondered for a moment if that was a softening he saw in Halley's expression. Or was it just a quirk of the sub-space connection? "Terrible times, and they call for desperate measures."

"I take it the wider battle isn't going well," Halley responded.

"We're suffering defeats," Marshall said. "Dropholes taken, enemy ships infiltrating deeper into the Sphere. The more drops they make, the more we lose track of where they might emerge next."

"We're pretty bashed around here," Halley said. "The blast knocked the *Pixie* from the sky. A couple of broken bones among the crew, but they've been fused. It's the damage to the ship that might take longer."

"We don't have longer," Marshall said. "We need you to find one of their androids, and take it alive."

"Right," Halley said, not even trying to disguise her skepticism. "You mean one of those androids that just self-destructed in a massive nuclear blast?"

"One of those. Yes."

Halley nodded, smiling. "Why us?"

"Because you're out there. You have the *Pixie*. You're the best I have. If we find one, discover how its self-destruct works, it might give us the advantage we need. And... I'll admit that assigning you the mission was my

184

idea, as you have Palant and McIlveen with you. My hope was... is..."

"Yautja," Halley said. "Your thinking is that we can team up."

"They did storm in to rescue you," Marshall said, "and I've been led to believe they've remained in the vicinity. Is that the case?"

"Yeah, they're still close," Halley confirmed. "Palant and McIlveen had some small success communicating with them after the battle. They're as hard to read as ever, but they admitted that they've been shadowing us, ever since the peace treaty with Elder Kalakta, with orders to ensure Palant's safety."

"So Kalakta's taken a shine to our Yautja expert," Marshall said, smiling. "Maybe that will help."

"I can't see us teaming up with the Yautja," Halley said.

"Yet where you and Palant go, they'll follow."

Halley nodded slowly. "And how are we supposed to find one of these androids. You know, the ones with nukes in them?"

"Look for another Fiennes ship."

"Seriously?" Halley asked.

"Major, I couldn't be more serious," Marshall said. "At the moment they seem to be everywhere. Take advantage of that." Without waiting for a reply he signed off, then leaned back in his chair, enjoying a moment of silence.

He feared it might be his last for quite some time.

# 1 4

## JOHNNY MAINS

Othello, *Outer Rim*
*November 2692 AD*

He knew the sound, and it brought nightmares into his waking world.

"Xenomorphs!" Mains whispered. "We have to run."

"We can stand and fight," Durante said.

"Eddie, listen to me—we have to *run*!" Mains hissed. "Even if there are only a few of the damned things, and we shoot them down, the sounds will bring more, and more." He knew this from experience. He also knew that they were in a giant hold containing tens of thousands of people, most of them impregnated with Xenomorph embryos.

Fighting the beasts in their own nest would be suicide.

"We... we know where to go," the one-armed woman said. The three newcomers were still staring at them with open shock and wonder, but now wasn't the time for questions and explanations.

"How do you—"

"We've survived for over a standard year," the burned man said. Behind him, from far along the corridor, the scuttling sound was coming closer.

Mains and Durante shared a glance. Mains nodded.

"We'll follow you," Durante said to the woman. "Any bullshit and we'll blow you into a smear." It didn't seem to faze her.

"You're really from outside?" she said, but Durante raised his weapon and pointed it at her.

"Now!" he said. She just glanced at the weapon. Mains wondered what terrors she had faced, that she could be so calm.

"This way," the man said. "I hope you'll fit." He looked Durante up and down before heading to the right. He and the two women led the way, with Mains, Lieder, Durante, and Moran following, and Hari bringing up the rear. They skirted the edge of the big hold, passing several thick branches and hundreds of gel pods, each nursing a human held in suspension.

Mains noticed a couple of pods where the gel was clouded and the person inside had shriveled, shrunken into the size of a child and quite obviously dead. In one, a body floated along with a deceased baby Xenomorph, the gel clouded with black blood set in solid waves. But most people seemed alive, fit and healthy, except for the feathery remains of the facehuggers that had impregnated them, and then died.

The sounds behind them continued, and Mains guessed the Xenomorphs would soon be upon them. The three people they'd met looked terrified, but perhaps it was all an act—a way of luring them into a trap where they'd be taken down by the beasts, stripped of weapons and clothing, forced into a gel pod, and then impregnated. He'd had nightmares of becoming a breeding ground for Xenomorphs. The suffocation, the pain…

He began to slow, ready to express his doubts, when

the two women in the lead dropped to their knees. With the man's help they eased up a panel in the floor. A stench rose up so shocking that Mains almost gagged, despite his suit's face mask. Eyes wide, they gestured inside, and the man hauled himself through first, moving effortlessly in weightlessness. Moran followed without pause.

"It's safe," Hari said behind him.

"How do you know that?"

"Because that way isn't." She indicated behind them, where shadows already danced across the doorway through which they'd accessed the big hold. "We've only got seconds."

They pulled themselves down through the hole, one by one, into the blackness. Durante had to contort to make it through. Hari came last. The women slid the panel back over the hole, then in the complete darkness one of the men whispered, "*Quiet.*" Despite a shallow layer of some sort of viscous liquid, their boots kept them tight to the floor, none of them floating in the zero gravity and knocking against each other.

Apart from their heavy breathing, there was silence. Mains's suit switched to infrared. The other Excursionists had done the same, but the three people they'd met had no such technology. They stood together, pressed close for comfort, eyes wide in the pitch darkness, as the monsters they hid from passed overhead.

Softly at first, Mains heard them. Their limbs connecting with walls, floor, and ceiling as they pulled themselves along the hallway. Then a soft, low hissing as they passed close by.

*Can they smell us?* he wondered. *Will they taste us?* But if they could, these people surely wouldn't have survived for so long.

One of the women still carried a metal bar, and at first

Mains had assumed it was a weapon, but as the sounds of Xenomorph pursuit faded above them, she twisted its end and a soft blue glow lit their surroundings.

"Oh, shit," Moran muttered. Mains heard others catching their breaths.

"Sorry," the one-armed woman said. "We didn't have time to warn you."

They were in some sort of drainage channel, just tall enough for Durante to stand in without crouching, narrow enough that if Mains reached out his arms, his fingertips would touch both walls. All of the surfaces were caked in dried material, streaked with rot. Droplets of fluid still floated, a thick jelly-like substance moving slowly in one direction and carrying with it more solid objects. Down here the stink was powerful, and it indicated what those objects were before Mains could quite make them out— even with the combat suit's face mask, and he had to concentrate so that he didn't puke.

He switched to his internal oxygen supply. A few deep breaths, and his stomach calmed.

Human parts drifted by. Arms with skin shriveled and gray, part of a head with an eye rolled up to white, a hand with fingers clawed like a dead spider. A lot of the flesh had rotted from these parts, hanging in pale clumps or unattached completely and slicked across the walls. Mains heard gasps of disgust and uttered one himself, but they all knew better than to knock these sickening objects aside. One gentle shove could send a limb bouncing from a wall. Exposed bone might scratch or bump. Any loud noise might give them away.

"We need to move," the burnt man said.

"Through this?" Hari asked.

"It keeps us safe," the man asked.

"How do you know?"

"It's worked for three months. Come on. It's not all this bad."

"What is this place?" Durante asked.

"Waste channel for the pods that fail," the one-armed woman said. "If a host dies, the pod's vented down here. It flows away."

"To where?"

"Somewhere none of us wants to go," the man said. "Please, we should move. We've got so many questions for you."

"Same goes," Mains said, "but I don't think we need to hide. We have a ship, and once we get back there we'll blast this place to hell."

"General Jones knows you're here now," the man said.

"How?" Lieder asked.

"He's not stupid. He'll be planning an assault." As the man led them along the rank tunnel, splashing gel-caked things aside and releasing more stench of rot to the air, he glanced back over his shoulder. "You should probably warn your ship."

"Who the hell is General Jones?" Mains whispered to Lieder.

"Battle of Kotto Plains, 2098," Lieder said. "She was four feet eleven tall. Killed thirteen enemy with a Samurai sword."

"Jesus. These psychos like their history."

They followed, but Mains didn't trust these people. Once of the Rage, now Founders again. He didn't know what any of that meant. All he knew was that they had discovered this monstrous ship en route to the Human Sphere, and whoever had built the *Othello* meant to use it for war.

\* \* \*

They reached a clean tunnel where the body-part-laden gel did not flow. It still stank, but it was dry and warm. It appeared that the three people had been living here for some time.

"You need to tell us everything," Durante said as they came to a stop. He'd already warned those left aboard the *Navarro* to expect an attack, and ordered them to take off and shadow the *Othello* until he called them back. It was an incredibly risky move for those left on board the enemy ship, but it was the call Mains would have taken. None of Durante's crew challenged the order.

Mains respected them hugely for that.

It was the one-armed woman who started talking. Her name was Sara, and once she began, the flow of words seemed unstoppable, as if this was a story she had been aching to tell for so long. It was amazing. Incredible, but Mains didn't doubt any of it. It made so much awful sense, and the more Sara told them the more his stomach sank, and hopelessness set in.

The Excursionists had been posted at the Outer Rim because there was always the fear that something terrible would come at them out of the void. Humanity had always been afraid of what it didn't know, and something that might exist in the darkness. Now that fear had been realized.

The most shocking aspect was that their doom had been seeded at the heart of the Human Sphere, so long ago.

The woman told them about the Founders and their journey out beyond the Sphere centuries before. Their discovery of *Midsummer*, what they found on board that strange alien habitat, and how they brought those creatures aboard their two remaining mother ships. She described the fall of the Founders, the death of Wordsworth, and the rise of Beatrix Maloney and the Rage.

All of these were events that had happened before they

were born, she claimed. Shipborn, they called themselves, but still Sara relayed the story with the certainty of truth. Their history was transparent. Wordsworth had always insisted upon that, saying that selective history was as good as lying, and that way lay dictatorship.

"So the Rage wants to go back home," Mains said.

"More than that," Sara said. "Maloney wants to conquer. She says it's about vengeance upon those who drove the Founders out in the first place, but that wasn't what happened at all. They left of their own accord. They were seeking new truths, exploration, and freedom of expression they couldn't find under the gaze of the rest of humanity. But now, with the Rage more powerful than even Maloney ever hoped, she's coming back to destroy, and to take control of the Sphere herself."

"Why?" Durante said.

"Because she's mad," Sara said. "Insane. She and the rest of the elders are more than three centuries old. They managed to slow the aging of their bodies, with the help of the life-giving compound they found on an alien world. But their minds did not fare so well."

"Yet you were brought up within the Rage," Lieder said. "What changed?"

"There's always been a strong contingent of Wordsworth supporters aboard *Othello*. The Rage elders aboard our ship didn't discourage Wordsworth memories as much as Maloney did aboard *Macbeth*, and over time a sort of underground movement was formed. An appreciation society—but it grew, and with it came a realization about what we were doing. The Founders were creative and open-minded people. They were experimenting with some incredible things, science that none of us shipborn can possibly understand—multiverse balancing, quark replacement theories, other things whose names are even a mystery to me—but the Rage has thrown that all away. The true reason for them fleeing the Sphere has been forgotten. Everything the Rage is doing now goes against what Wordsworth ever stood for."

"So what happened here?" Mains asked, returning the focus to the present. He knew what Sara said was important, and that she and the others carried intelligence that might be vital to the future of this war, but their immediate concern was survival. This information needed passing back to the Sphere, and to do that they had to return safely to the *Navarro*.

"Rebellion," Sara said. She looked away from them all, staring at the wall. Her two companions sat closer, sharing comfort. "Awful, bloody rebellion."

"You're alive, so you must have won," Durante said.

"You call this winning?" the man asked. His burned face was still wet with leaking fluids, his right eye a hazy, blind mess.

"Eddie, we need to get Sara and the others back to the *Navarro*," Mains said.

"Yeah," Durante agreed, then he spoke into the comms unit. "Bekovich, you there?"

"Here, boss."

"How's it looking out there?"

"All quiet. We left the docking bay, no problem, and we're shadowing the ship. Boss, there's more life-form readings now, and before we left we picked up more movement. Might have been you guys, but there were other areas, too."

"Right," Durante said. "Might need you to come and pick us up in a hurry. Still trying to establish exactly what's happening here, but meanwhile put a transmission together. Lock into Moran's suit cam and that'll tell you all you need to know."

"Already viewed some of it, L-T," Bekovich said. "It's unbelievable."

"Which is why you've gotta make the transmission clear," Durante said. "Keep channels open."

"What's our situation?" Mains asked Sara.

"Not good. The three of us are all that's left."

"Of the whole crew?"

"No. All that's left of the rebellion. The fight was quick and brutal. The Rage elders were wiped out, much of the crew killed. Escort ships clashed and were destroyed. The fight went on, smaller scale but just as violent. General Jones launched his Xenomorph soldiers against us, and we were all but wiped out. Now, it's him and a few Rage-loyal shipborn who control the *Othello*. Them, the Xenomorphs, and us. That's all that's left."

"Out of how many people originally?"

"A thousand," the man said. "Maybe more."

Lieder whistled softly. "So we're on a ship ruled by an android with delusions of grandeur and an army of Xenomorphs," she said. "How many does he have?"

"A hundred hatched, maybe more," Sara said, "but you've seen what the *Othello* carries. Kill one, and he hatches three more. That's why we've been on the run for so long, hiding, moving, hiding again. All control decks are sealed off, fully automated. If we could destroy the ship, we would have by now, but it's just become a matter of survival."

"So what's all this for?" Durante said. "What's the ultimate purpose of the *Othello*?" He gestured around them, pacing, and Mains realized that Sara and the other two were only revealing *parts* of their story. So much remained untold. They could never afford to trust these shipborn people.

Sara and the others exchanged glances.

"Sara," Mains said. He shifted his com-rifle, just a little. "What's the plan?"

"Have there been attacks?" she asked. "Assaults across a sector of the Outer Rim?"

Mains nodded. He thought of Patton, but decided not to mention the android and his ship of Xenomorphs. They had to gather intelligence here, not give it.

"That's Maloney," Sara said. "As we understand it, the plan was for her to make a lot of noise, while the *Othello* slipped into the Human Sphere, unseen and unnoticed. Once inside, the ship's programmed to split into a dozen component vessels, each one filled with Xenomorph soldiers, Rage commanders, and android generals. Surprise attacks, hit and run, and our main target was the Sol System."

"Old Earth," the man with her said, his one good eye suddenly filled with wonder.

"But your rebellion stopped it, right?" Moran asked.

"No," Sara said. "The ship's fully automated. General Jones is in command now, and all the damage we did to drive and navigational systems has been fixed by the Faze."

"What the *fuck* is a Faze?" Hari asked.

"Our maker," Sara said. "The fixer. The engineer. The beast."

"My day's just getting better and better," Lieder said.

"We know enough," Durante said abruptly. "We need to send all this info back to Tyszka Star. Meanwhile, we get off this ship and nuke it to hell. Any thoughts?"

Mains liked the way Durante invited input from his crew. The man was a decision maker, but this was unknown territory with plenty of intelligence they still didn't have or understand. He was wise to ask the opinions of others.

"Boss… so many people," Moran said.

"They're not people anymore," Sara said. "We harvested them from big ships we tracked and found, impregnated them. They're just birthing vessels for the Xenomorphs."

"They can't be saved," Mains agreed. "We'll be doing them a favor. Besides, we can't risk allowing this ship to enter the Sphere. There might be thousands here, but there are billions there."

"Bekovich, we're getting back to the docking bay," Durante said. "We might be running."

"Oh, we will," Lieder said. She glanced at Mains and he saw her fear, felt it himself, because they had been through this before. That time they had survived, but only because Durante and his HellSparks had showed up at the last minute. No one would be coming to rescue them this time. They were on their own.

But they were fully armed and suited, and they knew some of what to expect.

"You've been surviving here for a long time," Durante said to Sara. "You must know the hidden routes and crawl spaces."

She nodded, and looked suddenly scared. All three of them did, glancing at each other and drawing closer.

"What is it?" Mains asked.

"This ship is all we know," Sara said. "We were born on *Midsummer*, but we've lived most of our lives on board *Othello*."

Lieder looked around, sniffed the air.

"I thought you'd be pleased to leave."

"Boss!" Hari said. She'd been standing a little way along the tunnel, keeping watch, and now she was moving back toward them.

Mains listened, his suit amplifying sound, expecting to hear the dreadful noise of spiked footfalls. But it was something else.

Something splashing.

"They know you're on board," Sara said, panic slurring her words. "General Jones is preparing to fight."

"How do you know?" Mains asked.

Several globules of gel drifted into the tunnel. Each carried a stench with it, age and rot and fresh blood, and when the trickle turned into a surge, the body parts started to come.

"He's started the birthing process," Sara said. "The Xenomorphs are hatching, the pods are venting. We need to run!" She and the others stood and hurried in the opposite direction, insulated boots clomping softly on the deck.

Mains caught Durante's eye and they exchanged a silent nod. For now they would follow the rebels, but they still couldn't trust them, and they would have to prepare for a fight.

They switched on their lights. Something nudged Mains's hip and he looked down at the severed arm. It was tattooed, wearing an image he didn't recognize from centuries ago. Its ragged end was still bleeding. He kicked it aside as Lieder grabbed his own arm and squeezed.

"Johnny, we've got to go!" she said.

The entire group ran together. Durante was at the front, his com-rifle trained on the three rebels ahead of him. Moran and Hari brought up the rear.

A roar behind them signaled a sudden increase in the gel surge, and Lieder slipped, tipping back with her arms held wide. She splashed down into the mess, her impact causing a slow wave of further impacts that splurged gel up against the wall. Mains reached back, grabbed her, and pulled.

He was holding a man's arm. It was attached to a ruined, headless torso, torn across the stomach, chest open with shattered ribs pointing outward.

"Fuck!" Mains shouted, shoving the corpse aside.

Lieder splashed a little way from him, sitting up, then standing again, kicking body parts aside as she pushed through them. The gel was thick now, deeper, heavy and flowing all around, driven from behind by the weight of yet more. It was laden with lumps that Mains had no desire to see. The flow moved slower than water, the gel thicker, but its weight was substantial, shoving him forward every time he lifted a foot. He was forced to run, carried along with the sickening surge.

Sara's torch flashed ahead, lighting their way. The combat suits added their own lights, and the tunnel flickered with reflections from the gel's surface.

"Not far now!" Sara shouted back.

"L-T!" Hari shouted.

Mains tried to turn to see what was wrong, but his foot caught on something and he went sprawling. Just as his head passed into a floating mass of gel and shreds of flesh, he caught a fleeting, terrifying glimpse.

Moran was rushing toward him, his eyes wide. Behind him, Hari stood braced against the wall, com-rifle aimed back the way they'd come at shadows that danced, scraped, and swam toward them.

Then Mains was subsumed in a mass of the sick fluid, splashing with one arm, rolling, trying to kick himself upright without dropping his com-rifle. His suit gave him air, but he could still feel the sick warmth of the gel through its thin, sensitive material. Warm like blood.

Laser flashes flickered across his vision. Something grasped his heel and pulled, and Mains pushed against the slick floor, finding his feet and turning in one motion in case it wasn't a human hand.

His weapon was pointed at Lieder's face. She slapped his shoulder, then turned and started shooting.

Hari and Moran were firing along the drainage tunnel, laser blasts and nano-shot forming a deadly kill zone in the confined space. Soon, it wasn't only human body parts that bobbed and flowed past them. Slicks of acid bubbled, and Mains was glad for his suit's protective qualities.

But not everyone wore a suit.

"Sara!" he shouted. "Get out of the flow!' Ahead he could see Durante trying to shove the woman and her companions into a higher side tunnel. Sara pulled the burned man up after her, but the other woman slipped, gagging as gel washed into her mouth.

Durante pulled her upright and she screamed blood. Clawed at her throat. Smoke came from her mouth and nostrils, and as he tried to grab her she lashed out, knocking his hand aside and sending herself spinning against the opposite wall. Agony made her mad as the flesh, skin, and cartilage of her throat burned through and thicker, darker blood began to flow.

Mains turned away just as Durante put the woman out of her misery.

"Fall back, we'll cover you!" Mains shouted. Hari and Moran did so without looking back. The attack seemed to have paused, and further along the tunnel clouds of steam and smoke obscured where the Xenomorphs had died. Molten metal dripped slowly through the floating gel from where one of the HellSparks had unleashed a plasma burst.

Mains and Lieder aimed their weapons past the two retreating Excursionists, waiting until Hari and Moran reached them, then waving them on.

"L-T needs your help," Mains said.

"You two got this?" Hari asked. She was wide-eyed, wired, but she still sounded in control.

"Yeah," Lieder said. "We've met these fuckers before."

As the other two splashed toward Durante, Mains and Lieder backed away from the enemy. Mains flipped his suit from normal view to movement detection, but the gel stream and what it contained confused the reading.

Something scraped, just beyond their vision.

Gel slurped against the tunnel wall.

A shadow darted toward them.

They fired together, nano-shot followed by laser blasts. The stream erupted, smoking and burning, splashing from walls and ceiling and sending body parts splatting and ricocheting.

Another weapon opened up and Moran was with them, his firepower adding to the chaos.

Still out of sight, Xenomorphs screeched as they were blasted apart. The tunnel ceiling collapsed, metal groaning and melting as Mains let go three rapid plasma bursts. It was risky in such an enclosed space, but with what he knew about these bastards, there was no such thing as overkill.

"To me!" Durante bellowed.

They backed along the tunnel, more confident with their footing now. Mains tried not to imagine what the objects were that brushed past him, and he was glad when they reached the smaller side tunnel. Sara and the man were up there, a grim-looking Durante crouched low. "Come on," he said. "We'll have to fight our way back to the ship."

"We're relying on you two," Mains said to Sara and the man.

"No," Sara said. "We're relying on you. We've been trying to find ways to destroy the *Othello* for months, and now you're here."

Together, they crawled into the darkness.

* * *

Fifteen minutes later they emerged from the drainage tunnels and found themselves in a small storage hold. It contained several wheeled vehicles and other equipment, much of it rusted and decaying, tied down with heavy chains and magnetic locks. The place smelled of age. Some of the wheels still had mud on them, and Mains wondered what strange world it came from.

"Everyone okay?" Durante asked. There were nods all around. Sara and the man were close together, relatively calm now. Mains guessed they had seen many of their friends die, and one more wasn't a shock.

He smiled at Lieder and received a smile in response. He felt a surge of emotion, and perhaps he could call it love. He'd been in space for so long that he wasn't sure. It had a way of reducing a person, stark infinity crushing down on your soul. He railed against it, as they all did, but sometimes it was all too much.

"We need to move," he said. "Can't stay in one place too long. Sara, what'll happen now that the birthing's begun?"

"I don't know," she said.

"You don't know?" Durante asked.

"I'm a medic," she said. "I didn't deal with the nurseries. I hardly ever even saw them."

"We can assume the ship's crawling with little baby Xenos," Lieder said. "So the General will want to do whatever needs doing to get them under his control."

"They already are," the man said. No one had even asked his name, and he hadn't offered it.

"How?" Mains asked.

"The queen is genetically modified with the Touch."

"What's that?"

"The technology that links them telepathically to their general. Every egg she lays, every facehugger, every infant Xenomorph is already under its general's control."

"You… have a queen?" Mains asked.

"Not on board. Maloney had one on *Macbeth*, and until we parted ways there were regular shipments of eggs across to *Othello*."

"A regular production line," Lieder said.

"We need to time this right," Durante said. "How far to the docking bay from here?"

"Depends which one you landed at," Sara said.

"The one with an open fucking door!" Hari said. She moved toward the shipborn, drawing her combat knife. "I don't trust you. Either of you."

"Then you're a fool," Sara said.

"Listen, once we leave here and head for the docking bay—" Mains began, but then their ears were filled with a transmission from the ship. An agonized scream, rising, wavering, then being cut off. Something wet, tearing. A hiss.

"Bekovich!" Durante said. "What's happening?"

"Something got on board!" Bekovich shouted. "Something in the—" His words were swallowed by the sound of gunfire.

"Who the hell's shooting?" Durante shouted. They all knew what the results of gunfire might be in a ship as small and enclosed as the *Navarro*.

Mains's stomach sank, and he felt sick.

They heard the unmistakable sound of a Xenomorph's wild shriek.

"L-T, there are two of them, I'm coming in to—" A wet, meaty thud. Something sharp scraped against metal. Someone whimpered, muttering rapidly, their words lost to the sounds of violence. Then an explosion slammed through their headsets. A loud roaring followed, rapidly diminishing to dreadful, painful silence.

"Decompression," Hari said. "Someone let off a plasma grenade." She shook her head.

"Bekovich!" Durante shouted. When he saw Mains looking at him, he glanced away, knowing it was hopeless and that he had to take control. Just for a moment, Durante looked much smaller and lighter than he was, grief curling around him and crushing him down. Then he straightened and faced them all.

"Hari, Lieder, guard the doors. Moran, check for any other ways in here."

"Eddie," a voice said. Mains held his breath. It was the *Navarro*'s computer.

"Spike," Durante said.

"Eddie, it's not looking very good out here."

"So tell me."

"The crew are all dead. In the chaos, a plasma grenade was detonated, and the *Navarro* has suffered total decompression. There were three Xenomorphs on board. They're dead too. They seemed to melt down when they were killed. Their blood is everywhere, and it's eating the ship. There's nothing I can do."

"Spike, can you bring the ship in, land it in the bay you recently took off from?"

"There's nothing I can do," Spike said again. "Controls have been badly damaged, relay nodes are smashed, and the acid is… it's damaged the warp core and…"

It wasn't often that a computer spoke with anything approaching real emotion. Spike sounded scared, and it reminded Mains of Frodo, his computer on the *Ochse* that had given them as long as was possible before its drive failed and exploded.

"Core stabilizers are melting. *Navarro* is about to drop out of warp."

They all knew what that meant. Dropping out of warp in such an uncontrolled manner would smash the ship into a billion pieces.

"Are you sure you can't dock?" Durante said. "You have to try."

For a few long seconds, Spike did not reply. Then it said, "Oh, dear." A moment later, silence fell, and the *Navarro* was dust.

The marines and the two remaining shipborn stood in stunned silence.

"Well," Lieder said, "it looks like we're stuck without a ship again, Johnny."

"Getting to be a habit," he said.

"We usually get rescued."

"We just listened to our friends dying!" Hari shouted. She went for Lieder, but Durante held her back.

"Sorry," Lieder said. "Sorry."

# 1 5

## JIANGO TANN

*Space Station Hell*
*November 2692 AD*

"It's time to see past our hate," Yvette Tann said. "This is bigger than all of us. Bigger than anything."

"I know that," Jiango said. He was tired, sad, frustrated. Terrified. "I just wish none of this had come *here*."

Gently Yvette touched his face. They had always been a tactile couple, more so since their son had died. He sometimes thought they were constantly reassuring themselves that the other was still there.

They were sitting in Bailey's, one of the bars in Hell's big central core, and probably the hub of the whole station. Bailey's was spread over five levels with three bars on each, a brewing room, several restaurants, a holo deck, a gaming room, and four dance floors. As usual they'd chosen Floor Four, ostensibly the quietest of the bars but still a buzzing place, floors vibrating with the pulse of music from below. There was no day or night in Bailey's, no closed, only open. One day each year the whole establishment shut its doors for maintenance and cleaning, but otherwise it was maintained floor by floor, day by day.

Its clientele reflected the wide range of people who lived on Hell or merely visited, once in their lives or multiple times. A sign above one bar said, "We Serve Pirates and Popes," and although the pope claim was hard to substantiate, many were happy to believe it. Some people spent most of their life in Bailey's. A few of Hell's residents had been conceived there, and more than a few had died there. It was one of Jiango's favorite places in the whole Human Sphere.

Today it buzzed with excited conversation. There was a Yautja on board! Tall tales were being spun, animated discussions held, opinions mooted, fighting talk talked. News of the Yautja incursion had reached the station, and there were a couple of Hell-dwellers who had apparently lost family members in some of the attacks, but most people were excited rather than scared. Everyone was trying to figure out what Hashori's appearance on their station meant.

Most residents knew Jiango Tann as one of the regular council members, and he'd already had to fend off several interested parties.

"There's an announcement coming at midday," he'd told them all. Now they were five minutes from midday, and every holo screen in Bailey's was tuned to the Council's main channel. Tann had declined the invitation to make the announcement himself. He had enough on his mind without having to make himself presentable for a public broadcast.

"Come on," he said, grabbing Yvette's hand. "There's something we need to discuss, but not here."

"We haven't finished our wine."

"I don't want any more. I need a clear head." *And so*

*do you*, he thought, but his wife had already picked up on his meaning. Fear clouded her expression. She squeezed his hand, as if in confirmation of what he had to ask her. In truth she probably already knew, and that was why he loved her so much.

"Where do you want to go?" she asked, and the question brought him up short. For the moment he kept up the pretense, feigning to have misunderstood her question.

"Let's go to the gardens," he said. "We haven't been there for a long time."

Yvette sighed heavily, and together they left Bailey's just as the holo screens lit up. Outside they crossed the main plaza and headed toward the entrance to the green dome. There were six diamond tunnels stretching upward from Hell's main body to the green dome moored five hundred yards out. Three of them could be walked, while the other three were designed for transport of produce and water.

Halfway up the tunnel, Tann paused and leaned against the clear wall. He was panting hard, wishing— and not for the first time—that they could reduce the artificial gravity a little. Age was creeping up on him, and climbing the long, curving staircases was hard work.

"Just take a look at that," Yvette said. She was always the one to see wonder in things, and she had long ago taught Jiango never to take anything for granted. Indeed, this view always took his breath away.

Hell was in geostationary orbit several hundred miles from LV-301, the unnamed planet that had once been mined by workers dropping down from the station. That was before the station had been renamed Hell. It spun around its central axle, the spin creating the artificial gravity. Newer stations and ships had gravity generators designed around a core centrifuge, but Hell was of a much older and more basic design.

As they watched, LV-301 appeared above the station and slowly moved into sight, its pink and red storms a palette of color set aflame by the Scafell system's sun. It was majestic and beautiful, and the colors kissed the diamond enclosure, refracting red-toned rainbows, the beams slowly dropping as the station turned.

LV-301 had a circle of pale rings, the remnants of an asteroid that had been smashed to smithereens a billion years before. In the station's early life as WayStation 14, a few expeditions had ventured across the rings to search for precious minerals, but those found had been much too difficult and expensive to harvest. Now, the rings were objects of wonder, and Hell undertook a twice-yearly festival when they reached their northern and southern zeniths. They caught the sunlight now and glimmered in the darkness, jewels set into the landscape of infinity.

It was beautiful and mind-blowing, and Tann thought he and Yvette were of an age to appreciate that. Sometimes younger people seemed to take such sights for granted. For them the future was long and the darkness far away. A sense of mortality gave such sights an element of the sublime.

"They want it to be you," Yvette said, and it was a statement more than a question. "The Council wants you to take the android and the Yautja and hand them to the Company."

"No," Tann said. "They want it to be us."

Yvette smiled at him sadly. "At least we won't be apart."

"We never would," he said. "If it was just me, I'd have said no."

"But since it's both of us, you said yes? Without asking me?" Her voice had taken on a harsh edge that he recognized all too well.

"Asking you is what I'm doing now." He paused, looked up, and said, "Come on." They climbed three more staircases toward the next elevator point. When the doors opened a few people came out, nodding a casual greeting. Tann had seen them before, but they were like many people on Hell—passing acquaintances. He couldn't be friends with everyone.

In the elevator he leaned in close and kissed her cheek.

"You remember?" he asked.

"Of course," she said. "You remind me often enough." She was only pretending to be angry. On another world, far away and many years ago, they'd been trapped in a similar elevator when the station's power had gone down. They'd made love, hardly caring if the power came back and the doors opened, revealing them to anyone waiting to board. Such events made up the tapestry of a relationship.

"Pity it's an express elevator."

"Fifteen seconds would be long enough," she said.

"You hurt me, Yvette."

The doors opened, and they walked toward the security gate. Two dome employees scanned the chips in their wrists and waved them on.

"The blood roses are in full bloom right now," one said.

That gave the Tanns a destination.


Blood roses were used for many purposes, chief among them a medicine that could temper the dizzying effects of space sickness. Their stems were churned and used to fertilize the next crop, petals were shipped down to the Bailey's best restaurant to spice various foods, and their aroma was fed into the station's life support systems, offering an occasional subtle hint on staid, bland air. That they were also beautiful to behold made the blood rose fields a favorite place to visit for many of Hell's residents.

"So what's the plan?" Yvette asked.

"Really?"

"Oh, Jiango." She sighed, and he heard every sadness they'd ever experienced in that sound. Sometimes it was as if their son was always there with them, in each word spoken and every move made. Silent, unseen, he haunted their lives, and they wouldn't have it any other way. "If we could stay here and grow old together, I'd be more than happy with that, but I've always known that would never happen. Not with you and your sense of adventure. I'm amazed we've been here as long as we have, to be honest, much as I love the place. So if we *are* destined to leave, I'd rather us leave together, to hopefully do something good."

"You never cease to amaze me," Tann said. He meant it. Yvette was an amazing woman, and in his infrequent conversations with whatever his God might have become, he often thanked Him for such a blessing.

"So…" she said again.

"The plan," Tann said. "That's the interesting part. The plan is to hire a ship, and a crew, and get the woman and the Yautja into Company hands as soon as possible."

"Why hire a ship when the Yautja already has one?"

"Because they've already had a couple of near misses," Tann said. "They're being chased by a Rage army, and no one really knows whether they're still being followed. Could be it's the Yautja ship they're tracking. If that's the case…" He looked up through the sectional dome at the deep darkness beyond, the starscape shifting as the ship slowly turned. Far away lay the nearest drophole, and from what Liliya had told them, an army might be flying through there at any moment. An army the likes of which no one on Hell had ever seen.

The idea that they might come here was awful.

"If that's the case," Yvette said, "it's all the more reason to get the Yautja ship away from here."

"That's the other part of the plan," he said. "Trouble is, the Yautja's not too keen on the idea of separating from its vessel."

"That thing makes me cringe," Yvette said, and she shivered against him.

"Yet it seems intent on remaining with Liliya," Tann said. "Even though it's responsible for those wounds and scars she carries, there's some sort of loyalty thing going on between them."

"Why here?" Yvette asked, expecting no answer. Tann knew what she meant. Hell was a nice place, people here kept themselves to themselves, and they'd existed without any serious trouble for a very long time.

It was almost as if all the trouble had been saving itself for now.


Bailey's was the best place to find a ship, too. Two days following the Council meeting he left Yvette in their rooms to begin packing. Tann knew that the first things she'd gather would be the mementos of their son's short life, and he found it too painful to look at these objects, even now.

They had the commemorative cap from his passing-out parade with the Marines, the first pair of shoes he'd worn as a baby, and several recorded messages he'd sent them from places far away across the Sphere. Although he'd been delighted at becoming a Marine, he'd also been keen to keep in contact with his parents, and eager to visit them every couple of years, if his missions allowed. As time went on he'd seen them less and less, but they still held memories of those visits, clear and close.

While Yvette gathered the detritus of their family life, Jiango Tann had tasked himself with sourcing the fastest and most appropriate ship for their mission. He'd already perused a manifesto of ships and crews currently docked on Hell. There were the craft that used the station as a permanent base, and he knew most of them quite well. Of the nine ships, he wasn't sure any of them was really suited to such a journey. A couple of old tugs, an in-system cruiser, three ex-mining vessels, and some private ships too small and slow to undertake such a treacherous voyage.

Even the decommissioned Colonial Marine frigate wasn't suitable. Used by the station's indies, it was more than a hundred years old. It had an outdated warp drive and several ongoing mechanical problems that plagued its core. Its computer was notoriously cranky, only answering to the name Al and calling every crew member, no matter what their name or sex, Dave.

That left the complete strangers who were visiting Hell. One of the mining ships was a possibility, because it was modern and fast and specifically designed for frequent drophole travel. The one that caught his attention was the *Satan's Saviour*. Aside from the colorful name—curiously apt for where it had come to rest, for a time—it looked to be the sort of ship and crew he wanted.

They called themselves "autonomous exploratory salvagers." Some might have viewed them as indies, but in reality they were probably pirates, and as with all good pirates, Bailey's Bottom Bar was their favorite haunt. Not only was it on the lowest level of the establishment, it also serviced what some might view as the basest desires.

Its two dance floors were constantly abuzz with exotic dancers of both sexes, greased flesh catching poor lighting, pulsing music vibrating through the metal-decked floors.

Drinks stations served some of the roughest brews from Bailey's brewery, as well as selling booze imported by some of the visiting ships, and in the darker rooms at the back, private exchanges of credits, illegal substances, and bodily fluids were commonplace.

It wasn't the most salubrious of places, but the Council supported its existence because it provided a service. A selection of services, in fact, some of which made Tann uncomfortable. He and Yvette had only been there a couple of times—once while drunk, the second out of sheer curiosity. Based on those experiences, it didn't rank high on their list of favorite places.

As he walked through the Bottom Bar and exchanged nods with a couple of Hell's familiar residents, he scanned for the crew of the *Satan's Saviour*. Two women, two men, he'd seen the uniform they wore, and hoped the white stripes on dark material would stand out beneath the bar's neon glare.

He soon found them at an Acid bar. Acid was one of the wines produced in Hell's ancient engine room, a notoriously toxic brew. Hell's engines hadn't been started for over a century, and their pipes and ignition chambers, pistons and vents made for an excellent still. Perfected over decades, brewed from extraterrestrial fruit that resembled grapes, the wine was a surprisingly palatable creation, but its effects were legendary. He'd heard it suggested that some crews bought Acid to clean their ship's hulls.

Nevertheless, the four crew members were probably the least inebriated of all the bar's patrons—though that wasn't saying very much.

"Drink, old man?" one of the women said when she spotted him watching them. They were seated at a round table in the bar's far corner, hidden away from the displays of greased flesh that gyrated on a nearby dance floor, and protected from the thrumming music by a sound screen. Tann took her offer as an invite, and the second he walked through the sound screen the cacophony from the rest of the bar lessened dramatically.

That and their relative soberness indicated to him that they weren't just here for a night of debauchery. They maintained a constant air of seriousness. Perhaps even discipline.

Tann brought his own glass with him, primed with one of the Bottom Bar's weaker beers. He found that his aging frame didn't deal well with alcohol, and he no longer enjoyed the loss of control. Besides which, alcohol made him maudlin.

The pirates watched him approach.

The woman who'd raised her glass tapped the upholstered bench beside her and shuffled around, the four crew bunching up to give him room.

They seemed very open to company. That openness belied the looks in their eyes, expectant and suspicious.

"Nice place you have here," one of the men said. He was one of the tallest people Tann had ever seen, his deep black skin streaked on his left cheek with four parallel pink scars that ran from jaw to temple. He wore a constant smile, and his voice was almost a chuckle. Exuding good nature, Tann guessed the man could probably break his back with one arm and no qualms.

"Bailey's?"

"Hell," the man said. "Odd name, but I like the feel of the place. It's… undemanding."

"That's why I've been here so long," Tann said, raising a glass. All four pirates returned his toast and they drank.

"Music sucks, though," the other man said. Short, heavily built, bald, he must have been the oldest of the group.

"It does in here, but there are some music dens you

really should visit," Tann said. "O'Malley's Bar on the east arm is a great place for jazz, and Metros plays plenty of older stuff."

"You suggesting I'd like older stuff?" the man asked, and the two women laughed.

The one who'd called him over leaned on the table, hands clasped, and stared at him. She had stunning green eyes and long auburn hair, tied in braids with a dozen metallic clasps. Tann noticed that each clasp glowed with a soft red light, and he thought perhaps they were weapons of some kind. Homing bombs, perhaps.

He looked the others over, trying to assess how ready they were for combat. The tall guy wore an ammo vest beneath his loose shirt. The other woman had her withered left arm in a mechanical brace, a robot prosthetic that would link into her nervous system. The brace was heavier than it needed to be, contoured in several places with pods that might have been plasma charges.

"I hear you're after a ship?" the woman said.

"Who did you hear that from?" Tann asked.

She shrugged. "We have ears."

"I'll bet." He took a swig of ale, and tried not to look as unsettled as he was. These weren't pirates, he knew. They were indies disguised as pirates, a curious camouflage that put them on a level with some sort of Special Forces. Indies were usually very open about their origins and purpose.

"Hey, don't worry," the woman said. "We're harmless."

"Actually, I hope not," Tann said, and the tall man laughed again, a hearty sound that somehow put him at ease. "I'm in the market for some indies, and a fast ship."

"*Satan's Saviour* is the fastest and safest ship you'll find anywhere," the woman said, "but we're on an assignment right now, and I'd feel bad letting our employer down."

Tann sighed. He'd hoped this would be easy.

Since fleeing to Hell after Weyland-Yutani's alleged attempt on their lives, he and Yvette had sought and found a relatively simple life. Sitting here with this crew of indies reminded him again of that troubled time, when the death of his son was raw and ideas of revenge—or even an admission of guilt from the Company—had kept him on fire. As the years passed, he had been happy to let the blaze of his fury die down into a gentle simmer.

He didn't want it reignited. He was too old, and there was nothing to be gained.

Not against the Company, and not now that he was undertaking to seek out the very people he had once fled.

"Maybe I have the wrong crew," he said. "I'm offering a simple commission—"

"Simple?" the woman said, sitting upright. "From what I hear, whoever you hire might be carrying the most dangerous cargo in the Sphere."

"And what do you hear?" he asked, curious.

"A Yautja," the woman said. "An android woman being sought by the Rage."

Tann blinked in surprise. Hell wasn't a clandestine place, and the Council rarely tried to keep such secrets, but still this crew's knowledge came as a shock.

"I told you," the woman said, "we have ears. Now, let's introduce ourselves properly. I'll tell you about who we are, and what we can do, and if you want a resume I can provide you with that, too. Then it's all up to you."

Tann nodded and raised his glass in another toast. He glanced around, and found it strange, sitting behind the sound screen and still seeing the raucous insides of the Acid bar. A man and woman were on the stage, dancing to an exotic rhythm he could feel pulsing up through the chair and dimly hear on the air. Over by the entrance two men were fighting, so drunk that their fists flailed and a small crowd of onlookers cheered and jeered. Booze was bought from the bar, the wine itself bubbling down several thin pipes that came from the ceiling. People laughed and cried, shouted and whispered in each other's ears, and he and the indie crew might as well have been light years away.

"First, I'm Jiango Tann," he said.

"Oh, I know," the woman said. "My name's Ware. I'm the captain. This delightful lady next to me is Robo. Short-ass there is Hoot, and the tall bastard with the inane grin is Millard."

"Right," Tann said. "Real names, obviously."

"Obviously," Ware said. "We've been a crew for seven years. There were six of us to begin with, but that didn't last long. Now, we find that four is an ideal number. We're private hire, independent security contractors."

"Not salvagers, as your title on ship's manifest suggests?"

"We've done salvage," Robo said. She lifted her glass with her augmented arm, the motors running smoothly and soundlessly.

"We don't like the term indie, but if that's what you want to call us, that's fine. As you can see, though, there's only four of us, so we're not intended for the sort of grunt work that most indies get drawn into. Bodyguards, facility defense, bounty hunting, seek and destroy—we leave that sort of shit to others."

"So what's your sort of shit?" Tann asked.

"Millard says it best," Ware said.

"We're Special Forces when Special Forces don't want to go there," he said.

"So you do nasty stuff."

"Not necessarily nasty," Hoot said. "Not all the time. But usually illegal, and always something that our employers would never want linked to them."

"Plausible deniability, eh?"

"That's what I wanted to call our ship," Millard said.

"Yeah, but that'd be a bit of a giveaway," Tann said. Despite everything he found himself liking these people. They might have been indies, but there was no posturing, and their seriousness sat well with what they claimed to do. They looked like professionals, and that was refreshing. He'd met a lot of indies, and heard of many more, for whom employment was just an excuse to fight and get paid for it.

These people had certainly seen action—Robo's arm and Millard's mutilated face bore testament to that—but they didn't seem to wear their injuries as an achievement, or a badge.

"You're currently on a mission," he said. "The fact your mission's brought you to Hell doesn't make me feel all warm and fuzzy."

"Just stopping by," Ware said.

"No one just stops by," Tann said. "We're out of the way. That's why people like me live here."

The crew glanced at each other. Ware shrugged.

"We're looking for someone," Ware said. She circled the top of her glass with her finger, making it sing. Millard was staring right at him. For the first time, the tall man wasn't smiling.

"Me?" Tann asked.

"And your wife," Ware said.

"For who?" The shock was so profound that the question fell out, when in truth it should have been obvious.

"The Company, of course," Hoot said.

"What? Weyland-Yutani? They sent a bunch of mercenaries to find me?"

"We don't like the term—" Ware began, but Tann cut in.

"I don't give a *shit* what you like. You're guns for hire. What's your order, kill me?" He glanced nervously at

Robo's arm. She could probably shoot him while hardly moving, and he'd slump down dead, just another drunk in the Acid bar, unseen and unnoticed. Then they'd be away before anyone knew they were gone, leaving Yvette with a cooling corpse for a husband and no answers.

But it was ridiculous. Why would the Company bother with him? He was hardly on the "Most-Wanted" list, and he and Yvette had disappeared years ago.

"Look, we've got no love for the Company," Ware said, "but they pay well."

"Meaning what?"

"We're not a hit squad," Millard said.

"You're meant to take me back?"

"Just find out where you are. Put a trace on you. Make sure you weren't making a noise, doing anything… anti-Company."

"The biggest organization in the history of the Sphere wanted to track me down because I kicked off ten years ago. Unbelievable."

"Nothing about the Company is unbelievable," Hoot said, "and no concern is too small for them. Frankly, that's why the fuckers are still in charge."

"Hoot should know," Ware said. "He was Section Seven."

"Oh, great, thanks for that," Hoot said. "Now I have to kill you all."

The whole conversation had taken a turn for the surreal. Tann had come here seeking out this crew, only to discover that they were on Hell seeking *him* out. He was sitting at a table with four people who were very probably killers, and the Company had sent them to find him.

"Section Seven?" Tann asked. He'd heard mention of that name once or twice, but he didn't know what it referred to.

"Special Forces, reporting directly to the Thirteen," Hoot said. He'd been relatively quiet up to now, contributing only a couple of words here and there, but now he held Tann's gaze. He was a small man, innocuous, with little to set him apart from anyone else in Bailey's. Maybe that was why he'd been Section Seven.

"So what happened?" Tann asked.

"I left," Hoot replied, in a way that said the topic was done.

"Look, we've been here a couple of days, and we know you're no threat," Ware said. "We've done what we were commissioned to do. Tagged you, put a trace on you."

"How?" Tann asked.

"Don't feel bad," Ware said, ignoring his question. "Fact is, though, things have changed. Shit's happening out there, some of which I'm sure you know about."

"Shit that has nothing to do with Hell," Tann said. "Or at least it didn't."

"We're the ship you want," Ware said. "I assume the Council sent you with permission to offer certain payments."

"A million credits," Tann said.

Millard whistled softly. "That's five times what they paid us to tag you."

"That's all I'm worth to them?" Tann asked, smiling. Millard grinned in return. Jiango thought he'd probably grin if he'd been hired to slip a knife into Tann's gut, too.

"The past's done," Ware said. "We didn't have to tell you a word of this, but like I said, I've got no love for the Company. Truth be told, I support what you did. Hoot's told us a lot of stuff…" She trailed off.

"I don't want to know," Tann said. "Not anymore."

"We're the ship you want," Ware said again, "and we'll do it for free. Deliver the Yautja and the android safely, and we'll bill the Company. Sound fair?"

"Suspiciously fair."

Ware smiled and held out her hand. "Trust me."

Tann shook, but he had no idea who to trust.

"When do you want to leave?" Robo asked.

"As soon as possible," Tann said. "Today."

"What's the rush?" Millard asked, and Tann felt a pang of delight. They didn't know everything, after all.

"The rush is, an army you've never even dreamed of might be about to drop into the system, and none of us wants to be here when it does."


"And you trust them?" Yvette asked.

"As much as I'd trust any indies." He hadn't told her the real reason they were here. He would eventually, when they were away and time allowed, and it hardly mattered anymore. He saw no need right now.

*In her skin*, he thought. *In my hair. Swallowed with food, marked with a nano trace.* He'd heard about a skin application of nano bugs that could work their way deeper and establish a signal trace in a person's bones.

Somehow Ware and her crew had come here and marked him and Yvette for the Company.

*My clothing, my eyeballs. Maybe it's even just a saying, and they haven't physically marked us at all. Perhaps they've just found us, so that if the Company reassesses, and still wants us dead…*

But none of that really mattered anymore.

"Yes," he said a few minutes later, when their packed bags were ready beside their cabin door. "I trust them."

# 1 6

## ISA PALANT

*Deep Space, Gamma Quadrant*
*November 2692 AD*

They prowled the skies for the next nineteen days.

The *Pixie* had sustained some damage in the nuclear blast on LV-1657, as had a number of its crew. Some of the exterior layers of the ship's hull had partially melted, but the ship's computer Billy suggested a method of effecting a quick and rapid repair before leaving the planet. It was impromptu, but it would last at least until they could get the ship into a proper repair dock.

Some of its auto-guidance systems had been knocked out, but Huyck was a confident and keen pilot. Worse, however, its weapons array had been damaged. They still had access to mini-nukes and the laser, but the ship's particle modulator was out of action. Although unpredictable and sometimes inaccurate in use, it was also the most powerful weapon the Arrow-class ships possessed, and to fly without it in these dangerous times did not please Major Halley.

Everyone on board the ship had been bumped and

bruised when the android Rommel detonated. The explosion turned much of the cliff into shrapnel, rubble, and dust, then rolled the ship across the sky and into the nearby forest. It was a blessing they'd all had the chance to strap into their seats, otherwise it was likely they'd have all been dead. As it was, Palant and McIlveen sustained cuts and bruises, Halley broke her arm, Sprenkel and Bestwick each had cracked ribs, and Huyck shattered both wrists as he tried to wrestle control of the *Pixie* through its manual steering sticks.

Such injuries could be repaired, and before leaving LV-1657 the ship's medical pod had been used day and night to fuse and reset the broken bones. Bruising was still heavy, and they all were absorbing differing doses of painkillers.

Then the message from Gerard Marshall had come through, and the new mission could not wait for them to heal.

They used drophole Gamma 116 to jump across the quadrant. Halley's reckoning was that other dropholes would now be the target of any attacking ships. Her intention was to drop, assess the situation, travel to another drophole, drop again.

This time around the injuries Palant sustained weren't enough to set her back, so drops wouldn't be too demanding on her.

Complication arose as they approached Gamma 116.

There were two Yautja ships shadowing them.

Halley was well aware of their presence, and she assumed that was intentional on their part. She didn't pretend to like it, but she accepted that the Yautja elder Kalakta had taken it upon himself to protect Palant and McIlveen. One of the ships had stepped in at the last minute to help repel the attack on the BloodManiacs' base, and although she claimed not to trust them, Halley was at least willing to remain open-minded.

It was Palant who envisaged a future where the Yautja and humanity fought together side by side. Perhaps Kalakta had seen that, too, when the two of them were face to face making peace. Either way, he had sent the two ships to shadow theirs, and at the drophole they had to make an important decision.

The debate hadn't lasted for very long.

Palant and McIlveen prepared a transmission, and using their ever-evolving Yautja language program they had sent drophole codes and coordinates to the two Yautja ships.

An hour after dropping through to Gamma 65, the two alien ships followed them through.

Halley wasn't confident that they would locate a Fiennes ship. She told Palant that if they went looking for trouble, they'd never find it. Thus it was a long nineteen days, with the ship's crew mourning the loss of Nassise and Gove, and picking up sketchy transmissions about major engagements involving other Colonial Marine forces.

Halley's own 39th Spaceborne, the DevilDogs, were powering out toward the Outer Rim on a mission to protect two dropholes as yet untouched by the enemy. Halley and her crew wanted to be with their army, not here babysitting Palant and McIlveen. The *Pixie* was an amazing ship, but they'd have far preferred to be on their battle cruisers and frigates with the rest of their brigade.

That was what they had trained for.

*We're not Excursionists.* Palant heard it said several times during those long, troubling nineteen days.

Palant herself was adrift, and one quadrant of space looked like any other. She attempted communication with the Yautja who were shadowing them, but neither ship responded to her signals. She knew they were receiving them—they'd used the drophole coordinates she and McIlveen had sent, after all—but not once did they respond.

As much as she and McIlveen understood the Yautja, more than any other humans in the Sphere, they remained an enigma. Palant had forged peace between the two species at a time when war might have torn them apart, but every time she began to think she knew them, they became more mysterious.

It was on day nineteen when the first transmission came through from one of the Yautja ships. At the same time the other ship streaked past them, a thousand miles away and moving twice as fast as they were.

It took Palant and McIlveen several seconds to feed the transmission into their translation program.

```
Enemy ship ahead.
Vengeance is ours.
```

"Confirmation," Sprenkel said. "It's a Fiennes ship, but the trace reading is weird."

"Weird how?" Halley asked.

"The ship's dead," Sprenkel said. "Whatever happened here, I think we've missed it."

"I can get it on-screen," Bestwick said.

"Do it."

The viewing screen brightened, and in the distance they saw the tiny spot that was the Fiennes ship. Bestwick magnified, and as the image grew, so Palant felt her heart rate increasing. The destruction at LV-1657 was still fresh in her mind. She had seen many men and women killed there, the new war brought brutally home. Now it felt as though they were looking for trouble. As a scientist that was anathema to her—she should have been searching for ways to end the war, not seeking more violence. That was what people like Halley and her troops were for.

But by making peace with Kalakta, she had made herself visible, and also placed herself at the forefront of this conflict.

The ship growing on their screen was like nothing she had seen before. It also appeared to be all but destroyed. A wide debris field surrounded it, and large portions of the vessel had been blasted to dust, leaving gaping wounds in the hull and revealing the ship's innards. The whole vessel was in a slow spin. From so far away it reminded Palant of a large, dead fish she'd once seen on a beach on Earth, insides exposed to the air. She'd been a little girl then, and the idea that she was looking into a once-living thing—at parts of it that were never meant to be seen—had made her feel like she was party to a great secret.

She felt the same now, but the sense of wonder was replaced by fear.

"What happened here?" she asked.

"We did," Halley said. "Colonial Marine units are under orders to destroy any unknown ships heading into the Sphere, and that includes the Fiennes ships."

"But we're looking for an android," Palant said. "Wouldn't everyone else be doing the same?"

"We're doing that on Gerard Marshall's orders, and so we're as good as working for the Thirteen." Halley smiled bitterly. "It's the Colonial Marines fighting this war, and as usual Weyland-Yutani are looking to see how they can benefit from it."

"Catching an android will help *win* the war," McIlveen said.

"Sure it will," Halley said, "but they want more than just to win. They want to profit."

"But all those people…" Palant said.

"They're not people anymore," Halley said. "Huyck, take us in, but leave a good distance between us and that thing. Bestwick, see if you can pick up any record of a recent engagement in this area. Sprenkel, can you plot that debris field?"

"I can, but only down to a certain size. Anything smaller than Huyck's dick won't show up on scanners."

"Wow," Bestwick said, "that's small."

"Eat me," Huyck said. He flew them in toward the ruined ship, matching attitude, velocity, and spin so that they moved side by side. "We're seven miles out," he said. "Near as I want to take us until Sprenkel can get into gear and plot the debris spread."

"Nearly there," Sprenkel said. "Billy?"

The ship's computer checked calculations, and it confirmed the new overlap that appeared on their holo screens.

"We can fly close to the ship on the other side," Sprenkel said. "Looks like it was a hell of an assault. Explosions were mainly on this side."

"Any clues as to the ship's identity?" Halley asked.

"It definitely used to be a Fiennes ship," Bestwick said. "As there's no activity, there's no new trace to search— but Billy's picked up the remnants of an ion trail, and it might have been a ship called the *Cooper-Jordan*."

"Not any more," Halley said.

On the screen, one of the Yautja craft became visible, approaching the wreck from the other direction, drifting in close and then performing a slow circle around the ship. A few small laser blasts speared out to destroy debris, and then the second vessel joined it, hanging off the derelict's bow as if standing guard.

"Palant, can you find out what your friends are doing?" Halley asked.

The Yautja were constantly referred to as Palant's and McIlveen's friends, and they'd both grown accustomed to that, however untrue it felt.

"We can ask, but they haven't once responded to any of our transmissions. You know that."

"Ask anyway," Halley said.

"Snow Dog scares me," McIlveen muttered as he accessed their translation program. His words weren't quiet enough to keep them private, and Palant guessed he hadn't meant to, but Halley was too busy to pay any attention. Palant was pretty sure that she'd take no offense, regardless.

McIlveen prepared a message, their program translated, and he sent it.

There was no reply.

"What are they doing?" McIlveen whispered, but Palant didn't know. Sometimes she thought the Yautja were accompanying the *Pixie* as some sort of escort, while other times she feared the Predators were guarding them, ensuring that they didn't do anything that ran contrary to Yautja interests. Whatever those interests might be.

"I don't know," she replied, "but Elder Kalakta wanted peace as much as we did."

"You think?"

"It's worked, hasn't it?"

"Peace with the Yautja, yeah. But now we have the Rage."

"You think they're linked?"

"Maybe." McIlveen frowned. "It doesn't feel right, but we really don't know anything about the Yautja. Maybe they've nothing to do with the Rage—whoever or whatever the Rage is—but that doesn't mean their intentions won't clash with ours."

"Maybe they want the Xenomorphs," Palant said.

"We know the Yautja hunt them," he agreed. "We know they hunt *anything*, if they see potential for sport in it."

"Not sport," Palant said.

"Okay, then, competition. Still, maybe the Yautja want the ability to control these things as much as we do."

"We?"

"Weyland-Yutani," he replied, then added, "Humanity."

"Are they one and the same?" Palant asked.

"Don't you think so?" he asked. By his own admission a Company man, McIlveen had surprised her time and again with his dedication to what was right, and not just what was right for the Company. Even so, Palant harbored an element of doubt about him. She thought that was sensible, and trusting people implicitly had never been her strong point. That was why she'd spent a decade alone, submerged in her research.

She liked McIlveen, but the two of them had been thrown together by the Company, and she could never forget that.

"I don't know," Palant said. "Weyland-Yutani has a history."

"Don't we all," McIlveen said.

She left it at that.

"Okay, we're going in," Halley announced. "The ship looks dead, but that doesn't mean there's nothing useful on board."

"What about whoever did that to the ship?" Palant asked. "Wouldn't they have investigated? Taken anything of value?"

"It depends on how this happened," Halley said. "Some of that debris field is from another couple of smaller ships."

"Colonial Marine?"

"Doesn't appear so, but this thing might have had escorts, and there's no way for us to know whether any of them survived. Whichever Marine unit had a contact here and took out the *Cooper-Jordan*, they might still be involved elsewhere."

"So you really want to go aboard that thing," Palant said.

"You heard Marshall's orders," Halley said, looking across the flight deck at her. She smiled. "Believe me, I'd really rather not."

"I'm taking two weeks leave," Bestwick said. "Effective immediately. I'll just stay here. I'm halfway through a good book."

"Okay, suit and weapon up," Halley said. "Huyck, take us in."

With nowhere suitable to dock, they were faced with a dangerous space walk from the *Pixie* and into one of the damaged areas of the Fiennes ship's hull. None of the ship's external ports were active, so Billy scanned the ruined structure and pinpointed the most suitable point for them to gain entry. It would take some cutting, but the ship's computer suggested that they could be across to the hull and inside within an hour.

The two Yautja ships pulled back to a hundred miles distant, and were following the wreck and the *Pixie* with no overt interest. They would do what they would do. Palant only hoped that Halley and her crew would be ready if their actions became hostile.

She didn't think that would happen, though.

Halley decided that the full crew should go. Billy would maintain the *Pixie*'s station, and would be in constant touch with the crew. If they needed to move quickly, it would guide the ship in close, doing its best to fly near enough to the *Cooper-Jordan* to rescue them.

Palant and McIlveen weren't happy with performing a space walk in such hazardous circumstances, but they were both eager to get on board the ship. As scientists, their curiosity overrode their natural caution.

For Palant, this was somewhere she had never expected to be. Her life had been turned upside down, and her universe had expanded from her lab and the base where she lived to the whole of space. In a way she'd become a very different person since being rescued from Love Grove Base, forced to consider horizons she had long believed out of sight, and plunged into situations from which she had hidden herself for years.

She didn't want experience, though, she wanted study. She wanted her own niche from which to research the things that interested her. Instead, she had become someone important. That wasn't something she'd ever sought.

At least she had McIlveen, though. He was the closest she had to a friend, and in this new, wider, infinitely more deadly universe, she needed that.

Suiting up on the flight deck, she realized they were wearing spare combat suits that might have belonged to Nassise and Gove. None of the DevilDogs commented, and she was grateful to them for that.

At the airlock Halley turned to them both and presented them with weapons.

"No," Palant said, holding out her hands. "Really."

"Yes, really," Halley said. "Have you fired a laser pistol before?"

"Yes, but—"

"Then take it," McIlveen urged her. He had already taken one of the guns and he nudged Palant again. "Go on… no buts. We can't expect them to babysit us if we won't help ourselves."

Palant took the gun.

She'd fired one a few times, back at Love Grove Base, when out on one of her semi-regular excursions with her friend Rogers. He'd set up an old drinks can on a rock, and then let her fire away, missing the can entirely but blasting the rock to pieces. He'd called her a natural at not being able to hit anything she was aiming for. She'd taken that as a compliment.

"Extra charges in your combat suit belts," Halley said, handing them over. "There are a few things you should know about these suits. We'll all be in touch all the time. They'll protect you from damage, but only superficially. There are a whole slew of commands that mean you can use the suits to your advantage, but there's no time to teach you them now. Just be ready to react if the suit throws up a warning onto your visor. And keep your eyes and ears open."

Palant nodded, caught Halley's eye, and took comfort from the small, cool smile the Major offered her.

Then Billy drifted the *Pixie* closer to the ruined ship, and it was time to enter the airlock.

Six of them fit inside comfortably, and it was a strange sensation as air and sound bled away. Palant expected her breathing to change, but the suit was providing her air. Apart from an initial fogging across her visor, very little changed.

"Gravity off," Billy said. Weight left them and Palant started to lift, drifting into McIlveen. Their boots were fitted with electro-magnets, but it didn't make sense to initiate them until they were on the ship.

The outer door slid open.

Palant's breathing came shallower and faster. She

closed her eyes. She had never been adrift in space before, her trips on ships usually done within the confines of windowless environments, or in cryo-sleep. Faced with the cold, endless magnitude of space for the first time, she felt panic begin to crowd in.

Someone held her hand.

"Hey, it's all right," McIlveen said. "It's really pretty cool once you're out there."

"You've done this before?"

"A few times."

"Okay, moving out," Halley said, paying no attention to Palant's show of nerves.

Bestwick and Sprenkel went first, little bursts of gas from their combat suits driving them from the airlock and out into open space. Huyck followed. The three marines held their combat rifles at the ready, and even as they were drifting across toward the largest wound in the side of the *Cooper-Jordan*, they were swiveling their guns left and right.

"I'll take temporary control of your suits," Halley said. "It'll make it easier to guide you across." Moments later Palant felt herself shoved forward as her own suit's directional jets fired.

It took her breath away. One second she had the *Pixie* around her, the next there was infinity. Ahead of her lay the Fiennes ship, but looking up she could see only the endless void, speckled with long-dead stars and filled with dangers that even now sought to kill her. She gasped and took shallow, fast breaths, and her visor fogged again.

"Breathe easier," Halley said. "Deep breaths."

Palant tried. She focused ahead on the backs of the marines drifting in front of her, then glanced right at McIlveen. He was moving slightly faster than her, smiling as if this was the most natural thing in the world.

"Fifteen yards," Bestwick said. "Boss, it's a mess in here—you'll have to guide Palant and McIlveen in pretty carefully."

"I've got them," Halley said from somewhere behind her. Palant didn't want to turn around to see where the major was. Every movement could throw her off course, and even though the ship filled her whole field of vision, the idea of missing it and drifting off into space was horrific.

As they closed on the wreck they passed through some of the debris. Chunks of metal, melted and burned, were easily nudged aside. A couple of larger portions had already been shoved by Bestwick and Sprenkel, the wreckage spinning away above or below them. Palant wasn't sure how wreckage separate from the ship was still drifting with it. An explosion had obviously caused this hole, probably the impact of a laser blast from a Colonial Marine warship, and the explosive decompression should have blasted everything out into space.

There were several bodies, too. None of the humans wore space suits. The two Xenomorph corpses glistened, reflected starlight giving them the impression of movement.

Bestwick and Sprenkel reached the ship and grabbed an exposed section of damaged superstructure.

"Ten yards," Halley said. "Okay you two, I'm going to remotely fire a small retro burst from your suits, you'll then have to grab onto something as you reach the ship. Might be a bump."

Small streams of gas puffed from the chest panel of her suit, then Palant was nearing the ship just below where Sprenkel hung on. She hit softly, clung onto a curve of metal, and breathed a sigh of relief.

"Can we do that again?" McIlveen asked, and someone else laughed.

"Okay, can it," Halley said. "Huyck, Bestwick, start looking. The guts of the ship are exposed here, but there'll probably be blast doors closed inside. Let's see if we can find an easy way in."

"What about decompression?" Palant asked.

"We're searching for somewhere with blast doors close together," Halley said. "We'll make our own airlock. That is if the whole ship hasn't decompressed. If it has, we'll move on."

*If it has, all the dangers will have been blasted into space*, Palant thought. It was a nice idea, but somehow, everything that had happened didn't point at such an outcome. They weren't that lucky.

While Palant and McIlveen hung on, the marines worked to secure a way into the *Cooper-Jordan*. The damage in its side had exposed several decks, but much of the structure had been melted and reset by the staggering temperatures of the laser blasts. It was proving difficult to gain entry.

Finally arriving at something that resembled calm, Palant looked back the way they had come. The *Pixie* looked so graceful from this far away. She admired the ship, its flowing shape and pleasing curves. It was strange that a thing of beauty was built for war. It was the opposite of the ugly, functional Fiennes ship—one which had been built for peace and exploration.

How many people had died in the attack on this craft? She could hardly think about the numbers. Some of the Fiennes vessels had carried tens of thousands, and Halley had been wrong when she'd said they weren't people anymore. Even if they were impregnated with Xenomorph embryos, they still would have been alive, sleeping with their dreams. Killing them had still been slaughter.

"Okay, we're in," Halley said. "Work your way up here."

As she reached the opening, Palant watched Bestwick and Sprenkel venture into a darkened, twisted corridor. There they found a blast door that had escaped any bad damage. Sensors detected atmosphere beyond. They all gathered in the blasted space, their boots' electro-magnets were activated, and suit lights lit their surroundings. Huyck bypassed the door's controls, moved everyone aside, then opened them.

A surge of air burst out, freezing particles catching starlight as they drifted through the hole and away from the ship.

Palant followed the marines inside and Huyck closed the door behind them. Hanging onto exposed pipework, Huyck moved ten yards along the corridor, counted down from five, and then opened a second set of doors.

Air roared in, and with it came sound. Bestwick did a quick check, then confirmed that the atmosphere was breathable. Their suit masks retreated across noses and mouths, and Palant took in a deep breath.

"Holy shit," Sprenkel said.

"I'm gonna puke," Huyck said.

"Chill it, people," Halley said. "We've all smelled death before."

Palant felt her own gorge rise. She had smelled plenty of death, but nothing like this. She had worked with body samples and grown used to the scent of decay in a laboratory environment. After the attack at Love Grove Base, surviving for many days in the storage hangar with the other survivors, the stench of death had been their constant companion.

This was worse. A heavy aroma, meaty, rich, and hot, she could almost taste it on her tongue, and touch it on the tainted air.

"I don't want to see," she said, and although everyone

heard, no one replied. She had spoken for them all.

They moved along a corridor, cracked and warped from the attack, until they reached a heavy door leading deeper into the ship.

"Let's open it up," Halley said. Huyck bypassed the door's controls and it slid open, getting stuck halfway where the metal had warped. Motors whined for a few seconds, then died out.

McIlveen vomited. Bestwick leaned against a wall. Palant pressed her hand against her nose and mouth, trying to hold in the sickness, the disgust. But she failed. Bending next to McIlveen she too puked, eyes closed, preferring the acidic taste to the unbelievable smell that assailed them from beyond the doors. Their vomit splashed against the floor and then spread, globules coalescing and spinning back to impact their suits. It was disgusting, but couldn't be helped.

Palant instructed her suit to mask her face and feed her oxygen again, but Halley interrupted.

"We'll get used to the stink," she said. "And there's no saying when we might need the oxygen."

Her face was speckled with sweat, her eyes glassy. "Let's go. My guys, activate your suits' movement trackers and life sign monitors."

Palant held McIlveen's shoulder, squeezed, then shoved him gently after Halley. She didn't want to see what lay beyond the doors, had no wish to know what might cause such an unbearable smell.

But in reality she already knew.

Judging from the DevilDogs' reactions, none of them had ever seen so many dead. Even Halley stepped sideways to lean against a wall. Then she saw what she had almost touched and retreated to the small group. They huddled together around the warped doorway and looked upon a scene from hell.

The hold was large, but the combined lights from their combat suits proved powerful enough to illuminate most of it. Palant wished they were not. During the attack a firestorm had blasted through the hold, melting and twisting, making grotesque sculptures of the things, and people, it contained. Cryo-pods had exploded in the heat, hardened glass shattered and melting, then hardening again into obscure shapes. The people within the cryo-pods had been scorched, flesh and hair melted away and bones exposed to be blackened and broken beneath the flames. Palant hoped that they were still asleep or already dead when the firestorm came, but she couldn't be sure.

The heat had been so intense that it had melted metals and plastics, flesh and glass, and the molten masses had congealed in the zero gravity, flowing together and cooling again in converged, unnatural shapes.

Some debris floated free, and their entrance had stirred up the air. The things that drifted around the hold looked wet, but the attack had been some time ago. The dead people and body parts were cool and dry now, but for the rot that had set in.

A head touched the floor ahead of them, bouncing up again in horrific slow motion. It was a woman, most of her hair burned away and eyeballs melted, lips scorched back to give a broken-toothed grin. Palant could see her skull through her stretched scalp.

The more they saw, the less they wanted to see, but sick fascination kept them there for a while, probing the darkness with their lights.

"No sign of Xenomorph activity," Sprenkel whispered. The hold was a mausoleum to the dead, and none of them wanted to make a noise.

"Movement sensors useless in here," Bestwick said.

"Sprenkel, with me," Halley said. "The rest of you stay by the doors. Huyck, step outside to keep watch behind us."

"What are you doing?" Palant asked, but Major Halley did not reply. She and Sprenkel headed into the hold, approaching one mass of melted cryo-pod, human occupant, glass, and plastic. Palant could see a clawed hand sticking up, blackened to the bone, fingers curled like the legs of a dead spider.

"They're checking," McIlveen said, and then Palant understood.

Halley leaned toward the mess and pushed aside a hardened curve of reset glass. It broke off with a heavy snap and spun slowly across the hold. She tugged a knife from her belt and set to work.

Palant heard the meaty sound of cutting, then the heavy snap of bone. Halley's work released a heavier cloud of putrefaction, even worse than before. Sprenkel gagged and turned aside to puke, trying to aim the stream of vomit away from them all. Halley nodded at him to step back.

She finished the examination, and when she turned her dark skin looked gray, slick with oily sweat as if the decay could be passed on to her.

"Untouched," she said.

"What?" Bestwick asked.

"No Xenomorph implanted. No facehuggers present, not that I can see. Although I guess they might have been burnt to nothing."

"They were just sleeping?" Palant asked.

"Doesn't matter," Halley said.

"Doesn't matter?"

"No. The ship had to be under the control of the Rage, otherwise it wouldn't have been returning, and wouldn't have been attacked." She stood straight, and looked around. "We'll move on. It's a big ship, and there are other holds. Maybe some weren't destroyed."

Palant knew Halley was right, but she was sickened by the idea that the Colonial Marines had killed these people in their sleep. Bestwick seemed to be thinking along the same lines.

"Maybe we saved them," she said. "Maybe they were about to be implanted."

"Yeah," Palant replied. "Let's think that. It'll make murder feel better."

"It's fucking war, Palant," Halley said. "Now let's move on."

They backed out of the dead hold, Palant almost slipping on the floor made slick with her own vomit. Huyck closed the door again behind them, sealing off the horrific sights, but nothing could erase them from Palant's mind.

*How many people?* she wondered. *How many dead?* They were beyond counting, and their fate was cruel and wretched. Even if they had been dead when the firestorm swept through, what a vicious hand fate had dealt them. To be traveling for centuries, and then destroyed by their fellow humans.

Whether or not any of them had been impregnated, they had deserved better than that.

They moved deeper into the remains of the *Cooper-Jordan*, heading toward the bow which from outside had appeared the least damaged by the assault. Halley and her troops held their weapons at the ready, while Palant and McIlveen kept the laser pistols on their belts. They weren't used to handling weapons, and had no wish to shoot someone accidentally.

There was damage all around. Piping and ducting was melted and broken, bulkheads were warped from structural stresses and the effects of heat. The floor had given way in several places, and they had to switch off their magnetized boots to leap across the gaps. There was darkness down there into which none of them wished to fall.

Here and there were signs of death—blood smeared across walls, shreds of flesh caught on ragged, broken metal—but no more bodies. Whoever had crewed this Fiennes ship back into the Human Sphere was still unseen and unknown.

Palant's suit was looking after her, but there was so much about it she did not understand. Frequent displays were projected onto her visor, and she guessed that every marine was seeing the same images. Movement sensors, temperature and pressure information, life sign indicators—she recognized these, but there were lists of figures, graphic representations, and other color-coded information that she couldn't decipher.

They followed a long, curving corridor that opened eventually into a wider space. It was here that their surroundings began to change.

She had heard about Xenomorph nests, and read reports from people who had encountered them. There weren't many who had seen them and lived to tell of the experience. As a scientist she was fascinated with them, although it was the Yautja that caught and still held her attention. Nevertheless, as a human being, the Xenos terrified her.

Here, now, she had never been so afraid.

The place smelled acidic and rank, and something heated the air, producing a heavy and humid sensation that even her suit could not quite repel. Their suit lights played across the open lobby and focused on the six openings that headed off. Three of them had sealed blast doors, most likely leading back into where the guts of the ship had been torn out. The other three led toward the bow. Slick, black material surrounded them, appearing as if it had been grown instead of constructed. It was uneven, a surface sheen reflecting light and giving it a damp glow. The openings were heavy with the stuff, and it looked as if the deeper they went, the more clogged they became.

The more evenly spaced, too. Ridges of this new structure spanned like black bone all around the nearest corridor. Knots of it hung from the ceiling, spiny shapes that repeated again and again.

"This is a Xeno nest, Major," Palant said. "You know that, right?"

"I've heard about them," Halley confirmed. "Billy, what's your status?"

"Major, I have a status update," the *Pixie*'s computer said. "Both Yautja ships are docking on the ship. They've gone around the other side so I can't see them, and I'm not sure it's a good idea for me to go off-station."

Palant drew in a sharp breath. Yautja, on board this ship! She glanced at McIlveen, and he seemed excited, too.

"Not good," Halley said. "Okay, Billy, remain on station. We won't be long."

"We need to go, right?" Sprenkel asked.

"Not yet," Halley said. She nodded toward the nearest corridor. "Schematic shows another hold just through there."

"Even more reason to get the fuck out of here!" Sprenkel said.

"Private!" Halley said. "Everything aboard this ship is probably dead. Life signs are messed up, and even if there are a few Xenomorphs still alive, we can handle them. This ship might contain intelligence that will tip the course of this war, and if it does, it's up to us to find it. Do you understand?"

"Yes, boss," Sprenkel said. "I just don't want to die like Gove."

Palant glanced around, expecting a heavier reprimand from Halley, but the Major shook her head.

"You won't," she said. "First sign of trouble we use plasma grenades and get the hell out. Huyck, you got those doors we've already come through?"

"Programmed new access codes, my suit's ready to auto-open them."

Halley nodded. "Okay. Slow, careful, and heads up." She moved off toward the corridor mouth.

Palant followed close behind, hand on her laser pistol. She hadn't wanted it, but right now she was glad it had been forced upon her. She remembered how Gove had died. If it came to it, she'd make sure she didn't go that way.

Heart hammering, senses alight, Palant followed the marines into the Xenomorph nest.

# 1 7

## JOHNNY MAINS

Othello, *Outer Rim*
*November 2692 AD*

Whichever way they looked at it, they were fucked. The
truth of that was evident in the silence.

The HellSparks mourned their dead crew and lost ship,
and Sara and the male shipborn were the only survivors
of their rebellion. Mains and Lieder realized that their
rescue from UMF 12 had been but a brief respite, a last
breath before dying. But they were Colonial Marines, and
they couldn't let impending death distract them from
what they had to do.

As the echoes of his ship's demise played around
the storage hold, Durante stared at Mains for a moment
before issuing his orders.

"Okay, Moran and Hari, check this place for ways in
and out. Mine them. We need a few minutes to plan."

"Sir, we just need to reach the outside hull," Hari
said. "With our combined firepower we can blast a hole
through to outside, vent the whole fucking ship."

"Not certain enough," Mains said. No one argued,

because they knew he was right. "You said the *Othello* splits into a dozen vessels, right?" he asked Sara.

The shipborn nodded.

"Then a few holes in the hull won't suffice."

"My kingdom for a nuke," Lieder said.

"Roger that," Moran said. He and Hari moved away to secure their position, taking small plasma mines from their equipment belts.

"Okay," Durante said. "Main aim as I see it is to fuck this ship. With the Xenomorphs hatching, there's no point pussying around trying to destroy them."

"Right," Mains said. "The ship's gotta be toast."

"And don't forget where it's heading," Lieder said.

"Beta 37!" Moran called from across the hold. "Christ, we can't let it get there."

"Is that a drophole?" Sara asked, eyes wide.

"Yeah," Durante said, "and it's close. A day away, maybe a little more."

"That's where General Jones will make his move," Sara said. "That will be his only aim, now. He'll do everything to hunt us down, prevent us from doing any damage, but once we attack the drophole, *Othello* splits and one threat becomes a dozen."

"You know the target dropholes after that?" Mains asked.

"No," Sara admitted.

"Have we got any way to broadcast a warning?" Lieder asked.

"The *Navarro* was about to, before…" Durante trailed off. They still remembered the screams of terror and pain from the crew, the sounds of combat, the screeches and triumphant Xenomorph hiss.

"So we need to move fast," Mains said. "Eddie?"

"Yeah. As I said… find a way to fuck this ship." He

looked at Sara and the shipborn man. "Any ideas?"

"Maybe," Sara said. "It'll mean getting to the drive core."

"Blow that and the ship goes?"

"Only if we haven't dropped out of warp," Sara's companion said. "Once we're approaching the drophole and are sub-light speed, blowing the core will simply speed up the *Othello*'s splitting into smaller attack vessels."

"And you'd know this how?" Mains asked.

"I'm a ship's engineer," he said.

"How long before the drophole is the ship programmed to split up?"

"I don't know," the man said.

"Sara?"

Sara shrugged.

"So where's the drive core from here?"

"Aft," the man said. "But…"

"But?"

"It's where the Faze has settled." He looked terrified. "That's why we haven't tried it before. But now, with you, and your weapons, maybe…"

However much Mains didn't trust him and Sara, neither could hide their terror at the mention of the Faze.

"We need to stick together," Mains said.

"Yeah," Durante said, "but I don't like the idea of getting wiped out without a fall-back plan."

Mains shrugged. "Then we don't get wiped out. We fight, crawl if we have to. Get to the drive core and fuck the ship."

"Right," Durante said, smiling. "So we have a plan."

Silence hung heavy. They were discussing their own deaths, but for all of them it was an unstated, silent understanding. To Mains it felt strangely remote, a distant, meaningless event that had very little to do with him. He didn't believe in any deity, and despite science's wonders he'd seen nothing to indicate any sort of existence beyond death. It didn't frighten him. At least this way the way he died would be in his own hands. As a Marine he had often dwelled on going out in an heroic act. Not for the heroism, or to be remembered, but for his own peace of mind in that final, exquisite moment.

Or maybe it was because after UMF 12, and losing most of his friends and crew, he considered every extra moment borrowed time.

"Boss!" Hari called. "We've got incoming."

Mains called up a schematic on his suit visor, as did every other marine. He and Lieder worked effortlessly with this crew they barely knew, their training coming to the fore, years of experience flowing through their veins and making every action second nature.

"Sara, you two are our guides," Mains said.

"They're coming to kill us," Sara said.

The movement sensor in Mains's suit indicated intruders closing on the hold from several directions. They approached on the level they were on, and above and below. He counted at least thirty traces. They were coming in force, General Jones wasn't messing around.

"We choose our own time to die," Mains said. For the first time since they'd encountered the shipborn, Sara did not look scared.

"Moran?" Durante asked.

"Three doorways into this shithole," Moran said. "We've mined all three."

"There's service ducting, too," Sara said.

"We'll barely fit through there," Hari said.

"Which means the Xenomorphs can't get inside," Sara said. "They're bigger than us."

"They might be waiting wherever they think we'll emerge."

"We can't afford to make a stand here," Durante said. "Johnny?"

"I agree." The traces were closer, maybe a minute away. "We leave some surprises for the fuckers here, and get out through the ducting. If we're quick enough we can drop from the ducting and run like fuck before they know where we've gone."

It was a plan, but the ship was a mystery to them, their suit schematics confusing. Plans made on the run rarely ran smoothly.

Sara and the ship's engineer led the way to the service ducting in the ceiling. They had to stand on one of the wheeled vehicles, and Lieder tugged on a grating until it hinged down. She shoved Sara up through the opening, then her shipborn companion. Mains, Moran, Durante, and Hari followed, before Mains reached down and lifted her up after him.

*Every moment left alive is precious*, Mains thought. He enjoyed the pressure of Lieder's hand in his, their touch through the thin gloves, but he mourned the fact that they'd never feel each other skin on skin again. Their sex had gone from screwing to making love, and the passion of those moments came back to him now. Deep, intense.

"Come on!" she said, reaching for the swinging grating. It took two of them to pull it back up and secure it.

"Close," he said. He didn't need to. They could all see the traces on their movement sensors, converging on the storage hold, slowing, circling… and then the impact sounds began below.

"Move it!" Mains hissed, but they were already wriggling through the ducting ahead of him, combat suit lights barely visible because their bodies almost filled the compact space. The ducting was only a little wider than Mains's shoulders, and he had visions of it starting to slope, slick and slippery, and then narrowing…

He shoved his com-rifle ahead of him as they went. He was last, following Lieder. If the Xenomorphs did get in and somehow squeeze into the tunnel, he'd jam himself in there, shoot and fight, stab and tear them with his bare hands, giving the others every chance to move ahead while the beasts ate their way through him.

They would all be thinking the same way. They were Colonial Marines, and more than that, Excursionists. Every Excursionist signed up expecting to end their lives far, far from home, and often in violent situations. It was the manner of a death that defined a person, not the place and time.

From behind him came the first mine blast, followed by shrieking as a Xenomorph was smothered in blazing plasma. The duct shuddered. Several more explosions followed, more screaming, and then angry hissing as more creatures smashed their way into the hold. Clawed feet scampered, and then a different sound came as they swarmed across the old parked vehicles.

Mains continued moving. They were all doing their best to make as little noise as possible, shimmying on elbows and knees, pushing with rubber-soled boots, but they couldn't be completely silent. When he heard the animal noises cease from behind and below, he knew they were listening.

Mains paused, turned onto his side, slid the com-rifle down across his stomach. He had to jam it diagonally across the duct, and even then it only just turned.

"Johnny?" Lieder whispered through the suit's comms unit.

"Go," he said. He heard them crawling ahead of him.

From behind came a violent, rapid impact of something trying to smash through the access grille.

Mains aimed his suit light back along the duct. He could see the grille bending inward under each impact. He didn't think the Xenomorphs could fit inside.

A clawed hand burst through and tore the grille away, and he waited for the domed head to appear. He'd give it a plasma burst. It would be risky, as the white-hot flames might double back up the duct, but his suit should protect him against the worst of the conflagration.

Still nothing.

He frowned.

Something small appeared over the edge of the opening, then something else, and then a score of them were scampering after him, their footfalls kicking from the duct's sides to propel them forward, darting shadows like a disturbed nest of spiders.

Xenomorph infants. General Jones had initiated the birthing process, and already he was putting his new army to work.

"Plasma!" Mains said, and he fired a burst along the duct. It roared, and then he felt the metal around him heating, the suit's visor darkening but not quite enough. He squeezed his eyes shut against the glare and heard the high-pitched squeals of burning baby Xenos, accompanied by the anguished cracking of superheated metal. The surfaces around him shuddered, and for a terrible moment he thought the ducting might collapse and spill them all back into the hold.

"Come on, Johnny!" Durante called.

Mains turned and started crawling again, hauling his com-rifle by its strap so that it remained pointing behind him. The plasma fire continued burning, but it would soon fade away. Now that the Xenomorphs knew where they were, though, they would not give up their pursuit.

They never gave up. Death did not deter them—but

Mains and his companions now had an advantage.

Because death did not deter them, either.

He scampered quickly, listening for movement behind him and checking the motion scanner readings on his visor. There was movement all around, but it was only them in the duct. For now.

"Durante, we've got to get out of here," he said.

"Already on it."

Then Lieder was facing him. She reached back and grabbed his hand, pulling Mains through into a larger dispersal pod.

"Up there," Sara said, pointing at a narrow duct that sloped upward.

"You're sure?" Mains asked.

"Leads to the next level," she said.

"Fifteen yards, then we can get out into a corridor and run like fuck," Hari said.

"Story of my life," Lieder said. "Let's do it."

This time Moran volunteered to bring up the rear, taking a couple of plasma grenades from Hari. He grasped her shoulder, and their foreheads touched. Mains wondered whether there was something between them. It didn't matter. They were Excursionists, and there was something between *all* of them.

"Don't hang around," Durante said to Moran.

"Right."

Sara and the engineer went first, followed closely by Mains and Lieder. The others came behind. The duct was smooth and layered with a film of slick, greenish slime— detritus of centuries of conditioned air flow, Mains assumed. They had to shove through by crouching with their backs pressed against the ceiling and heavy boots pressing against the floor.

Just as Sara reached the end, and Mains heard a cover

being shoved aside ahead of him, the first shooting came from behind. Laser blasts first, then the heavier, booming impacts of plasma shots. Moments later a shattering explosion shook them all as a plasma grenade detonated.

"Hurry!" Durante shouted, his voice almost swallowed by the grenade's echoes.

Mains scrabbled from the duct and pushed himself to the left, rolling, coming to his feet to see Sara and her companion hunkered against the wall. He looked to the left, then the right, and saw that they were in a small, dark corridor. Empty. Lieder came through next and he pointed left. She crouched and covered that direction.

More explosions sounded from below, and light flared from the open hatch as Hari and Durante clasped the edges and propelled themselves through.

"Moran?" Mains asked.

"He's coming," Durante said. "Which way?"

Sara pointed to the left.

Mains checked the movement detector and saw nothing that way. Behind and below them, the signs were swarming.

"We need to go," he said.

"No!" Hari said.

"If he's coming, he'll catch up," Durante said. "Mains is right. If it takes all of us staying behind for one to reach the core, so be it. You know that."

Hari pursed her lips, then she was the first to lead their way along the dark corridor. Suit lights lit the way, and on their visors the movement detector flickered as it probed the space ahead of them.

Mains followed close behind Hari. She moved quickly and quietly, weapon at the ready—the consummate warrior. If she was mourning Moran, she didn't show it.

A couple of minutes later another, larger explosion came from behind them, slamming the floor upward, dropping the ceiling, fracturing walls and spilling a boiling wash of flames along the corridor. Durante and Lieder fell on the two unsuited shipborn, trying to protect them against the flames.

Mains ducked and closed his eyes. He knew that the suit could protect him for a while, but instinct still took over. He felt the air simmer around him as he was surrounded by fire, and as the roaring flames retreated he heard screaming.

The engineer was on fire. He'd been behind Mains, and Lieder's small body had only partially protected him. He rolled back and forth and Lieder slapped at him, trying to extinguish his burning hair, shouting at him to keep still, and then Mains saw the shapes climbing from the ruptured floor and he stepped past Lieder and opened fire.

The com-rifle juddered in his hands as he unleashed a burst of nano-shot. The thousand microscopic specks impacted on and around the two Xenomorphs rising through the flames, stuck to their hides, and blew them apart.

The man was still screaming.

Mains checked the movement sensor and saw nothing close by. No Xenomorphs, no Moran. He dashed back to where Sara was crouched by her companion, not quite touching his bubbled face and melted eyes, crying. Durante was there, too, and Hari, and Lieder was already pulling the laser pistol from her belt.

"No," Durante said.

"Yes," Lieder said, and she fired one shot through the man's ruined face. He jerked once and was still. Sara fell back and screamed.

"I would have done it," Durante said.

Lieder stood and pulled Sara away, holding her around the shoulders. She was rigid, her eyes were wide and her mouth was open, though no sound came out now. Her limbs relaxed a bit, and at Lieder's prompting she began to walk. As they moved along, they leaned their heads together. Mains wondered who needed most support.

"We can't lose her, too," Mains said.

"Yeah. She knows the way."

"Moran?"

Durante looked along the corridor and shook his head. "He turned his comms off four minutes ago. He knew he wouldn't be following us."

"So let's take the fucking head start," Hari said. "Come on!"

They started running. Hari went first, followed by Lieder and Sara. Mains and Durante brought up the rear. Mains switched his motion scanner to probe behind, reloading his rifle as he went. He had plenty of laser charge and nano-shot left, but he was already low on plasma. The ship was huge, but he didn't think they had so far to go. The drive core wouldn't be as far back as the engine room.

He watched Lieder ahead of him, and every step he took reinforced the idea that this didn't have to be the end. Blowing the ship was the priority, but surely there was a chance they'd survive. There must have been some facility for escape—lifeboats, escape capsules. Maybe they'd be able to drop from warp and change direction, fly the ship into a star and escape beforehand. If *Othello* was designed to split into separate attack craft, perhaps they could escape in one of them.

There was so much allied against them—including the android General Jones they had yet to meet—and so many variables, which meant that no outcome was certain or written in stone. Moran had already sacrificed himself to improve their chances.

Dedicating themselves to die couldn't be the only way. They had to keep all options open.


At first Mains thought the voice coming through his comms unit was Moran, groaning as he struggled through burning corridors and past fallen ceilings to catch up to them. He felt a flood of delight.

*They're just animals*, he thought of the Xenomorphs. *We out-gun them, we're smarter, and we're Excursionists, doing what's right*. The Rage were the bad guys, there was no doubt about that. The bad guys always lost.

Then the strained voice turned to a deep, throaty laugh, and a chill traveled down his spine.

"Keep running," the voice said. "Keep running fast. It's good training."

"General Jones, I presume," Durante growled.

"Dead Marine, I presume," Jones said, mocking Durante's voice. He was surprisingly good at it. Perhaps an android could adapt his voice box in order to impersonate.

"Sending your toy soldiers, instead of fighting us yourself," Lieder said.

"Well, I *am* a general."

"Generals are normally good at tactics," Durante said. "You don't seem to have any idea what you're doing." He signaled to them all, pointing ahead. They continued jogging along the corridor, checking sensors. Perhaps the android general knew exactly where they were, perhaps not, but every yard they made would count.

There was a pause, then that deep laughter once again. Mains thought it sounded on the verge of madness.

"General Janicile Jones was one of the bravest women the British Paratroop Regiment ever produced," the android said. "She led her army on an assault of Mount Erebus on Mars, during the Martian uprising at the end of the twenty-first century. The battle lasted for three months. The rebels lost almost half a million soldiers, while General Jones's losses were substantially less. Her tactical forethought meant that every assault on the rebel stronghold was conducted in a different manner. The enemy could not learn her habits because she had none.

"Seven times she was pressed to take out the rebels in an aerial assault, and seven times she refused. Not only were they holding more than a thousand prisoners from the Mount Erebus deep-set bases, but their stronghold also contained all nine of the Martian cubes. Back then, they were the only alien artifacts in human possession. General Jones was not prepared to risk either the prisoners or the cubes, so she launched her final assault across the allegedly impassable Kotto Plains.

"During the attack her battle truck was destroyed. She alone survived, and badly injured, she led an assault on the bunker that had taken them out. Clothing burnt from her body, skin blistered, breathing apparatus down to the last three percent of air, she used her Samurai sword to kill all twelve bunker defenders. In the base of the bunker they discovered the entrance to a network of caves and tunnels. General Jones lived long enough to see Mount Erebus retaken, and the hostages and cubes saved.

"She died a hero's death."

"Very fucking profound," Hari said, "but that general was a woman."

"I'm an android. I have no gender."

"You sound like a guy to me," Lieder said. "One eager to big himself up. You must have been manufactured with a really small prick."

They laughed. It couldn't be helped, and Mains

doubted it would aid their situation at all, but it gave them a boost in the direst of circumstances.

"I'll bet you're really modeled on General Nath Jones of the 9th Terrestrials," Durante said. "Screwing one of his privates, caught with his pants down during an attack, fled across a battlefield naked, stepped on a mine. They found his balls hanging from a tree."

More laughter. Mains joined in, keeping his eye on the movement tracker on his visor, trying to figure out if the general was smarter than they thought.

"Enjoy your final few moments of humor," the android said, then the transmission ended.

"Well, he sounded nice," Hari said.

"If he's listening in on everything, we can use that," Durante said. "Just follow my lead."

"Which way?" Durante asked Sara. She pointed to the right. A few yards along the corridor there was a staircase leading up. Their suit lights cast strange shadows there that shimmered and danced.

"Okay," Durante said, "switch to secure channel seven."

They switched channels. Mains knew that channel seven was no more secure than the open channel they'd been using, but Durante was relying on that.

"Mains, you and Lieder take the right tunnel, but double back after two minutes. We're going left. Join us at the next junction."

"Roger that," Mains said.

Durante signaled that they should start using hand signals. The Colonial Marines were taught a complex system of signals and signs for use where comms units gave out, or for close-quarters situations where silence was of the essence. Mains only hoped he remembered the language now.

Durante pointed at Hari and Sara, signaled right, then he, Mains, and Lieder followed.

At the staircase Hari went first. *All clear*, she signaled. They followed, pausing at a switchback, checking, moving on again.

Mains and Lieder shared a glance, and smiled.

*We're getting closer*, Mains thought, but it wasn't a comfortable idea. Strangely enough, it seemed as if the Xenomorphs had stopped chasing them, and he couldn't figure out why. *He must know where we're heading.*

Whatever was happening, they were rapidly running out of time... and luck.

At the top of the staircase Hari signed that they should halt. They paused, breath held.

*What's up there?* Durante asked.

*Large lobby, dark, several routes in and out. Elevators*, Hari replied.

Sara looked back and forth between them, eyes wide. Lieder reached out and touched her shoulder, and Sara seemed to relax a little, taking comfort.

Hari gave the thumbs up and stepped out into the lobby. They followed close together, all keeping an eye on their visor displays.

Sara froze. Sniffed the air.

"Oh, no," she said.

Mains's suit visor came alive. Movement exploded all around, and several warnings vied for attention at the same time.

Hari screamed and started firing, her laser blasts spraying wild as something dropped on her and smashed through her suit, bursting from her chest in a spray of blood. The Xenomorph lifted her up on its tail and she screamed some more, swinging her rifle around and firing directly into the creature's mouth. It collapsed, she fell on top of it, and as it burst apart she rolled to the side. Its tail still impaled her, and it came apart as the Xenomorph melted down.

Hari tried one more scream as the acid blood flushed inside her, but she had no more breath.

Durante darted to Sara, holding her tight with one arm while he opened up with his com-rifle.

Lieder and Mains were shooting, too, back to back, their vision clouded by alerts and movement, their suits lining up target after target, so many overlaid that they simply turned a slow circle, firing laser and nano-shot all around the large lobby. It was all they could do to keep track of Durante.

Mains aimed upward at the ceiling as panels fell aside and dark shapes plunged down toward them.

*Comms on!* he thought, and his comms flickered into life again in time for him to hear General Jones's laughter one more time.

"Too many!" he shouted.

Lieder did not reply. He could feel her pressed against his back, and see the reflections of her gunfire.

The lobby was a chaos of darting and floating Xenomorphs of all sizes, from infant to fully grown. Laser blasts slashed across the space, nano-shot exploded far too close to the marines for comfort. Mains felt his suit holed in a dozen places by one blast, the hardening of the shell preventing fatal damage, but he and Lieder were flung sideways. Seconds later a plasma grenade exploded a few yards from them.

Durante screamed. It was pain, and rage, but outright defiance, as well. He and Sara were aflame, floating around the lobby and sharing the blazing plasma with Xenomorphs, laser shots still blasting out from the conflagration, and soon he could scream no more. Part of the fire fell aside, spitting and sparkling as Sara's unprotected flesh melted down and she joined the rest of her crew at last.

Durante lasted a little while longer.

Mains knew that this was the end. He staggered to his feet and shot Durante, just to make sure. Then he programmed his com-rifle to launch every last plasma charge, aimed—

Lieder grabbed his arm and pulled.

"With me, Johnny!"

He stumbled backward, not questioning what she was doing. As he felt the floor disappear from beneath his feet he pulled the trigger.

The opening before him lit up like a sun as five plasma charges erupted in the lobby. The explosion shoved against him, sending both of them tumbling down the elevator shaft.

Johnny Mains closed his eyes.

# 1 8

## ISA PALANT

*Deep Space, Gamma Quadrant*
*November 2692 AD*

Their surroundings had changed. Gone were the metal decking and walls, replaced by uneven surfaces, slick and solid. Their magnetic boots ceased to work and they started to drift, pulling and nudging themselves along.

The marines were much more used to working in zero-G, and Palant couldn't help being impressed by their almost balletic movements. She and McIlveen bumped and spun clumsily, sometimes holding onto each other, sometimes pushing away. It was tiring. On top of the constant fear, it made their hearts hammer. Her suit even issued a warning, and she took several deep, slow breaths to try and calm down.

The lights threw shadows everywhere, and every shadow might have been danger. Palant saw spiked, cruel tails swishing out of hidden corners, sharp limbs protruding from walls, teeth punching across light beams. She heard the hiss of charging creatures as her suit whispered along any surface, and the stamping of feet when McIlveen tripped and twisted, his sudden movement arrested by Sprenkel. As they moved further along the corridor the atmosphere grew heavier, skeins of mist absorbing light and exuding a soft, ghostly glow.

"Life signs ahead," Sprenkel whispered.

"Got it," Halley said. "No major movement, though."

"Any movement at all?" Palant asked. She was thinking of Xenomorphs, but also of the two Yautja who might even now be aboard the *Cooper-Jordan*. She wouldn't be the only one entertaining the idea that they had chosen this fraught time and dangerous location for a hunt. She didn't think it likely, but could not be sure.

"Some," Sprenkel said, "but very small. I'd guess it's debris in the next hold."

"Which is close," Halley said. "Come on, let's hustle."

They moved ahead, fast but cautious, and soon an opening appeared on the right. They ducked through the opening into the deep, wide space of another darkened hold. No larger than the burnt-out one they had just left, this one was in a better state.

But there was still something very wrong.

Lines of cryo-pods circled the tubular chamber all the way around, leaving an open space in the center. Shards of glass floated everywhere. That explained the signs of movement on their sensors, but on closer inspection, it wasn't only glass.

It was blood. Congealed, hardened, clots of old, dried blood drifted all across that strange space, in a constant weightless dance with the smashed glass.

"Oh, no," McIlveen said. "Every one. Every single one."

"There must be over two thousand in here," Bestwick said. "We're dead. We're fucking dead. They've let us come this far and—"

"Shut up, Private!" Halley said. "You two, you're the

scientists, is this what we think it is?"

Palant and McIlveen pushed themselves from the doorway to the first line of cryo-pods. Palant did not want to look inside, but McIlveen beat her to a pod and checked, and she couldn't let him face it alone.

The man probably never even woke up. Naked, he was still strapped down for his centuries-long journey, his skin wrinkled and withered from sudden exposure to an atmosphere. The pod's clear cover was smashed and splattered with blood from the inside. His chest was a mess—ribs protruding, chest cavity open and exposed to the elements. The sight reminded Palant of the gutted ship floating in space, the dead fish on the beach.

"And the next one?" Palant asked. They pushed off together and checked the next pod. Then the next. Every one was the same. Occupant dead, their chest burst open from the inside. Pod cover smashed. Blood splashed.

Xenomorph vanished.

"We need to leave," Palant said. McIlveen nodded, and she knew that the marines had heard her, even though they did not answer. She turned around and launched herself back toward Halley. It was a clumsy maneuver and she struck the Major, both of them drifting into the wall beside the door opening. "We have to leave, *now*," she said urgently.

"Maybe they're dead," Halley said.

"Can you even see how many people there are in here?" Palant asked. Her voice was rising, panic growing.

"We need to find something!" Halley said.

"Forget what Marshall said," Palant urged. "He's not out here."

"I'm not doing this for Marshall." Halley seemed surprised at the very concept. "I don't give a shit about him. I'm doing this to try and end the war. You've seen those things first-hand, seen how powerful they are. Imagine them getting further into the Sphere. Imagine them landing on one of the inhabited planets. Weaver's World or Addison Prime. Millions of people."

"Or Earth," McIlveen said. "Billions."

Halley blinked in shock, glancing past Palant at McIlveen then back at her again. "I know you're scared," she said. "I know we're in danger here, but it doesn't matter."

Palant let her go and shoved softly, drifting back from the Major.

"I know you're scared," Halley said again, this time to all of them. "So am I."

From somewhere out of sight came a long, low hiss, and then a thudding explosion shuddered through the ship.

"What the hell—?"

"Movement!" Bestwick said. She was out in the strange corridor, glancing both ways as her suit projected the sensor readings onto her visor. "Both directions."

"It's like the walls have come alive out there," Sprenkel said, joining Bestwick at the opening. Another blast followed, and something screeched in pain.

"That's a Xenomorph," McIlveen said.

"Stay close!" Halley said, pointing at Palant and McIlveen. She looked around the hold, appearing to assess whether it was a place they could defend. It was too large and filled with shadows, and every pod would provide a hiding place for a beast with sharp edges and teeth.

"Okay, Palant," she said finally, "it sounds like your Yautja friends are on a hunt. We break left and head back the way we came. Bestwick, you've got point."

"Oh, super," Bestwick said, but she headed off.

Imbued with a new sense of restrained panic and urgency, the others quickly followed.

Palant pushed off from the wall and struck the

doorway, gloved hands slipping on the slick surface. The dark material felt like contoured plastic, yet she couldn't help feeling that there was something softer underneath. It was like a carapace surrounding a huge insect's moist insides. She pushed. There was no give, but condensation settled on the dark veneer, moisture that burst outward in slow-motion splashes each time she hit a surface, shoved again, and moved on.

Huyck brought up the rear, expertly moving backward so his suit lights illuminated their retreat.

More hissing came from ahead. Then, from around a slow bend, a flickering red laser shimmered across the walls before winking out again.

"Yautja targeting laser," McIlveen said.

Three loud blasts followed, shaking their surroundings. Something screamed, a sound cut off by a heavy, swishing impact.

"I think—" Palant began, but Sprenkel's voice silenced her.

"Above!" he shouted, kicking back into Palant, splashing the ceiling with his light, showing the Xenomorph uncurling from the uneven, shadowed surface and lashing out with its cruelly barbed tail. Someone shouted in pain as Sprenkel opened up with his com-rifle, sparkling laser shot lashing across the corridor and ceiling.

The Xenomorph split in two, then erupted into a spreading haze of body parts and acidic blood.

Palant's suit immediately encircled her head again, face mask enlarging into an all-over helmet just as droplets of acid speckled her chest and shoulders. It sizzled, but did not penetrate the suit.

More gunfire came from behind her. Huyck fired laser, then unleashed a hail of nano-shot back along the corridor. The explosions were loud in the confined space, shrapnel winging past them all. Palant felt impacts all across her back and only hoped none of them had penetrated.

*How do we get back to the* Pixie *if our suits are holed?* she wondered, but that was a worry for later. They had more immediate concerns.

"*Plasma,*" Huyck called. Palant felt her suit hardening, her visor darkening as the marine fired three plasma shots back along the corridor, melting the strange black surfaces with loud popping, crackling sounds.

Ahead of them, the shadows came alive as three Xenomorphs charged. It was a terrifying sight, but the confined space was perfect for a burst of nano-shot. The marines opened up, and then so did the creatures, spilling insides, splashing acidic blood, bodies melting down under their own strange self-destruct mechanism.

Then they were running as they splashed through drifting remnants, and Palant's suit buzzed an unknown warning.

"Can't take much more of this acid," Sprenkel said.

"Just run!" Halley shouted.

Palant saw the red flicker of a targeting laser again, then they turned a corner and the Yautja stood before them, battle lance held across its chest, blaster aiming right at them.

Halley kicked into the wall to stop, one hand reaching out and grabbing Palant.

"No," Palant said. She shrugged off the Major's hold and shoved, drifting slowly forward.

The ceiling was low enough that the Yautja had to stoop. It was wearing full battle gear, and in a score of places acid bubbled and spat. A smear of bright green blood was splashed across its chest plate. Its helmet was scarred with evidence of older battles, and a trophy belt hung across one shoulder and the opposite hip. It held skulls, scraps, and other gruesome mementos.

The Yautja tilted its head at Palant. Then it turned and kicked off, back through the corridor and into the open space beyond.

"Come on," Palant said.

"We're following that?" Sprenkel asked.

From behind them came the haunting sound of many limbs clattering across the black surface.

"We're following that," Sprenkel said. "Go!" He turned and lobbed a couple of plasma grenades. Weightless, they quickly disappeared in the dark corridor, and when they exploded a few seconds later Palant caught a brief image of a dozen Xenomorphs consumed in plasma fire, limbs thrashing, heads lashing left and right as the white-hot conflagration melted them down.

They drifted across the wide space and followed the Yautja into a different corridor. It wasn't the way they'd come, and a schematic flickered up onto Palant's visor— an uncertain representation of the blasted ship, many areas left blank where the suit's computers could not scan. It looked as if they were heading around the burnt-out hold in a different direction.

She wondered at the Yautja's motives in leading them on. If it and its comrade had come onto the ship to stalk and hunt the marines, the killing would have begun by now. It carried evidence that it already had encountered Xenomorphs, and it was in full combat dress—lance and blaster, knives at its belt, spikes along its forearms, armor sizzling with acid-blood. Whether it was leading them to safety or something else, she did not know, but they were going away from the nest and the thousands of dead people.

*Thousands…*

Though this ship was blasted, adrift, and dead, it might yet be home to monsters beyond counting.

"Billy, we'll be coming in fast," Halley said.

"Roger, Major."

"Okay, guys, we're heading back."

"No prizes to take back to Mister Marshall?" Bestwick asked.

"It's too dangerous. Getting ourselves killed—"

The Yautja swung into a doorway, bending down to grab something out of sight. As they reached it Palant surged ahead again, eager to be close. There was something intoxicating about this creature's appearance and movement, its actions and hidden meanings. For her the Yautja represented all that was mysterious about space, and if she'd been told it would be her and a Yautja, alone on the ruined *Cooper-Jordan* forever, she would not have been sad.

The alien heaved something into view, and as their lights converged on the shape, Palant gasped.

*It's tearing them apart!* she thought, but then she saw the splash of milky-white fluid arcing across the corridor to impact the far wall, and she understood.

"Android!" she said. Even after what they'd witnessed on this ship, still it was a shock seeing a human-like body in such a state.

The android was smashed, ripped, torn. One leg was missing below the knee, the other crushed into pulp. One side of its torso had been torn open as if something huge had taken a bite from it, leaving trailing organs and internals hanging out. One arm was a mangled mess, and its head was almost detached from its body, held on only by a few opaque tubes and a silvery spine.

Yet it was still blinking, damaged limbs twitching. Palant imagined every remaining facet of its computer brain struggling to detonate the nuke contained somewhere in its torso.

Halley appeared beside her, weapon raised.

"It's as if it knows what we came for," she said. "Ask it if—"

"I don't know Yautja," Palant said. "It's just a program."

"But I'd be willing to bet it knows about the self-destruct capabilities of that thing," McIlveen said from just behind them.

"Why would you bet that?" Halley asked.

"It has one itself."

The Yautja shoved the android their way. Palant gasped and pulled aside, disgusted. Bestwick and Huyck caught the floating mess, shoving it to the floor and aiming their guns.

It blinked up at them, mouth twisted in pain or a sneer. Its one good arm slapped on the floor like a dying fish, flopping on the ground. Milk-white blood flowed from its wounds and clouded the air.

When Palant glanced back, the Yautja was just a shadow far along the corridor.

"Move out," Halley said. "Bring this thing with us."

"We have one," Palant said.

"Yeah, Marshall will be delighted." Halley looked at her. Something silent passed between. A fear, a doubt. Then they moved on, and Palant knew there was more to be discussed.

But not here.

"Company!" Sprenkel said. He started firing behind them again, spraying the corridor with laser fire, slicing a Xenomorph in two, then firing a hail of nano-shot that embedded in the walls, ceiling, and floor before exploding.

Bestwick and Huyck brought the battered android with them.

"You think it's trying to detonate?" McIlveen asked.

"It would have done it by now," Palant said.

"You're sure?"

She paused. "No." It was a gamble—they all knew that—but they could learn so much from this thing that they could not possibly leave it behind. Even the Yautja had known that.

Marshall knew it, too. He knew what the Company could glean from the tech this android carried within it.

They worked their way back through the ship, Sprenkel launching occasional rearguard actions when Xenomorphs found them. They were a tight unit, and they made it back to the place where they'd entered the ship, and did so unscathed.

There was no sign of the Yautja.

Into the airlock formed by the two blast doors, they vented the air and prepared to start drifting back toward the *Pixie*. Xenomorphs smashed against the doors, but only for a few seconds.

Then all was silent.

"It's as if they know there's only vacuum out here now," Palant said.

"I'm sure they do," McIlveen said.

Sprenkel stood guard while the others drifted across to the *Pixie*, and fifteen minutes later they were all on board.

Sprenkel and Bestwick sealed the android into a suction bag, a clear container that was used for vacuum packing equipment and clothing to make the best use of space. Its damaged limbs were drawn in, body compacted, head held on a tilt with its eyes open. It was so tightly contained that it could not blink, and Palant felt its strange gaze upon her as they strapped it down in the rec room.

She wished they'd turned it over before securing it to the hull.

"We need to blow that ship," Halley said.

"Fucking right," Sprenkel said.

"Good work back there, guys," Halley said. It might have been the highest praise Palant had heard the Major give her crew, and she saw them all bristling with pride.

"Palant, McIlveen, you'd best message your friends and tell them of our intention."

As the crew hustled to the flight deck, Palant and McIlveen accessed their program and prepared a short transmission. Minutes after sending it, the two Yautja ships lifted from behind the Fiennes ship, and seconds later they accelerated away.

By the time the *Pixie* had swung around into an attack vector, fifty miles from the crippled Fiennes ship *Cooper-Jordan*, the Yautja vessels were a thousand miles away.

"Ready?" Halley asked.

"Three nukes," Sprenkel said. "Fore, amidships, aft. There'll be nothing left but dust."

"Hit it."

They hit it.


With artificial gravity on the *Pixie* enabled, Palant felt weighed down with greater worries than ever before.

Huyck remained on the flight deck, keeping careful watch over their trajectory in case they needed to compensate for the *Pixie*'s damaged guidance systems.

The rest of them gathered in the rec room—some seated, some standing—with the android at the center of their attention.

It remained strapped to the wall in the vacuum bag. The bag flexed and writhed, very slowly, and the android's damaged body and leaking wounds made for a grotesque sight.

"It doesn't look like it'll take kindly to interrogation," Bestwick said.

"It looks like something the Yautja Woman puked up," Sprenkel said. He glanced at Palant. "No offense."

"None taken," Palant said. The Yautja had given them this catch. They all knew that.

"So, what now?" Bestwick asked.

"Now, we get this thing to a Company lab," Halley said. She was pacing the room. Palant had already seen her doubt, and now it was palpable.

"They won't get anything from it anyway," Sprenkel said. "What a mess."

"They'll get plenty from it," Palant said. "Marshall has our best scientists at his disposal. ArmoTech labs are filled with people itching to get their hands on this."

"So they'll find out how it ticks, right? How it controls the Xenomorphs? Help us win the war?"

"Yeah, help us win," Palant said. "Then what?"

"What do you mean?" Bestwick asked. "Then we take out the Rage, whoever or whatever they are. Clear up the mess."

"And they start singing songs about us?" Palant asked.

Bestwick raised her eyebrows but said nothing.

"Then the Company will have something they've been after for a long, long time," Halley said. "A Xenomorph army, under their control."

"Yeah, but that's a good thing, right?" Sprenkel asked.

"How in any way would that be a good thing?" Palant asked.

"'Cause… well, Weyland-Yutani are human, and they're in charge. This'll make them even more powerful."

The rec room fell silent. The android squirmed, one eyeball rolling wetly against the tight clear packaging as if trying to see them all.

"Even more powerful," Palant said.

"Are we even disputing this?" McIlveen asked. He'd

been quiet up to now, watching the exchange. "What we've just been through on that ship, what we saw, we can put a stop to all that."

"Yeah, you know the Company better than any of us," Halley said. "ArmoTech will be coming in their pants if we tell them about this."

"*If* we tell them?"

More silence. Palant stared at the android and saw hate in semi-human form—an alien, unknown power stewing in its own leaking juices and its desperation to kill them all. Whatever was behind it had such advanced knowledge, which they used only for war. She wondered how peace might benefit from such science. Or if it ever could.

"McIlveen, you and I can take this thing apart and find what we need to know," Palant said. It was a brash statement, loaded, heavy with an idea that she knew the crew would find hard to accept—disobeying orders.

All attention focused on her. She was confident of being able to do it, but just voicing the idea suddenly made it ten times more daunting.

"We'll need to find a suitable lab, but we can do that. It'll be quicker than getting it into Weyland-Yutani hands. We can find how these things control the Xenomorphs, how they self-destruct, maybe even come up with a way of triggering it ourselves."

"But that's not what we were ordered to do!" McIlveen said. "Isa, we're under orders. And these are Colonial Marines, not indies. In the Marines, you follow orders."

"They didn't follow orders when we sent that first transmission to the Yautja," Palant said. "If anything, they could have been court-martialed."

"No," Halley said, "we did what was right."

"Yes, you did what was right, and stopped a war," Palant said. McIlveen shifted from foot to foot, looking from Palant to Halley and back again. *I don't really know him at all*, Palant thought. She'd grown to like him far quicker than she usually grew close to anyone, but perhaps that had been brought on by the desperate times in which they found themselves. He'd seemed like a Company man with sense, not someone blindly following orders.

Now, she wasn't so sure.

"We have our orders," he said again.

"We do," Palant said, "but imagine what happens if we follow them. We hand this thing over to the Company, they backward engineer it and retrieve whatever tech it carries, win the war."

"Yes!" McIlveen said, nodding.

"Then we face a Weyland-Yutani that can field armies of Xenomorphs. A Human Sphere policed by those things. Uprisings put down by monsters that don't think, aren't afraid. You know the old saying—with power comes responsibility. From what I know of Company history, what we *all* know—"

"Fuck this," McIlveen said. The laser pistol was in his hand.

Palant laughed. It was so unexpected, so ridiculous, that she stood and took one step forward, still smiling in disbelief.

McIlveen swiveled only slightly as he turned the gun on her.

"Really?" she asked. "Milt, really?"

Nobody moved, but Palant felt a shimmer of tension run through the rec room, a thrumming of potential violence.

"Do you know what could happen if you fire that in here?" Halley said.

"So don't make me fire it," McIlveen said. "Billy, plot a course for the nearest drophole."

The ship's computer did not answer.

"Billy!" McIlveen said. His face dropped as he realized what he had done, how he had doomed himself, but beneath that was a deeper fear. Fear of failure, perhaps.

"What did Marshall promise you?" Palant asked.

It was almost as if McIlveen hadn't heard.

"You going to hold that gun on us for the next forty days?" Palant asked.

"No," McIlveen said. "Not all of you."

Palant gasped softly as she realized what he'd said, what he meant, but Marshall's man was already squeezing the trigger, turning the laser pistol on Major Halley and squinting against the flare to come.

Nothing happened.

Huyck stepped through the doorway from the flight deck, clinched his left arm around McIlveen's neck from behind, and plunged his combat knife into the man's back. McIlveen's eyes bulged as he slumped. Huyck let him go, tugging the knife out and slicing it quickly across his throat. Then he kicked McIlveen onto his stomach and bent to wipe his blade on the twitching man's jacket.

"My God," Palant said. She wanted to turn away, close her eyes, but she was suddenly terrified of these soldiers. Bestwick was still seated, expression unchanged as she watched McIlveen bleeding out. Major Halley was retrieving the laser pistol.

"Not a misfire," Palant said.

"Of course not."

"Did you not trust me either?"

Halley came to her and plucked the pistol from her belt holster, tossing them both to Bestwick. "Guess we'll never know."

"You've just killed Gerard Marshall's man," Palant said.

Halley ignored her. "Billy, set course for the nearest drophole."

"Where are we going?"

"You mean what you said?" Halley snapped, the only sign of the immense pressure now bearing down on her. "About being able to find out about that thing?"

"Yes. Given the right lab, equipment, and time."

"And you can do it without him, right?" She nodded to McIlveen, motionless and dead in a spreading pool of his own blood.

"You could have asked me that thirty seconds ago."

Halley grunted, then stepped over the body and onto the flight deck.

Isa Palant closed her eyes at last.

# 1 9

---

## L I L I Y A

*Space Station Hell*
*November 2692 AD*

Liliya was dreaming.

She rarely slept. She needed occasional downtime so that her systems could run diagnostics and perhaps reboot, and there were times when she felt what she supposed was "tired," but sleep was an entirely optional function. As such, her brain had a sleep mode that she could switch into if desired. It mirrored a human's sleep in many regards, but still ensured that a small part of her remained conscious and alert.

She called it her "standby mode."

Over the decades she had learned to master this human-like sleep aspect of her old, old mind, and she took pleasure in allowing herself to sink into those mind-freeing realms. For an android, control was everything. In her efforts to make herself as human as possible, Liliya enjoyed surrendering control, and allowing true randomness to steer her mind.

\* \* \*

Wordsworth is walking beside her along a long, wide corridor. It's like nowhere she has ever been before—white walls, clean floor, a sterile environment the likes of which is never seen on a ship. It's so bright and clean that she finds it dazzling, yet Wordsworth seems accustomed to such brightness.

"Not this," he says. He's pointing to a doorway. She hadn't even noticed that there were doors, but now that he indicates this one she sees a whole wall of them, set at intervals all along the corridor, stretching into the far, hazy distance.

He's still pointing at the door, waiting for her to step forward and see what lies beyond.

There is no window. Instead, there's a small viewing eye to which she has to press close in order to see what the door shuts off. There's a small room beyond. Perhaps it's a cell. Inside sit Roberts and Dearing, the man and woman whose deaths she was directly responsible for on the *Evelyn-Tew* centuries ago. Even though they cannot know that she's there they look up, meeting her gaze. They don't appear to be sad. There's hardly any expression at all.

"It was an accident," Liliya says, backing away from the door.

"Not this," Wordsworth says again.

"I didn't mean it," she says. "It was an accident. It had to be done, otherwise I would never have escaped the ship and—"

They are walking again.

Wordsworth is silent, and she's not used to that. He is always talking, a man filled with boundless enthusiasm and grand dreams. Some of her most precious memories involve just the two of them, sitting in his suite on board *Macbeth* discussing where they are going, and all that they have left behind. He carried a great sadness—he never called it regret—about leaving the Human Sphere, but insisted that they were going toward something better. That has always been Wordsworth's intention. Something better.

"Not this," he says. They're at another door, exactly the same as the first. He's pointing again.

She steps to the door and looks inside. The room is much larger than the first, and it is almost entirely filled with a monster. Liliya is not surprised at its presence. It turns its massive head as if sensing her, hissing, its huge mouth extruding another set of teeth, curved head gleaming with condensation as its suspended egg sac deposits another egg to the floor.

"Beatrix said it was for security," Liliya says, wondering how she could have been so naive. "An army for protection. Not war."

They are walking again.

The corridor never seems to grow shorter, and she can see many more doors along its length. She wonders if she has truly done so much wrong in her life, and the idea makes her despair. Liliya has always wanted to be a good person. The good part of that should have come naturally, and she has been working on the person part for what feels like forever.

"Not this," Wordsworth says. Inside this room lies Erika, the Founder become Rage person who Liliya had murdered in her escape from *Macbeth*.

"Not this." A much wider scene, a view that could not possibly fit inside one room, waves of Xenomorphs dropping from a cloudy sky onto a facility of some kind, unfurling, charging, killing the poor ranks of defenders who do not have a hope.

"I never intended—"

"Not this." Behind this door lies Wordsworth, blood

flowing from his slashed neck. Beatrix Maloney stands above him, blade in one hand, Wordsworth's security pass in the other. There is nothing on her face. No expression, no eyes, no skin, but Liliya knows for sure it is Maloney. She has always known.

"I'm trying to help," Liliya says despairingly. "I'm doing everything I can to help."

Wordsworth starts walking again, but then he leans against the corridor's blank white wall and slips down. Liliya is terrified that he is dying again, there in front of her, right now—but in fact he is crying, and somehow that is worse.

Liliya has let him down.

"I'm trying to help."


She was snapped from her dreams and into reality, and her android's mind switched instantly to the here and now.

"Did you hear me?" Jiango Tann asked.

"What?"

"I said there're indications that the drophole has been activated. No sign of who's used it yet, but it might be the ones chasing you."

*So soon!* Liliya thought, and she glanced across the room at Hashori. They'd moved them to a larger space, at least, but the two of them remained under house arrest. There were guards. Nothing was being left to chance.

She had never seen Hashori asleep. She wondered what the Yautja had been doing while she faux-slept. Watching her, perhaps. Guarding her.

"It's them," she said in Yautja, and Hashori stood to her full height, picking up her battle spear and heading for Liliya. As she did, two guards entered the room behind Tann.

They leveled their weapons at Hashori. The Yautja stood beside Liliya and paused, clawed hands clasping tightly around the spear. The pressure was palpable, potential violence simmering in the air.

"When do we leave?" Liliya asked.

"As soon as possible," Tann said, "but the ship we're using is still being prepared, and it might be a few hours."

"We might not have a few hours!"

"The drophole's almost a light year away. It'll take them weeks to get here."

"You don't know them," Liliya said. "You don't know their ships, their capabilities. If Alexander somehow knows where I am, he could be here in a matter of days." She translated the exchange for Hashori.

"We should leave in my ship," Hashori said. "Follow me."

As the Yautja turned for the door, two more guards appeared, guns leveled. They were big guns. Two were aimed at Liliya, two at Hashori, and she had no doubt that these people would use them.

"What did Hashori say?" Tann asked.

"That we should leave in her ship."

"It's not big enough."

"I'd agree with you there," Liliya said.

"That's not going to happen," Tann said. "You can understand why, can't you?" The older man seemed twitchy and unsettled, and Liliya could tell that confrontation troubled him. He seemed like a good man. This situation had landed in his lap when all he wanted was peace and quiet, but she could not change what had happened. Neither could Tann.

"I can understand," Liliya said. She reverted to Yautja. "Hashori, we can't leave in your ship. They won't allow it."

"Then I'll fight them until—"

"They are not your enemy," Liliya said.

"If they stand in my way, they are enemies."

"No!"

Hashori turned quickly, leveling her spear at Liliya. The guards behind Tann came in closer, looking nervous but determined, and she could not guess at how unsteady they were. They might shoot at any moment.

If their first shot did not kill Hashori, there would be a bloodbath.

"Please," she said. "Hashori. These people want what we want."

Hashori lowered her spear slowly, staring at the guards until they, too, backed down. She consulted the device on her wrist, breathing slowly and deeply.

"Perhaps a brief wait is a good idea," she said, uttering what might have been a chuckle.

"Come with us," Tann said. "We'll get you to the *Satan's Saviour* and leave as soon as we can. The crew is almost ready, and as soon as the ship is prepped—"

"If it's nothing vital, we should leave right away," Liliya said.

Tann sighed, then nodded.

"What's wrong?" Liliya asked.

"This place," he said. "It's become my home, and now it's under threat."

"All the more reason to hurry."

Still under guard, they left the room and set out for the main docking arm.

Two hours later they were seated in the *Satan's Saviour*. It was a large ship, sleek, built for speed and war. The crew eyed them curiously, but Liliya sensed only a little fear when they looked at Hashori. Maybe they had encountered Yautja before. Perhaps they had fought one.

Jiango and Yvette Tann were there, also, grim and silent. She felt very sorry for them. Soon she might ask more about what had brought them to Hell, and why they were so sad to leave—but their story would not affect events either way, and these events were larger than all of them.

Ware, the ship's captain, had arranged seating for them in the open space behind the flight deck. As she was going through pre-flight checks with her crew Millard, the tall man, brought an image up on the main screen before them.

"Captain, something's happening," he said. Liliya suspected he was a man prone to understatement.

The screen showed a holo of a space battle. Nuclear blooms grew, expanded, and faded. Laser blasts seared across the darkness, splitting reality itself before darkening to black once again.

"How far away?" Tann asked, shocked.

"About ten billion miles," Millard said.

"We have to leave!" Yvette said, looking at Liliya and Hashori. "However they're following you, we can't let them come to Hell. It's a good place. They're *good* people! They don't deserve this."

"Something else," Millard said, and this time he seemed more animated. "Captain, five ships just dropped out of warp a million miles from the station."

"Oh, no," Tann said.

"They're broadcasting," Millard said, and Liliya had not expected that. Even she was amazed at how quickly Alexander had arrived from the drophole, but she was convinced that he was beyond instructing her to stop. This was search and destroy.

Hashori said something. It was too quiet to hear, and

Liliya had to ask her to repeat it.

"What did that thing say?" Captain Ware asked. Others turned her way, waiting for Liliya to translate.

*Maybe this isn't the end*, she thought.

"She said, her comrades have arrived. Those new ships are Yautja, and they're here to help."

Hashori stood. "I will join them."

"We've left it too late to run," Tann said. "Hell will have to fight."

# 2 0

## ISA PALANT

*Gamma Quadrant*
*November/December 2692*

They blasted McIlveen's body into space. It was a disposal, not a funeral, and no one offered to say any words over the dead man. Isa Palant considered it, but then she realized that she hadn't really known him at all. She didn't know whether Milt McIlveen held any religious beliefs, where his family lived, not even if he was or ever had been married.

He had been a friendly face and a wise voice to her, and he had come at a time when she was facing what had been the biggest and most exciting challenge of her life. She'd been grateful for his help examining the Yautja corpses on Love Grove Base, and after the explosion there the two of them had something in common. They had both been survivors.

Not any more. McIlveen had shown his true colors, and his foolish move had resulted in his own death.

Palant wished she could unsee what she'd seen, but McIlveen had brought on that violent death himself. If

Akoko Halley had trusted him as Palant had, McIlveen would have killed one or more of them, and held a gun to any he left alive.

As it was, now Palant was still in good, strong hands. Akoko Halley and her surviving DevilDogs—Sprenkel, Bestwick, and Sergeant Major Huyck—were on the right side. She had no doubt about that, and she'd trust them with her life.

In fact she already had, many times.

"Goodbye to bad stuff," Sprenkel muttered as they watched from the *Pixie*'s rec room. The airlock closed and re-pressurized, and McIlveen drifted away from them forever.

"So what now?" Halley asked.

"You're asking me?" Palant responded.

"Isa, you're the one who said you can experiment on that." The Major nodded down at the remains of the android, vacuum-sealed in a clear wrapping, and now strapped to the foot of the wall in the rec room.

"I can."

"So where do we need to go?"

"I…" *I don't know*, she wanted to say, and that was the truth. Palant had spent so long at Love Grove Base that her knowledge of other destinations was sparse.

"You need a lab," Halley said. "We're all in agreement that it can't be a Company lab."

"Well, not now," Palant said.

"You think what we did was wrong?"

"No, not at all. In fact, it… it was brave of you."

"Brave?" Halley asked.

"You've gone rogue," she said. "AWOL. For all the right reasons."

"Yeah," Halley said, breathing out slowly. "Yeah, there goes my promotion."

"There are certain things I'll need," Palant said.

She stared at the android, wondering at the incredible technology it carried, wondering also how she could extract it. *I have to know exactly what it is before I even go looking*, she thought. *But if I can't go looking properly, how will I ever find it?*

"What things?"

"Basic lab equipment, but other things, too. Let me…" She squatted beside the battered, torn android. The clear wrapping was pulled tight across its body in every place, but its one good eye still moved and bulged.

"We're heading toward the nearest drophole," Halley said. "You think about what you need. If you can, maybe you can tell us what facilities might have it, and we can perform a location search. Meantime, I need to speak to my crew."

"Of course," Palant said. They'd all just signed their own death warrants with the Colonial Marines and Weyland-Yutani. Of course she needed to speak to her crew.

Major Akoko Halley went through to the bridge, leaving Palant alone with the android.

It was wet, shifting even beneath the pressure of the wrapping. Trapped fluid formed bubbles against the surface, and its exposed innards looked like fresh meat waiting to be cooked. She didn't like its eye. She reached out to turn the bound being around, but the eye seemed to open just that little bit wider, pupil dilating in excitement. Maybe it wanted her to touch it.

Instead, Palant stood and turned her back on the android. It made her uneasy. All the things that eye might have seen… they haunted her, and the idea of working on it, alone, was daunting.

But she had to do her best. A huge responsibility sat with her, made larger by their reluctance to take this thing to the Company. She had to discover everything about the android, and she was confident that she could. She'd spent much of her adult life alone while examining the physiology of the Yautja, and she would translate that knowledge onto this. She had to face the responsibility head-on.

There was still blood on the floor from where McIlveen's throat had been cut.

"There's nothing safe this side of the nearest drophole," Halley said. "Couple of research stations orbiting planets, a bigger space station with medical research facilities, but they're all linked to subsidiaries of Weyland-Yutani."

"We could still go there," Palant said. "They don't need to know who we are, or what happened."

"I can't risk it," Halley said.

"Pride?"

"Partly." The Major looked put out, and Palant was instantly sorry for offending her. Of course she had pride. "Mostly because I don't want to be forced to kill other marines. If we get to one of these places and they've been assigned Colonial Marines protection, we might be faced with a tense situation."

"And if that happened, you and your crew wouldn't fight."

"I didn't say that. I said I don't want to be faced with the choice—but look, these places we've found are all on the chart, all listed in deep-space manifests. They have histories, sponsors, company details, even contact information."

"We want something more off the grid," Palant said.

"That's what I thought."

They were drinking whiskey. It was false stuff manufactured on the *Pixie*, a chemical concoction that resembled the original only in strength and increased harshness, but it gave them a buzz. Palant was surprised at seeing Major Halley loosen up a little beneath its influence.

Huyck was still flying the ship, while Sprenkel attempted repairs to the damaged auto-control systems. It wasn't essential, but it kept him busy. Bestwick was sleeping in her bunk. They all needed rest, but Bestwick was the only one who'd managed to close her eyes and drift away. Everyone else was too troubled by what they had seen, what they had done.

From the mumbles and occasional shouts coming from the sleeping quarters, Bestwick was also haunted.

"Those two Yautja back there," Halley said. "That was weird."

"Wouldn't be surprised to find they were still with us," Palant said.

"No trace of them on our scanners."

"If they don't want us to know, there won't be." Palant had been trying to assess the Yautja's motives in helping them on the Fiennes ship, and she could find none other than simply wanting to help. The Rage had launched massive attacks against Yautja interests—habitats, as well as planets—and it would probably always remain unknown just how badly the Yautja society had been affected. As a species they were an enigma, and to even pretend to understand their reasoning was a mistake. But she could conceive of no other reason why the Yautja had aided them against the Xenomorphs and handed over the android.

"We need to decide where to go once we hit the drophole," Halley said. "That's if we're not reported AWOL by the time we get there."

"Marshall," Palant said.

"Yes. He'll probably try to contact us before we reach the drophole. We could tell him McIlveen was killed by

Xenomorphs, we could even lie about having the android. Tell him there was nothing useful on board."

"But he won't believe us."

"I don't think so, no. We boarded an enemy ship. We must have something of value."

"So?"

"So he'll direct us to the nearest Company facility for debriefing."

"And when we don't show…"

Halley nodded, turning her glass slowly on the table. The fluid inside reflected amber and gold, almost like real whiskey.

"If he tries to contact us, we don't answer," Palant said. "He's hundreds of light years away. It's not as if he can reach across space and grab us."

"Gerard Marshall has a very long reach," Halley said. She swigged her whiskey, hissing at the harshness and the burn.

"Major!" Huyck was calling from the flight deck. "Get up here, now. You too, Yautja Woman."

Palant was on her feet with Major Halley and through to the flight deck in seconds. In a way, she already knew what to expect.

The main holo screen was operational, and it showed the two Yautja ships. One seemed to be on station ahead of the *Pixie*, the other was performing a distant orbit of both ships.

"Any threats?" Halley asked, slipping into her captain's chair.

"No, but I've gone weapons hot."

"Drop them," Palant said. "Quickly."

"Seriously?" Huyck was looking at Halley, not Palant. The Major nodded.

"Weapon systems cold," Huyck said. A chime sounded

through the ship and several combat screens folded back into the walls. "Hope you're right."

Moments later another sound filled the bridge.

"What's that?" Palant asked.

"Contact request from the Yautja," Huyck said. "Full holo."

"Put them on," Halley said. She turned to Palant. "You're up."

It took twelve days to follow the two Yautja ships to the asteroid. It was an unnamed, unnumbered chunk of rock drifting between systems, twenty light years in from the Outer Rim. The Yautja relayed coordinates to the *Pixie* in stages, disappearing, meeting them again a couple of days later, moving on in short jaunts. It made the crew jumpy, but as time went on Isa Palant was growing more and more excited.

The Yautja had promised a research facility. They knew what she needed, and Kalakta's implication that the two species might work together now seemed to be bearing fruit. With little to do aboard the *Pixie* as they traveled from point to point, Palant started to imagine what might be waiting for them at the end of their journey.

The asteroid was large, its forty-mile diameter giving it more the dimensions of a dwarf planet. Yet this asteroid had no star. Some time in the distant past perhaps it had orbited a sun, but now it drifted in deep space, on an endless voyage across the void like an orphan who had never known its parents. It carried with it several insubstantial asteroids far too small to be called moons.

The Yautja contacted them again, and Palant used the

research she and McIlveen had carried out to reply.

"We're landing on the asteroid," she said.

"Really?" Halley said. "There's nothing there."

"They told us to follow."

They followed. Over the course of their journey here much discussion had been held about what they were doing, whether it was right, and what monstrous mistakes they might be making. But the Yautja had presented no threat or aggression, and Palant and Halley were both convinced enough to follow. They couldn't find any ulterior motives in what the Yautja were doing.

The Yautja transmitted approach vectors, and Huyck checked them with the ship's computer.

"Perfect landing vectors," Billy said. "We'll be approaching the asteroid's widest point—its notional equator—and an area of ravines and mountains. I can't detect anything artificial, but that doesn't mean there's nothing there."

"Thanks, Billy," Halley said. "That's a lot of help."

"My pleasure." Billy seemed not to be programmed for sarcasm.

Huyck steered them in, with the Yautja ships escorting them three miles off their port and starboard. It was only as they neared the asteroid that the first unusual readings started coming in.

"Boss, there's something else down there," Sprenkel said.

"Of course there is," Palant whispered. She was in a seat once occupied by a dead member of the crew, unable to do anything but observe. Something was happening here, something amazing, and she couldn't hold back her excitement. She knew that the others felt it, too, in different ways. While she viewed this as an amazing opportunity, they saw it as a challenge, perhaps even a threat.

She hoped that would change.

"There…" Halley said. But she didn't need to say any more, because they all saw.

Down in the network of valleys and low mountains marking the asteroid's equator there were unusual shapes. A few small surface structures became apparent, and then three large hangar doorways opened in a valley bed, spilling bright light and mystery.

The Yautja ships angled down and headed toward the openings.

A message chimed through to the *Pixie*. Palant keyed it in for a translation.

```
Follow. You can do your research here. We will
help.
```

Halley looked across at Palant, and Isa was pleased to see her excitement reflected in the Major's eyes.

"A Yautja base, well within the Outer Rim," Halley said. "We should report this."

"But they're showing us secrets," Palant said.

"And making certain we can't share them," Sprenkel said, looking at the controls. "All transmissions are blocked."

"After all this, we *have* to trust them," Palant said. The crew remained silent. She could almost hear their thoughts churning, knowledge and experience fighting against orders and training.

"We will," Halley said. "For now. Huyck, take us down."

They drifted down through one of the open hangar doorways and the doors closed above them, enfolding them in light, hiding them away from the Human Sphere. As the *Pixie* settled, Palant could only wonder at what might come next.

She looked back toward the rec room where the android was held prisoner. It was time to learn his secrets.

# 2 1

## JOHNNY MAINS

Othello, *Outer Rim*
*November 2692 AD*

"Johnny."

Mains didn't want to open his eyes. Everything was too calm, too relaxed, and he was floating in peace, arms and legs stretched out. He opened his mouth to breathe and cool, stale air rushed in.

"Johnny!"

He turned his head to either side, but did not open his eyes. When he turned, the light changed, darker to the left and right, brighter when he looked straight up. For some reason he couldn't feel the sun on his face.

"Johnny…"

This time the voice was weaker. Mains frowned. Sounds came in from outside, disturbing the tranquility. A heavy, regular creaking. The roar of flames. The screams of dying things.

Johnny Mains opened his eyes.

The shaft above him was tall and dark but for the rectangular fire blazing on one wall. Flames floated across the space, then receded again, curled around the opening's edge, flowing down the walls like melting butter. Fire in zero-G was quite beautiful.

"L-T..." the voice said, and Mains sat up, groaning, feeling pain all across his body. Lieder was propped against the wall just out of reach, and her left arm was twisted at an unnatural angle across her chest. She was breathing short, sharp breaths.

"Gemma," he said.

"Jesus, no one's called me that in years," Lieder said. "You there? You with me?"

"Yeah." Mains nodded, the action causing pains to flare and die down again. His suit was doping him, applying painkillers to his bloodstream. He wondered what the damage was.

Looking up, he knew that it didn't matter. All that mattered was that they had to move.

"They've gone," Lieder said. "Sara, Durante, Hari... just gone."

"Took a few with them."

"It's not a few we have to worry about. It's a few thousand."

Mains stood, magnetic boots locking on. He reached for the wall and leaned against it. His left leg felt weird, but it had been heavily numbed by his suit. He took two steps toward Lieder and his leg clicked.

"Help me up," she said. He helped her, and for a moment they leaned against the wall with heads touching through the thin suit masks.

"Come on," he said. They searched for their weapons. Lieder retrieved her com-rifle, but Mains couldn't find his. Maybe he'd dropped it above, just as they tumbled through the open elevator doors.

He looked up. Flames still roared, plasma scorching

across the elevator shaft with each fresh gust.

They used their knives to force the doors open on this level, then jumped half a yard out of the shaft. It was dark, quiet, and their suits showed no movement nearby.

They also showed what appeared to be a large, open space just twenty yards away and one more level down.

"Another hold?" Lieder asked.

"Let's see," Mains said. At the back of his mind was the hope he'd been clinging to, an idea that perhaps this didn't have to be the end. He and Lieder had survived again, and maybe there was a reason for that. Mains had never been one to believe in fate. Perhaps he'd taken a blow to the head.

"Can you walk?" he asked.

"Fuck you, L-T. You're the one with a broken leg."

He looked down and saw that she was right. His left leg twisted at a strange angle, moving oddly with every step he took.

"Oh," he said.

"Not sure I'm much use to you, though," she said. "My arm…" The limb was still held across her chest, shoulder pulped and forcing it there.

"Got another one, haven't you?" he asked.

Lieder grinned and hefted her com-rifle. The grin was more of a wan smile. Mains held out his hand for the rifle.

"I'm a better shot than you, even with one arm," she said.

"Yeah, okay. True. Come on."

They moved out, heading into darkness given life through their infrared vision. Movement appeared at the edge of their sensors. They hurried, Mains's leg starting to hurt even through the numbing and the flow of painkillers. He knew that the suit would balance the requirements—painkilling against mobility and alertness.

Soon, the pain would be allowed through so that he could continue to handle himself.

They reached another staircase and drifted down, pulling on handrails, and avoided touching the stairs. Lieder moved past him. She waited at the closed doorway below, rifle at the ready.

Mains touched the handle and nodded to her.

One… two… three…

He opened the door and she slipped through, panning the space beyond with her rifle. Nothing moved. Not in front of them, at least, but behind and above the movements were coming closer, converging on their position.

It was a hangar. Two ships stood on mooring decks, held in place by safety arms. They were half the size of the *Navarro*, but bristled with weapons.

"Fucking jackpot!" Lieder said, and Mains felt hope rising once again.

"Hurry," he said. "They're coming closer. Hurry!" He knew that they were in no position to hold off a wave of Xenomorphs, not now. They were both broken. Lieder's ammo was probably low, and all he carried was a laser pistol and a couple of plasma grenades. He mourned his old shotgun.

"Fuck you, General Jones," he muttered. He wondered why the android general wasn't mocking them anymore. Maybe it didn't know that they had survived.

They crossed the hangar to the nearest ship, skirting around the other side to where a door stood open. One side of the hangar was an external wall, which he guessed would drop away at a given command. If only they could understand the commands, know how to fly the ship, how to shoot—

*We won't know*, he thought. *We couldn't use that weird ship docked at UMF 12, and we won't be able to use these*. But that didn't matter, because at that moment he saw the first movement across the hangar as doorways burst open. Xenomorphs streamed in. Dozens of them, then scores, large and small and all drifting directly at them, pushing from walls and floor, claws reaching, teeth extruding.

Lieder gave them a burst and several creatures went down, then she was up into the ship and reaching for him, hauling him in after her, playing her light around as she looked for a door control.

"Fuck fuck fuck!" she shouted.

Mains drew his laser pistol, waited, and when the first dark shapes came close enough he shot them down. He fired quickly, carefully, and dropped seven more Xenomorphs before the door slammed closed.

Moments later, the impacts began on the other side.

Low lighting turned on inside the ship.

"Cockpit," Mains said. He and Lieder helped each other up and they bumped through to the small cockpit. Beyond, the shadows were alive. Writhing, twisting, dancing, the whole of the hangar was filled with Xenomorphs. There must have been hundreds of them out there, maybe more.

The first of them launched at the small ship's windows, bouncing from the diamond-hard glass. More thudding came from the doors behind them.

"How long will this hold?" Mains asked.

"Dunno. Look." Lieder stood at the small control pillar and touched some of the controls. Nothing happened.

"What do you think?" Mains asked.

"Looks… different from the ship we were on at UMF 12. More human. Gimme a minute."

"I'm checking out the weapons hold," Mains said. "You figure out how to fly this baby, and we'll take off and nuke the fuck out of *Othello*."

"I like your thinking, L-T."

"That all you like about me?"

She threw him a strange look. Sad, wistful. Mains turned away because he could feel the same expression on his own face. *We're not getting out of this*, he thought. *We both know it. We both know this is the end*.

He moved toward the back of the ship, still holding the laser pistol. The impacts were coming from all around now as Xenomorphs clung onto the hull and thumped against it, butting, biting, scratching. The idea of them breaking in was ridiculous—this ship was an attack craft built for deep space travel, very probably with warp capabilities. Still, if they kept bashing like that, for hours or days…

The weapons hold was small and compact, and filled with canisters, charge-bulbs, and an array of fist-sized objects that could only be nukes.

Mains touched one, almost feeling its potential coiled within.

He turned to rush back to the cockpit and Lieder was there, pressing into him and reaching back to close the door behind her. They were crushed into the weapons hold.

"What?" he asked. She looked terrified.

"They cracked the viewing window," she said. "They're killing each other, using acid to melt through the crack. They'll be inside in moments." She looked past him and down at the nukes.

"What do you think?" Mains asked.

Lieder shoved the com-rifle at him, pushed past, and picked up one of the nukes. She left it in the air before her, gently turning it this way and that.

"I think I can hot-wire this," she said, "but I've only got one good hand. You'll have to hold it for me."

As they worked together, neither of them spoke of

what they were doing. The future was seconds long, minutes, an hour, but they didn't discuss what existed, or did not exist, beyond that. Mains had confronted death many times, and considered it many more. It had never held fear for him, and now he found himself strangely at peace with the potential.

Gone in a flash, not screaming and melting, torn apart, agonized.

"This is so shit," Lieder said.

"No, it isn't," Mains said.

Something was inside the ship. Their movement sensors were overwhelmed. A Xenomorph started butting against the door, the impacts shaking the entire bulkhead wall.

"We don't have long," Mains said.

"I know," Lieder said. "I think I'm done." She leaned back and Mains looked down at the object in his hands. Its guts were out, wires and filament, virtual connections splayed like a living thing's innards. At its heart, the small globe of matter that could cause such destruction.

"Really?" he asked.

"This," she said, touching a small glass sphere. "One crack, three seconds, then... I think it'll set off all eight nukes."

"All of them?"

"Think so."

"One would be enough."

"No such thing as overkill with these things."

Every word they spoke was interrupted by the smashing sounds from outside. The air itself reverberated, hurting their heads.

Mains reached behind his ear and disconnected the com-suit's mask, pulling it from his face. Lieder did the same.

"You're quite a soldier," he said.

"Christ, Johnny," she said, leaning in to kiss him. He felt her hand stroke the back of his, feeling for the device he still held. The smell of her breath, the touch of her lips, the sensation of skin on skin made him feel so human.

The glass sphere cracked between her fingers.

"Wait—" he said.

"We've got long enough," she said.

And she kissed him again.

# 2 2

## GERARD MARSHALL

*Charon Station, Sol System*
*November 2692 AD*

"Try again," Gerard Marshall said.

The computer tried again. It seemed to him that it paused, just for a moment, as if irked at being questioned. But that was impossible. It was only a computer, not an AI.

"No contact made," the computer reported.

Marshall swilled his third glass of whiskey and stared at the empty holo frame. "Try again."

A pause.

A blank screen.

"Still no contact with the *Pixie*," the computer said. "I've tried a range of sub-space frequencies."

"Is our equipment all serviceable?"

"Of course."

"Check it."

Another pause. Marshall was certain the computer was growing impatient with him. Or maybe it was him projecting his own impatience and concern.

"Confirmed," the computer said. "All systems are

fully functioning. The sub-space transmitter is online and all in the green. Everything is working as it should."

Marshall took a drink. "Maybe it's the tech," he said. "It's cutting edge. New, expensive. Expensive stuff always goes wrong."

"It's not the tech," the computer said. "The *Pixie* is not receiving the message. Even if the crew did not wish to reply, indicators would show that the message was being received."

Marshall stood and paced his suite. He knew what he had to do, but wanted a little more time before doing it.

"Sir, I think you should accept the possibility that the *Pixie* is lost."

Marshall stood at the wide window and sighed. Outside he could see part of Charon Station's north docking arm, and the two big ships currently docked there. One was a Darkstar resupply vessel, almost the size of the station itself. The other was a Spaceborne frigate.

The sight of these ships should have made him feel safe.

"I'd like to speak to General Bassett," Marshall said.

"Connecting."

The holo screen chimed, then faded in with a blue glow. Bassett appeared, standing at a complex wall display with his hands behind his back. The connection established, he turned.

"Hello, General," Marshall said.

"Gerard." Bassett walked close to the screen. Behind him, the display was constantly changing, different constellations fading in and out, red lines and green spots appearing and disappearing like so many births and deaths. "I assume you're calling to inform me about the *Pixie*."

Marshall tried to hold back his surprise. Bassett smiled.

"Come on, Marshall. Let's not pretend."

"It's not certain that it's lost," Marshall said.

"No, but I think we have to assume that's the case," Bassett said. He looked tired. Marshall had never seen him rattled, not even when his own son had been killed. At the time they'd believed the incident was connected with the Yautja incursion, but now it seemed likely that the saboteurs were somehow in league with the true aggressors. The Rage. There had been no contact or communication with them yet. Only violence, destruction, and death.

Marshall guessed that the General was hardly sleeping.

"It's a minor setback," Marshall said. "Palant might have been our link to the Yautja, but I believe the peace treaty will stand."

"Maybe, maybe not. The Yautja don't concern me anymore."

"At all?"

Bassett shook his head. The screen behind him changed once again, displaying a vast network of points and curved lines that looked like a chaos of spider webs.

"So what's the latest?" Marshall asked. "Barclay will be in touch again later today, and we'll need to update him together."

"As if he doesn't know everything already," Bassett said. "As if *you* don't."

Marshall was shocked by the General's unusual outburst. He was usually the face of professionalism. He really *was* tired.

"Paul, contrary to what you believe, I don't have eyes and ears everywhere. That's why I'm here, on this station, with you. I'd much rather have a planet underfoot, but I'm here so I can be close. I'm the conduit for communicating military matters to the Thirteen. If I knew everything that was happening, I wouldn't need to ask you—and I suspect you're the only person who has the *complete* picture."

"You're trying to flatter me, Gerard?" the General asked, and he actually smiled. That was rare. It made him look more exhausted than ever.

"So tell me," Marshall said.

"Come to my suite," Bassett said. He nodded at Gerard's hand. "I've some single malt. Better than that piss."

Fifteen minutes later Marshall had been escorted through the bustling war room and into General Bassett's suite. Bassett already had two glasses poured, and he handed one to Marshall before nodding at the big screen. It was still cycling through images—maps, schematics, graphs, other representations of events that Marshall could hardly decipher. He watched the General watching the screen, wondering how one man could bear such a weight.

"How bad is it?" Marshall asked.

Bassett raised an eyebrow.

"Come on, Paul. You didn't ask me up here to share your precious single malt because of my sparkling personality."

"Okay, Gerard. It's bad." He waved a hand and the huge screen faded to gray. "We've lost nineteen dropholes across the Gamma quadrant."

"Nineteen? Christ."

"We suspect a dozen more might also have fallen to them. We've lost contact, so we have to assume the worst."

"Only the Gamma quadrant?"

"For now, yes. We're taking them on wherever we can, but like I've said before, their technology is ahead of ours. Their ships have defensive shields, and when they land—on space stations or habitat—the Xenomorph hordes are overwhelming."

"What about the Fiennes ships?"

"We've taken out a couple, but at great cost. They have escorts."

"And your forces have retrieved nothing useful from the ships they've hit?"

Bassett looked sidelong at Marshall. "Generally, if you nuke a ship traveling at a hundred million miles per hour, there's not much left."

"So the dropholes," Marshall said.

"They could be jumping deeper and deeper into the Sphere. Some dropholes have reported ships dropping in and then rapidly disappearing. Others report nothing. Some dropholes much deeper into the Sphere have fallen silent."

"It's a true invasion," Marshall said. He was stunned. Until now, the conflict had seemed contained, a skirmish across a wide sector of the Outer Rim, only just bleeding into the Sphere. Maybe he hadn't wanted to allow himself to believe.

"Which will be repelled," Bassett said. "During every contact we learn something more. We're gathering intelligence."

"Yet if it all goes bad…" Marshall said. He'd mentioned before about shutting down selected dropholes. Bassett's reaction had been one of shock, and that was understandable. The Thirteen had the ability to remotely shut down dropholes from several points throughout the Sol System and beyond, but the process was destructive. Once a hole was closed, the chance of opening it again remotely was small. It would take travel to that drophole location and a full overhaul of systems, and that would take years.

"No," Bassett said. "You know you can't do that. Shut down all six hundred Gamma quadrant dropholes and you doom everyone out there to die a cold, lonely death. You'd set the Sphere back centuries, stranding people hundreds of light years apart with only ships to travel between those points. The Human Sphere now is a coherent whole, even though it is huge. We're one civilization spread over this portion of the galaxy. Shut down the dropholes and you turn one civilization into hundreds."

"I know the implications," Marshall said.

"What would it take?" Bassett asked. He wasn't requesting it happen—he was terrified at the prospect, and Marshall guessed the General wanted to know how likely the horrific action might be.

"It would take the agreement of every one of the Thirteen," Marshall said. "It's a doomsday scenario, Paul. We're not stupid."

"I know," Bassett said. He shook his head, waved his hand, and brought up the big screen again. Data flickered across it, fading in and out.

"Can you get this under control?"

"Yes," he said.

"You sound certain."

"I have to be." Bassett scanned the screen, taking in data and details that Marshall couldn't even begin to understand. The General drained his glass.

"I have to be."

# 2 3

---

# B E A T R I X   M A L O N E Y

*Outer Rim*
*November 2692 AD*

They had taken the drophole three days ago. Rage attack ships performed the action, killing many, but capturing almost a thousand of the moon's population and shipping them back to the *Macbeth*. They would provide food for the Xenomorph queen, and fresh hosts for her countless eggs.

And so the Rage continued to grow.

Beatrix Maloney floated her hover platform closer to the center of the room. She drifted into and through the floating image of the *Othello*, that old companion ship to the *Macbeth* which had been sent its own way many years before.

"And you're sure?" she asked again.

"Yes, Mistress. It's the first confirmed transmission we've received from *Othello* in seven years. It was an automated signal, programmed to be sent under certain severe circumstances, and we can confirm that it was at the moment of *Othello*'s destruction." Kareth seemed nervous.

Maloney wasn't surprised. He had brought her

the worst news, yet he knew she would not shoot the messenger. She wasn't like that. She was a good leader. Not kind, perhaps, but fair and forgiving. Kareth and Dana would not have remained her dedicated caregivers for so long, if that were not the case.

Maloney closed her eyes and willed herself to relax. Her bio levels were raised again, and her suit was busy dealing with those symptoms. The life-supporting gel bled into and through her—she could feel it, she could sense that mysterious alien compound fixing her from the inside out. She was always being fixed. Hers was a constant battle against death, which stalked any normal human from the moment they stopped growing.

Death was so unfair.

Wordsworth had told her that, one day early in their journey out among the stars. He'd gestured all around them, at the infinity of wonders they had yet to touch, and his frustration and sadness had been palpable. *"So much still to know,"* he'd said sadly, *"and I've touched hardly anything."* It was ironic that he had died by her own hand. Unfair, perhaps, in the grand scheme of things, but his vision had been limited.

Her own vision was still wide open, and each day brought her closer to succeeding in her ambitions.

"It doesn't matter," she said.

"Mistress?" Kareth sounded shocked. He'd been young when the *Othello* left them, and that sister ship had taken on an almost mythical status among the shipborn. They would meet again, Maloney had always promised. Their battle would be fought, and at the same time the *Othello* would penetrate the Human Sphere and fight its own battle. Deeper inside, more secretive. While Maloney and her ships made plenty of noise, the *Othello* would strike at the heart of human society, and when victory was theirs, the two ships would meet again, their crews mingling like old friends, celebrating their triumph and planning for the future.

A future with the Rage in control of everyone, and everything.

"I said it doesn't matter," Maloney said again. "Plans can change. Leave me. Let me think."

Her helpers left her in the room, the door whispering shut behind them, and Maloney drifted across to the window. It cleared at her touch and offered a view out into infinity. She never tired of looking.

She had instructed the *Macbeth* to orbit the drophole, angled so that her viewing window always stared out into the Human Sphere.

"Somewhere out there I'll meet my triumph," she said. Then she closed her eyes to plan.

"It's only a pause," Maloney said. "Just as long as it takes us to transport the Faze down to the drophole and set it to work. It will do its thing—rebuilding, improving, refining. Perhaps thirty days, perhaps sixty, and then the drophole will be countless times better than it was before."

"To what end?" Challar asked.

"I'll get to that," she said. "In the meantime, while *Macbeth* is paused here, we push our attacks to a new level, expand the front. Until now we've targeted dropholes and Colonial Marine installations. Strategic military targets across Gamma quadrant. It's time to reveal what our armies can truly achieve.

"I've chosen Weaver's World in Beta quadrant as the scene of this demonstration. General Mashima can drop his force there within the next twenty-eight days, transported on board his Fiennes ship *Aaron-Percival*. He'll be accompanied by six attack ships and a storage vessel carrying our entire store of Xenomorph eggs. I've ordered him to launch a full assault on the planet and its defenses."

"To what aim?" Challar persisted.

"You sound shocked," Maloney said.

"Surprised."

"There are more than seven million settlers on Weaver's World," Maloney said. "Mashima will give his Xenomorph army free rein on that planet. The slaughter will make it the center of the Sphere, and our enemies will draw attention, divert forces, and give us the time to wait here while the Faze does its work."

"And when the Faze's work is finished?"

"Then *Macbeth* will make the deepest jump ever attempted."

"Dropholes have only ever been capable of jumping ships ten light years, perhaps twelve," Challar said.

"I know that!" Maloney snapped. She was excited rather than angry, filled with the buzzing certainty that the *Othello*'s loss would not be the disaster she had feared. Indeed, it had prompted her to make some radical decisions.

Perhaps in a way, it would make everything better.

"This deep jump, Mistress," Dana asked. "To where?"

"To their center," Maloney said. "While battles are fought across the Outer Rim, and Weaver's World dies, we'll take our invasion directly to the Sol System. The *Macbeth* will drop in and split into a dozen attack craft, pierce their heart, cut off their head. That's how you win a war."

There was a flurry of comments, but Maloney ignored them and drifted across to her viewing window once again. Out there, too far away to see, lay Sol, and Earth.

Home.

Soon, she would be ready to drown it in blood.

# ABOUT THE AUTHOR

—————

TIM LEBBON is a *New York Times*-bestselling writer from South Wales. He's had more than thirty novels published to date, as well as hundreds of novellas and short stories. His latest novel is the thriller *The Hunt*, and other recent releases include *Coldbrook*, *The Silence*, *Alien: Out of the Shadows*, and *Predator: Incursion*.

He has won four British Fantasy Awards, a Bram Stoker Award, and a Scribe Award, and has been a finalist for World Fantasy, International Horror Guild, and Shirley Jackson awards. Future novels include *The Family Man*, a new thriller from Avon, the conclusion of the *Rage War*, and the *Relics* trilogy from Titan Books.

A movie of his story *Pay the Ghost*, starring Nicolas Cage, was released in 2015, and several other projects are in development for television and the big screen.

Find out more about Tim at his website
**www.timlebbon.net**

# ALIEN
## SEA OF SORROWS

BY JAMES A. MOORE

In the future, no one can hear you scream...
A direct follow-up to *Alien: Out of the Shadows*, this
adventure reveals the far-reaching impact of events
seen in that novel. It shows the continuing malevolent
influence of the Weyland-Yutani Corporation, and
their inexorable efforts to weaponize the Xenomorph
known as the Alien.

# ALIEN™
## RIVER OF PAIN

BY CHRISTOPHER GOLDEN

Concluding the all-new, official trilogy set in the
*Alien* Universe!

When Ellen Ripley finally returned to Earth, she
learned that the planet LV-426—the planet from
*Alien*—has been colonized. This novel will reveal for
the first time the fate of the colonists, of the Colonial
Marines who accompanied them, and how there
came to be one survivor: the girl known as Newt.

**TITAN**BOOKS.COM

# ALIEN
## THE OFFICIAL MOVIE NOVELIZATION

### BY ALAN DEAN FOSTER

The crew of the *Nostromo*, a commercial deep-space mining ship, investigates a mysterious signal. Landing on planet LV-426, they discover a massive extraterrestrial and a nest of strange eggs. They bring back to the ship an Alien which, as it grows, stalks and picks off the crew, one-by-one, until only Ellen Ripley remains.